First printing

Cover Design by Ananda McIntosh,
Harmonic Creations

ISBN: 0-9685876-3-1
Published by: Miracle Creative Productions
www.awakendreamer.com
Printed in the United States of America

Dedication

We Were Blind But Now We See

Amidst charred skeletons of half believing
nightmares, the stark silhouette of comfortable
dreams smolder, crumbling under the weight
of an endless illusion.

We come with saddened hearts to the funeral
Pyre of a dream we can scarce believe was
never real.
A mist blinded us to our true estate and
doomed us to an acceptable pain.

We sensed a greater, lighter path could be
chosen, but ages of complacent adjustment
to our discontented existence bound us to
our dream of quiet despair.

To shake us from our endless gloom we chose
and created apocalypse and as one we have
marched onto the battlefield of specters long
dead, but still alive in our dreams.

We locked arms in our vigilance to fight an
unreal enemy and were astonished to find
never were we apart beyond our foolish
thoughts of separation.

We were blind, but now we see.

Forward

" ...there is no death, only 'the shuffling off of the mortal coil' as grandfather Ibrahim loved to quote. We are spiritual beings having a very short physical experience, all, returning to a lighter dream in the blink of an eye. And there we remain until another round of physical experience allows us the opportunity to come closer to fully awakening from the dream of separation - separation from the God that lives within us all. *Every great belief system and religion has in its origins this same truth - we are one with God and we have fallen asleep to this truth.* We come again and again and yet again until finally we awaken to this great truth to sleep no more.

Introduction

2095

"Nanny Bashira, my life instructor told me yesterday that long ago there were people who didn't believe in *angels*. Do you remember any of those silly people, nanny? "Huriyyah asked. She walked over to the kitchen table where her nanny was making a pitcher of her favorite drink and sat down at the table. Then she adjusted her school tunic so that its emblem was straight. The emblem was a series of three triangles. Each triangle was smaller than the last and fit tightly inside the larger one. In the center of the smallest triangle were the letters TSG.

Huriyyah was a precocious seven-year old going on forty-seven. She accepted nothing on face value. Her instructor told her from the beginning of her life training studies, 'always pass new information from the outside world through the filter of your inner guide.' She preferred to call her inner guide *Jacob* after the ancient seer. She had been told that he was a sage who could read the true meanings behind the symbols in the world and in dreams.

Huriyyah liked asking questions but she didn't always wait for the answers. She often went on chattering as if she were speaking to herself. Nanny Bashira knew there was much value in this practice and simply allowed her granddaughter to exhaust her curiosity before attempting to answer her questions. Frequently, it would not even be necessary to reply since Huriyyah often came upon her own answers. Nanny Bashira was a very wise woman and knew the value in simply playing the part of a perfect sounding board.

"Jacob told me he prefers the word *'messenger'* better than *angel*. He says it's a more accurate way to describe what angels actually *do*. He asked me how I thought messages or angels appear to people, and I wondered about it for a while. Then I told him that people who haven't learned how to use the *light messages* that come from their inner guide get messages on their *compu-cards*, the same way many years ago people used to get messages on their computers through the Internet, or in those paper packages that came to the door everyday."

She paused for a moment trying to visualize why a weird system like paper packages was used to communicate. Nanny Bashira could feel her thoughts and smiled as Huriyyah asked herself why people would use such a slow method to speak to each other when it could take weeks before they got their answers back. Huriyyah shrugged her shoulders as if there was no use trying to figure out nonsense and continued with her dialogue.

"I told Jacob that when I wanted to have some fun, I would only use the slow way to get messages and interpret the *mirror messages* the Great Spirit sends to us from everything in our world. She told him that's why she called him Jacob, because he was a master interpreter of symbols.

"I told him, 'once, before I knew you Jacob, a black bird showed up at our home everyday for a week and tapped its beak on the window over and over again. I began looking for something dark that flies and keeps interrupting my playtime. I finally decided it was scary thoughts that sometimes fly through my mind one after another and upset me.' He said the message told me to be more careful not to allow those pesky little ideas into my mind.'"

"Huriyyah continued and said, "whenever mummy and me are flying someplace in our auto cruiser and we see the same words or numbers on license plaques, we have fun figuring out what the *great Spirit* is trying to tell us. The other day we saw the word *blue* come up four times in ten minutes on license plaques on different auto cruisers. Then an eagle flew right in front of us and almost hit the windshield. We were on the way to the book store and when we got there, right in the front window was a holo-book about Native American Indians called 'Blue Eagle', so we knew that Jacob was telling us to buy the book and play the program."

Huriyyah shifted in her chair and took a sip of the lemonade that Nanny Bashira had placed in front of her while she was speaking. "That's the easy stuff Nanny, but I like to know things right away so I usually talk directly with Jacob. Sometimes its hard trying to figure out what Jacob is trying to tell me though. I don't always understand his messages, all I know is that they are always right - even if I don't understand them and do something other than what he suggested I do."

"Listen closer my little angel." Nanny Bashira said. Huriyyah nodded.

"I know, I know. My life instructor tells me that all the time. Listen to your inner guide, listen carefully to your inner guide. Maybe if he called it Jacob too I'd listen to my life instructor better." She laughed. Nanny Bashira smiled.

"Jacob asked me if I notice other ways the Great Spirit sends people messages. I said I could think of two more. He asked me what they were and I told him that when people are showing their love for each other the Great Spirit is speaking through them. Jacob seemed very pleased that I already knew that. I was a little surprised that he didn't know that I knew that." Nanny Bashira raised her eyebrows at Hurriyyah's pride. Hurriyyah lowered her head and grinned impishly.

"Then I told him about my favorite messengers - real Angels like you nanny. Jacob said even now that everyone knows angels or messengers are real, a lot of people still don't recognize them, even when they are standing right beside them. He said it had to do with *poor tuning*. I asked him what he meant and he told me about the sound boxes people used to listen to. I think he said they were called *radios*. They would turn a knob and different channels came on as the knob moved a dial forward or backward. And just like the *media chips* we wear on our ears, they could hear the messages of music or people. 'The problem was,' he said, 'when people didn't get the dial in exactly the right place the messages would come through full of *static.*' I asked Jacob what static meant and he said it is the opposite of *harmony.*"

Huriyyah took a long drink of her lemonade and shook her head. "Nanny, how could people live in the world without harmony? For just a minute I had a scary thought when Jacob told me that. I remembered something dark that once happened. It didn't happen to me, but I just knew about it, so I asked if this thought was from the *Great Record* and Jacob said that it was." Huriyyah trembled as she recalled the memory again. Nanny Bashira placed her hand on her granddaughter's hand and told her to be still for a moment. The trembling subsided immediately. She thanked her nanny then said,

"Nanny Bashira, Jacob told me that if I really wanted to know what it used to be like for people to live without harmony I should ask you."

Nanny Bashira remained silent for a moment to determine if Huriyyah was really finished speaking. She could see by the questioning look in her granddaughter's eyes that she was ready to hear what her Nanny was going to tell her. She smiled at Huriyyah and said.

"As usual my little angel, Jacob has spoken truth to you. *Tuning in* was once a big challenge for the people of this planet. People on one side of the planet understood some of what the great Spirit was telling them about how to live a happy life and people on another part of the planet also understood, but just like the channels on the radios, they didn't know how to tune together. There was great static. "Huriyyah shivered as she tried to visualize a world full of static. Nanny Bashira continued.

People everywhere were taught the very same truths about the Great Spirit and how to live a happy life. They understood and followed much of what they were instructed, but there was so much static that they could not believe that people who were listening to a different channel were listening to the same teaching about the great Spirit. That's why the world lived without harmony for a very long time.

"Huriyyah my love, I feel its time to tell you a story that happened long ago. It happened at the beginning of this century and for most of the people in this great country of America, it was the biggest static they had seen in their whole life. You must hold onto my hand very tight while I tell you the story little angel, otherwise just the vibration of this old energy will take hold of your mind and contaminate it. That is how the ancient world created static in their world - contaminated thoughts."

Huriyyah looked nervous at first but knew that her nanny loved her very much and that she was a real Angel so nothing bad could happen to her if she just held onto her nanny. She nodded in agreement and nanny Bashira began her story

One

1920 -1945

Ibrahim Amal Faiz was born in the small southern Palestine town of Ma'an on February 22nd, 1920. He uttered the name "Allah" as his first word at only six months of age. To his parents who were simple peasant farmers who could barely feed their family of four children, Ibrahim's relationship with God was firmly established on that blessed day.

Whether it was what they believed to be Ibrahim's inside track with heaven or an attitude of expectant good fortune, Abdullah and Dalia Faiz soon found themselves and their family living in the port town of Aqaba at the southern most tip of Trans-Jordan. Abdullah's brother, Fahed had found him work on a ferry boat that regularly ran back and forth to Egypt carrying passengers and cargo. Abdullah soon made friends with several merchants who exported their goods to Egypt, the drop-off point to many others parts of the world.

By the time Ibrahim was eight years old he was working in his family's business supplying pottery to merchants exporting olive oil. The boy was a good worker and a quick learner and his deep devotion to Allah endeared him to one and all. By the age of twelve he could quote chapter and verse of the Qur'an with the passion of a faithful cleric. The boy's unusual zeal for Islamic tradition, gained for his family the respect of many important officials in the newly emerging government of Trans-Jordan.

However, the gifts of Allah brought with them a heavy price for Ibrahim. In his seventeenth year, Ibrahim and his family were on their way to visit relatives in the new Palestine during the holy month of Ramadan when their automobile was hit head on by a bus that had moved into their lane during a blinding sand storm. Everyone in the car was killed except Ibrahim. He spent the next two months convalescing in hospital and although his body healed, as the only survivor a deep-seated guilt had taken up residence in his heart.

The lingering self-reproach drove Ibrahim deep into the business world. His love of Allah and the original tenants of the Qur'an prompted him to divert much of his growing wealth into charitable ventures. He focused his attention on families oppressed by poverty or those suffering the loss of loved ones. At the time he believed he was reconciling the emotional wounds of his family's violent death as well as any conflict the Qur'an might have had with his penchant for material success.

He established a network of orphanages around the country, built a mosque in his birthplace of Ma'an and established the *Jordanian Family Relief Association*. By the time he met Nadira he was twenty-five years old and as a result of his zealous drive to purge himself of his inner torment controlled one of the largest export companies in Jordan.

Ibrahim married Nadira in the winter of 1945 in a grand ceremony that hosted hundreds of friends including powerful government officials and well respected men of business. But again the cost of Allah's gift was high for in the year that followed Nadira died giving birth to their son Mikha'ill bin Ibrahim Faiz. With happiness and power firmly in his grasp Ibrahim believed Allah had seen fit once more to bring him to his knees.

Two

Smokie's eyes opened slowly as he regained consciousness. He had no sense of feeling and the total absence of light had a disorienting effect on his perception. In the darkness, everything seemed to be coming from within his mind. A single moan echoed from the recesses of his unbounded body. Was it he that made the sound? He couldn't be certain. The muffled noise of crushing rock emanated from somewhere inside his awareness. Up and down did not exist and for a while Smokie was in a state of euphoria.

Gradually his senses began to reawaken and he began to feel dizzy but without a frame of reference he had no fear of falling. His disorientation continued for several minutes, then an ugly and terrible picture slowly materialized, filling the panorama of his mind.

Smokie found himself standing in the middle of a holographic rerun of the horror that had brought him to this moment of darkness. On every side he saw scenes of people running in terror through streets choked with white clouds of paper floating to the ground like giant ghostly snowflakes. The wildness of hundreds of flashing lights and sirens wailing like banshees created a theater of madness. Wave after wave of shock and disbelief reverberated through panic filled corridors as thousands of hysterical people scattered like rivers of ants.

"Don't worry, *pink lady* with Smokie." A voice beside Smokie said. It was the utterance of a small female child, perhaps four or five years of age. Calm immediately rippled through his boundless body like a soft warm shiver.

"Where are you?" Smokie asked. He felt a small hand slip into his.

"Meereka here."

Three

October - 5 - 2001

Dr. Heathrow opened a leather journal, oiled and weathered from years of intimate use. He scanned the inspirational notes he had scribbled to himself after a vivid dream the night before, then glanced at the three people sitting in the front pews. The incredible events that brought the small group together raced through his mind. He felt the pressing weight of unfinished business like a specter glaring at the group from the wings of the chapel. He shook off the uncomfortable emotion and gazed in the direction of Benny and Smokie. 'No, I don't think so.'

He turned toward Francine who was sitting by alone. A flutter of emotion passed through his belly. He suppressed the old feelings and decided he would address his question to her.

"Francine, what do you think Abe Lincoln meant in his first 'Inaugural Address' when he said; *"The mystic chords of memory, stretching from every battlefield and patriot grave to every living heart and hearthstone, all over this broad land, will yet swell the chorus of the organ when again touched, as surely they will be by the better angels of our nature?"* Benny raised an eyebrow when he heard the quote. "As Francine considers her answer, I want to draw your attention particularly to the last few poignant words: *"the better angels of our nature."*"

Francine considered the powerful words of a President about to draw upon the deepest resources of his soul as he guided his young country into the heat of bloody self-discovery. She struggled, embracing the essence contained in the compelling words Lincoln wished to convey to his countrymen on that special day he spoke them.

Something unfamiliar, almost ecstatic came over her as she rolled the words over and over again in her mind, *'better angels of our nature...better angels of our nature.'* She could feel their passionate beauty wrap around her. She was about to reply when a loud thump echoed throughout the vaulted hall. Everyone turned toward the gallery. "The noise came from somewhere up stairs Doc." Benny said, pointing toward the balcony.

Exhilaration swept through the tiny gathering. "Smokie, check it out for us, will you please?" Dr. Heathrow asked, smiling gently at the young man.

14

"Sure thing Doc!" Smokie gleefully jumped from his chair and headed for the stairs leading to the balcony. The support group was using a vacant chapel in St. Paul's Cathedral. The ancient structure was situated directly beside *Ground Zero* and had mercifully been spared. Now, just yards away from the gapping wound, the cathedral had become a Mecca for multitudes of lost souls desperately searching for some meaning behind the senseless act that leveled the great towers.

Built in 1766, St. Paul's was the oldest church in New York City. It had been the focus of prayer by every President dating back to Washington and seemed the perfect location to wrap Lincoln's famous inaugural speech around the agonizing inner journey each member was taking.

The ancient stairs moaned as Smokie headed for the balcony. Bumping and scrapping sounds echoed from the balcony as he struggled with whatever had caused the noise. Several anxious moments elapsed and just as Benny was about to see what was happening, Smokie began lumbering down the stairs. The steps bowed under the weight of his heavy treasure. He emerged from the stairway sweat pouring down face.

"Look what I found." he exclaimed in delight. Smokie lifted the unwieldy object from his shoulders. He turned it over in mid air then gently laid it on the marble floor. Everyone gathered around. A moment later there was a staccato of gasps.

Dr. Heathrow stood with arms folded on his chest shaking his head and smiling. When the commotion subsided he asked, "My friends, what are we to make of this strange phenomena? Moments after asking Francine to give us her evaluation of what Lincoln meant when he spoke of *'the better angels of our nature,'* an old wooden statue of an angel seemingly falls from heaven to join us."

No one spoke. Then Francine pointed to a small object attached to the feet of the angel. "What does that plaque say?"

Everyone leaned closer to get a better look. The paint had faded but the date that had been etched into the plaque could still be read. "April 12th - 1861." Benny said as he gently ran his fingertips over the ancient letters.

"What did you say? April 12th, 1861, is that what you said? Dr. Heathrow asked with a stunned expression on his face.

Benny nodded. Then he noticed the look of shock on Dr. Heathrow's face. "What's the big deal about April 12th, 1861?"

Dr. Heathrow hesitated. He couldn't quite get his mind around the incredible coincidence. "It's the day the Civil War began, a few days after Lincoln uttered the very words we are discussing."

"What do you think it means Doc?" Benny asked.

Dr. Heathrow shook his head without answering. A moment later little Meereka reached up to the wooden statue, placed her tiny fingers on the folded hands of the wooden angel and whispered,

"Pink lady want to help save flowers."

"Did you hear what Meereka said?" Benny asked. Everyone looked sympathetically at Benny.

"Tell us what she said Benny." Francine asked gently.

Benny looked from side to side. "You all heard her…didn't you? She said '*Pink lady* want to help save flowers."

"Meereka? Meereka is…" Dr. Heathrow put his fingers to his lips and interrupted Francine before she could finish.

"What flowers do you think Meereka is trying to tell us about Benny?" He asked

"I'm not certain but over the last three weeks she made several drawings with flowers in them and I'm certain she sees much more in this lifeless statue than we do." Benny's eyes rolled up and he stared at the ceiling for several moments. Something had occurred to him. He looked down at the child standing beside the statue. "Can Benny and Franny look at your beautiful pictures Meereka?"

The sweetest smile radiated from her face. She nodded her approval and took Benny's hand pulling him to the pew where she and her brother had been sitting before the excitement began.

The name Meereka was short for *miracle child*. Her given name was Teresa Rodriguez, named for St. Teresa, the saint of children. Soon after little

16

Teresa's own incredible healing, people began calling her the miracle child. She was only 12 months old at the time and had just begun speaking her first few words. When she tried to say her new name it came out *Mee-re-ka*. Soon, everyone who knew her amazing story accepted the abbreviation and the name stayed with her.

Despite the total remission of the HIV virus in her body four years before, now and at age five Meereka was not growing up like other children. Some thought her condition was a side effect of the deadly virus she had contracted at birth from her infected parents. But hers was not a physical condition. At least that's what Benny and his mother Maria believed.

Six months before her phenomenal healing, Meereka's father died from an Aids related heart complication. Thankfully, the HIV in her mother had so far remained inactive. Maria believed it was her devotion to Meereka that kept the devil form her own door. Since the blessed day Meereka was healed, the same September day in 1997 when Mother Teresa passed from the world from heart complications, Maria had prayed continuously to the Holy Mother that she would be spared until Meereka grew up and could be cared for by someone who would love her as much as she did.

Maria believed that in some divine manner, Meereka's life had been spared through the Holy Mother. In her mind the grace of God was with Mother Teresa and by her devotion to the Mother and by naming her daughter after St. Teresa her daughter had been healed.

Benny was not at all religious and scoffed at the idea, yet he could not deny the fact that the morning of the day Mother Teresa died, Teresa had barely been breathing, deathly ill with an Aids related disease. The doctor warned them the night before that little Teresa would likely not survive another day. Benny and his mother sat by her side and watched helplessly as the life in her tiny body ebbed away. Above Teresa's crib hung a large round clock with a picture of a huge Angel overshadowing two children as they walked together in the dark. At precisely 10:30 am EST, the exact moment Mother Teresa made her transition in Calcutta, India, little Teresa began breathing normally. By the next morning she appeared completely healthy.

When Maria heard the news about Mother Teresa's passing she knew in her heart little Teresa had been spared. A week later the doctor confirmed what she already knew, Teresa was inexplicably healed, totally free of the HIV virus. Nothing could shake Maria's conviction that the Holy Mother had intervened in some way and from that day forward she prayed a novena to the Mother for little Teresa and herself to be under the protection of the Holy Mother.

As Teresa grew and began talking she spoke in short, broken sentences when she spoke at all. At first it seemed the normal evolution of a child learning to talk. But as the months passed Teresa, now known as Meereka, frequently appeared lost in her own little world. By the time she was two years old the doctor sadly explained Meereka was autistic and recommended she be placed in a state funded facility. Maria would not hear of it. She believed Meereka had been spared for some special purpose that would one day be revealed. Until that day Maria would console herself by peeking into Meereka's world through a steady flow of colorful crayon drawings the little child made each day.

"Look at this." Benny exclaimed, holding up two of Meereka's pictures he had found in her knapsack. "See the flowers? One's got several tiny white blossoms and the other just a single pink one." Both pictures had what appeared to be a solitary black box or perhaps a house surrounded by a gloomy gray background. In a pale yellow window there were two flowers, a large one with white blossoms beside a small rose-colored flower. There was no flowerpot or vase. One of the two pictures had a round white circle just above the black box or house.

While Benny and Francine studied the drawings Meereka looked on in silence, then the picture with the white circle slipped from Benny's fingers and landed on the wooden angel. Meereka knelt down, pointed to the white circle on the drawing and with a hushed reverent tone said, "Pink lady fall down again."

"Did you hear what she said?" Benny exclaimed. "Pink lady fall down again." All eyes were on Benny who had crouched down beside his little sister and was embracing her affectionately. All but Smokie looked on in sadness as he asked her,

"Meereka, little princess, is this pink lady?" He pointed to the white circle hoping she might help he and the others understand the importance behind the fallen angel and how it related to her drawings.

She touched the white circle on her drawing. Then she repeated what she had said before, "Pink lady want to help save flowers."

18

Four

It was unusual for David to be home when Francine was drinking her morning coffee. He was the archetypal workaholic. This particular morning was an exception. Francine knew that spending time with her certainly was not one of her husband's priorities. This had to be an oversight nothing else could explain his presence at the table.

"Gerry's coming over Fran. Were taking the company helicopter to Martha's Vineyard this morning." David muttered from behind his New York Times.

'Hem. Not an oversight - an actual plan - fascinating.' She thought. 'Why is he not leaving from the heli-pad at the office I wonder?'

"Mechanical problems." He mumbled, answering her unspoken question.

"Aha! There it is - I knew it." She whispered with a cynical smile.

"What did you say Franny?" David asked. He didn't wait for a reply. "Can't be too careful. If there's anything I'm afraid of, it's going down in flames because of some stupid human error that could have been corrected with just a little professional foresight." David was all business and had an almost desperate need to always be in control. If he could put his arms around an issue to insure it was flawless, he'd do it. His reach was global, so invariably he found himself butting into a lot of things that his staff could easily handle on their own. The habit made him few friends, but then real friends were an unnecessary burden David took great pains to avoid.

David's father had been a successful Wall Street broker who lost his fortune, his reputation and his family in the bottom of the bottle. "The old man didn't have the chops - not enough discipline." David ranted to the financial butterflies that constantly fluttered around his ongoing flow of deals. "Could have gone the distance if he'd just had the damn discipline - gives a man control over his destiny."

"What are you up to today Fran - enabling the looney's I suppose?" He asked without masking his contempt for her work. Francine long ago insulated herself against the sting of David's cruelty. He placed no value on

19

anything less than perfection, particularly people he considered to be what he referred to as; *low-life-losers.*

'Are there no prisons - are there no work houses?' Echoed in Francine's mind whenever he went into one of his loser rants.

"I had a strange dream last night dear." She said.

"Really! Tell me about it. David exclaimed laying aside his paper. Francine knew the subject of dreams would get his attention.

When David was sixteen his father hit bottom and his mother decided to leave. While David hated what his father had become and especially hated the opportunities he had wasted, he loved what the old man had accomplished before Johnny Walker lead him down the path of destruction. He understood his mother's frustration but believed if she had just hung in, the old man's flame would have re-ignited. After that, his whole life became a quest to make up for his father's failure to win his mother's approval.

The night he and his mother left, David had a dream. In it he was walking across a bridge on a railroad track in the dark when a train began whistling in the distance. He was half way across and knew he couldn't make it to the other side in time to miss being hit by the train. As the whistle grew louder and the train's head light grew bigger and brighter, a dangling rope appeared just above his head. He grabbed for it but it slipped from his hands. He tried again and again but kept missing it. Just as the train was about to end his life he caught hold of it and was pulled to safety.

The next day David dropped out of school and went in search of work. He found an ad in the paper placed by a *light* bulb manufacturing company located on Bridge Street. Just as he arrived for his appointment a *whistle* blew from the plant in back of the offices. When the secretary ushered him in to see the manager she introduced the man as Mr. *Rope.* The man extended his hand and said,

"Hi there young man, my personnel manager tells me you're a fella that could use a *lifeline.* If you don't mind hard work and discipline this opportunity could be just the ticket for you." From that moment on interpreting dreams and following the insights he received from those interpretations became a passion for David. It didn't matter where they came from - office boys, corporate enemies, even his wife, he'd listen to them all looking for clues as to what his next step was to be.

The obsession would have tarnished his credibility if it were not for the fact that the decisions he made as a result of his interpretations frequently bore fruit.

"I don't know how you do it David and I don't care, just keep doing it." The president told him at the first brokerage firm he worked for. David literally dreamed his way into a partnership with the company. Eventually his insightful analysis of dreams helped lead him to the summit of the corporate world.

"C'mon, c'mon, tell me. Gerry's going to be here any minute." He was grinning like a little kid. A long forgotten feeling tickled her. Just for the moment, she allowed herself to revel in it again.

"I was in an apple orchard at blossom time. There was row after row of trees with the most beautiful blossoms. As I walked between the trees I saw a sign that read 'East Orchard.' I felt drawn in that direction so I followed the pull of it. When I arrived, there was another sign that read 'Middle.' It too pulled me. As I reached what I felt to be the middle, there was a single tree set apart from the rest. On it there was a blossom of unsurpassed beauty. I moved closer and noticed a bee approach the blossom. It landed on it, burrowed within it for nectar, then flew off into the sky. A moment later the bee mysteriously plummeted to the ground and landed at my feet dead." As Francine continued telling her dream to David a deep sense of sadness she could not identify come over her. A single tear came to her eye, falling in her coffee with a splash.

David's eyes had glazed over. She knew he was in the gap between thoughts where dreams revealed their mysteries to him. Two full minutes of silence passed while Francine sat immobile, fearful she might break the spell if she moved. Still in his trance-like state David spoke three words. "Yasmine is pregnant."

Immediately Francine knew he was correct. East, middle, Middle East, blossom, bee, fertilization. Then she shuddered. "The bee is dead." She called out in terror.

"Not yet I feel, but soon." Just then the bell rang and David jumped up as if nothing unusual had occurred. "See ya tomorrow Fran. I'll try to make it for the summer closing celebrations tomorrow at the Club." He threw her an indifferent kiss and headed for the door.

Five

1997 -2001

Benny grew up in a rundown tenement - a Slumlord heaven. Now twenty-two, he had been the father of the house for over five years, the first year while the specter of Aids shrouded his family and claimed his dad's life, and the last four years as the chief bread winner while his mother waged her own battle with the disease. Meereka was the shining light in his world. She anchored not only his hope for a better life but also for a world that reflected love.

At eighteen Benny had a run-in with the police that helped pave the way for his passion for detective work. He had a part time job walking dogs in lower Manhattan. One night while performing his duties, he was caught in the crossfire between two rival gangs fighting over drug territory.

He was crossing a deserted street when two black Mercedes screeched around the corner and stopped dead in front of him hitting one of the three dogs he was walking. What followed next was absolute chaos. Six Hispanics with guns drawn spilled out of the two cars while four black men emerged from a nearby alley armed to the teeth. Before Benny could utter a word of protest he was whacked across the side of the head with a gun. He crumpled to the ground falling beside the wounded Labrador.

Although bloodied and in shock his fist remained clenched to the leash that held the remaining two animals. Unlike their fallen brother, both dogs were full grown Dobermans and their relentless barking created the perfect cinematic background racket for the savage gunfight that ensued. Had Benny not been semi conscious, lying in the gutter, he would most likely have fallen victim to the hail of bullets that killed seven of the gang members and seriously wounded the other three. How the Dobermans escaped injury was a miracle.

It was several hours later while resting in the prison ward of the hospital that he first met constable Larry MacDonald of the 1st Precinct in Manhattan. The constable was in his late twenties, had flaming red hair and a toned six foot eleven body. He looked more like a player for the NBA than a beat pounding cop.

"Rough night huh kid?" The constable said in a matter-of-fact way. "Most of your friends have taken up residency in the morgue tonight."

"What...what friends?" Benny groggily replied as he gradually began to awaken from the sedation he had received when he arrived at the hospital.

"Guess the med's haven't worn off yet kid!" The constable said.

Benny's eyes were beginning to focus as he took in his surroundings. He was enclosed on three sides by white curtains. There was a single table and chair to his left where the giant constable had settled himself. Benny's head was heavily bandaged and he had a large ace bandage on his left arm where he'd sustained a nasty cut from a sewer grate when he was knocked to the ground. His right hand was cuffed to the bed.

"Lucky kid is what cha are, a very lucky kid." The constable said.

"You call this lucky? Benny croaked as he pointed to his head and yanked on the handcuffs.

"Hey man, do ya know what happened ta the dogs...I mean are they okay...are they okay?"

"You mean the two black beasts and the wounded Lab?" The constable asked.

"Yah that's 'em. Are they okay? I'm responsible for 'em." Benny said anxiously.

The carrot topped giant surveyed Benny's face like he was doing a CAT Scan. He was considering Benny's possible involvement in the evening's mayhem.

"So give me their names kid." He snapped.

"Their names, their names? Why in God's name do you want to know that?" Benny demanded. He was still slightly drugged and it had not yet occurred to him why the officer's was questioning him.

"Hemmm. Just give me their names if you don't mind young man." He asked again with less censure.

"Whatever. Ruffus and Gladiator are the Dobs and Angus is the Lab. Satisfied? Are they okay?" He demanded.

"As a matter of fact they are, 'sept for Angus, he's got a broken leg but he'll survive." The constable replied.

"Whew! That's a relief. They're my buddies and old man MacDonald would croak if sumthin happened to his babies." Benny said half laughing.

"That's for sure!" The constable said forgetting himself. Benny was not too out-of-it to notice the familiarity.

"Sounds like you know the old man." Benny pried. Before the constable could say anything Benny pointed at the officer's badge that read: PC Lawrence MacDonald. The constable nodded and said,

"Uncle Angus, just like the Lab."

"No kidding, I didn't know his first name, its jus Mr. MacDonald to me." Benny said. He thought about the old man's love for his babies then asked the constable if Mr. MacDonald was very upset.

"Uncle Angus is in canine heaven right now. We won't hear anything but dog hero stories for the next six months. You gave him a reason for living tonight...or should I say the thugs that shot up lower Manhattan did." He laughed. "You're his new champion kid."

"Champion? Who me?" Benny looked confused. "All I did was get caught in the crossfire of a couple of local posy's is all." Benny replied indifferently.

"Not really kid, you held onto the Dobs through the whole ordeal and laid across Angus in the process. We were pretty certain you weren't involved but had to check you out anyway. Just procedure you understand, just procedure." The Constable explained as he leaned over Benny and unlocked the handcuff.

"Ya, Ya sure. Forgetaboutit! I'm just glad my four legged buddies are okay." Benny yawned before passing out.

Six

September - 10 - 2001

"Amy, I can't get out tonight for San Fran. I'm taking the 8:00 am from Newark so it looks like I won't make it back for our dinner date at *Windows*. I'm sorry baby." David sighed halfheartedly.

"Oh no David! I can't believe it. Not on my birthday!" Amy pouted. She milked the moment for a few more seconds then laughed. "That's okay sweetie, I'll want you all the more the day after," she paused for a moment then added, " but you'd better make it up to me."

David was feeling somewhat relieved. It would be much easier to break off their affair on a less auspicious occasion and he could delay the torture of the moment one day longer. "God I hate this part." He thought.

"Sure baby, sure. It'll be great!" David lied poorly. "Listen, Francine is just in the next room so I better cut it short. I'm real sorry baby. I'll call you from San Fran tomorrow. Luv ya...bye, bye."

"Good night my love. See you in a couple. Luv you too." Amy replied after the phone went dead.

"Well, I guess its just me, Clifford and twenty one candles tomorrow night." Amy moaned.

"How's that sound to you Clifford?"

"Meeeow." Clifford leaped from the back of the sofa onto Amy's lap and did his little get-comfortable circle dance, then laid himself down and turned on his motor.

"At least your one man I can always rely on to come when I call." She giggled. Just then the portable phone, which Amy had placed right beside her leg rang and Clifford jumped a foot in the air digging his claws into her legs.

"Oooooch!" She yelped. "Damn it, that hurt. Hello, oowa..."

Startled, her best friend Rachel exclaimed, "Amy, Amy, what's wrong are you okay honey?"

"Yes, no prob, Clifford just left a notch in my thigh, that's all." She whimpered. Clifford was hiding under a nearby chair with his head poking out from under its skirt. "You lunatic cat." She laughed, "no more catnip cocktails for you fella. I'm puttin you on kitty-valium from now on."

Rachel laughed. "Nice! Intoxicate your cat why don't cha. Poor Cliffy, is that how you treat all your men?"

"Ooooh!" Amy lamented. "David can't make it for my birthday tomorrow night. I wish I could put some Valium in his soup, maybe he'd ease up a bit...stop and smell the roses for a change."

"Honnney! When are you gonna get with it, these guys never settle down. Nothin satisfies em. He's the top honcho for an international company, he's got a beautiful brainy wife and he *still* needs something on the side." Rachel said in an exasperated wake-up tone.

"I know, I know. But he treats me like a queen when we're together." Amy groaned.

"Queens don't have to play second fiddle to anybody honey. You deserve better, when are you gonna finally see you're worth it?" Rachel didn't wait for Amy to qualify her inadequacy.

"Listen, now that your free, on...your...birthday...lets get together and have a blast.

"As long as we don't meet up with any of your Jesus freek buddies. I don't need any more sermons about goin to hell if I don't get rid of the adulterer." Amy said defiantly.

" I'm sorry about that. They're really wonderful folks ya know...sometimes they just get a little carried away. You'd think so too if ya met them under different circumstances. I guess we shoulda just gone for coffee the first time instead of a revival meeting." Rachel giggled.

"No kidding Rach. Anyway, sure! Why not? Let's do the town together. Where shall we go?" Amy asked

"Tell you what...I finish in the Towers late tomorrow so why don't we go upstairs to *Windows?*"

"Oh, I don't think so Rach. That's where David and I were supposed to go. I think it would only depress me to be there." Amy replied.

"Well, where else could we go? You deserve to have a wonderful day someplace special, not just cuz it's your 21st but because *you are very special* and I love you. Rachel exclaimed.

"Oooo Rach. You got me all teary eyed now. I love you too. And you too Clifford." She said nodding Clifford as she reached for a tissue.

"Let me think about it hon and I'll call you back later okay?" Rachel suggested.

"Rach."

"Yes Amy."

"Thanks for being my friend. Luv ya, bye bye."

"I luv you too. Talk to ya later hon, bye." Rachel said.

Amy placed the phone on its cradle that she had placed on the end table out of Clifford's view. He cautiously crept from the safety of his hiding place and looked from side to side then stared up at

Amy.

"Its okay you coward. C'mon up." She said while patting her lap. Clifford seemed to understand the lap-patting signal and with a single leap returned to the warmth of his mistress' legs. He gave her a single bthurrrr and settled in again.

Amy ruffled his ears and began petting him as she thought about the simplicity of a cat's life.

'God, I wish *my* life was as simple as Cliff's. Just look from side to side, leave the past behind and peacefully ease into the security of a relationship with someone I know will always be there to take care of me.'

"*Pink lady* with you now." An unfamiliar voice in her mind softly uttered. At the same moment

Clifford began a particularly loud purr.

"Huh? That's a weird thought. Sounded almost like a little girl speaking to me. Hem, strange." Amy reflected.

"Not you...*pink lady*." The childish voice added. Clifford's purring grew louder.

"What the hell?" Amy said out loud, turning from side to side. Clifford remained fixed in the comfort of kitty heaven purring peacefully in stark contrast to the wild drumbeat in Amy's chest.

She shivered and her body stiffened as her skin began to tingle. Her breathing came in shallow bursts. Then, without warning an invisible blanket of calm enveloped her and she slumped back, deep into the sofa. She sighed as if the weight of the world had slipped from her mind. Breathing deeply Amy fell into peaceful reverie.

For a moment all thought dissolved then a white screen appeared before her inner eye. As she watched, a children's drawing formed on the screen. First a stick character of a girl showed up. She had yellow hair and a sad face. Then beside her a pile of stones or rocks materialized. Finally a large white circle stood out from a gray sky. The vision lasted for several seconds then she drifted off to sleep.

Seven

September - 10 - 2001

After David's abrupt conversation with Amy ended he slouched down into his bar stool and stared silently into his glass of Johnny Walker. The ice melting in his glass mirrored the cold ache in his veins. A shudder of depression raced through his heart. He shook himself, picked up his glass lightly touching his lips, paused for a moment and downed it in one go. He grimaced slightly as the intense heat of the liquid flushed down his throat. He waited for the intensity of the feeling to subside then peered down the length of the bar and lifted his glass to the bartender.

"Be right with you Mr. Bryan." The bartender said. He stopped what he was doing and headed toward David picking up a bottle of David's favorite scotch on the way. "Another Mr. Bryan?" David grinned sardonically and raised his glass in reply.

The bartender poured him another and David nodded indifferently. "Damn! Of all the bars in this town I have to pick the one that's got a bartender with the same name as her cat." He muttered under his breath.

An attractive young woman sitting two stools away thought David was speaking to her. "What's that? Did you say something?" David was in no mood to chat with anyone but as he turned and glanced at the girl behind the voice he changed his mind, straightened himself and grinned at her with renewed appetite.

Rebecca should have been offended by the way he ogled her but David had a magnetism that disarmed certain kinds of people. Invariably they sensed in him something that compensated for his boorishness. The last decade had been a wild ride for David, success after success. With every successful deal he cut for his company his sense of invincibility grew, along with his air of superiority. His attitude didn't go unnoticed by his colleagues but the blacker the bottom line got, the more they turned a blind eye to his arrogance. It was a kind of subliminal blackmail in which the sting of abuse was softened by a cushion of cash.

The business world tolerated him as a pompous wunderkind but socially he lived an arid life. His wife Francine hardly knew the man he had become and saw him less and less as he leapfrogged across the globe doing deal after deal. Since his appointment as CEO of one of the largest

29

software corporations in the world, she had become little more than an accessory at business functions. Granted, she was exceedingly bright and in her late forties still a strikingly beautiful woman, but she was not enough to fill David's haunting sense of emptiness.

A world-class womanizer, he felt barren and unfulfilled, yet in no way penitent. His perception of virtue had become twisted and led him down the path of dubious side deals that, if brought to light would certainly topple his ivory tower. But he had become oblivious to the warning signs that disaster was stalking him. Still, every now and then a nagging feeling scratched at the mask of invulnerability he wore and for fleeting moments he felt there was something loftier within himself begging to be acknowledged.

'I guess like attracts like.' Rebecca thought. Then in unison both she and David asked, "Do we know each other?" They stopped short and began giggling. Then David noticed the United Airlines broach on Rebecca's jacket and remarked that he often flew United. Rebecca allowed for the possibility they may have met onboard a flight, and asked him if he usually flew out of Newark.

"I do, and as a matter of fact I'm flying out of Newark tomorrow morning at 8:00 o'clock." He replied.

"No kidding, I am too. I'm on flight 93, is that your flight?" She asked hopefully.

David reached inside his suit pocket, pulled out his ticket and examined it. "Same flight alright." He said.

"You look like the kind of fellow that always flies first class. I'm not on duty tomorrow, maybe we could meet for a drink or something in Frisco." Rebecca suggested unabashed.

"We just might do that." David said as he unconsciously slipped the ticket into the side pocket of his jacket. His fingers touched a folded piece of paper and he pulled it out to examine. It was an old email for Francine directed to his private address. He had received the email the previous the week and forgot to pass on to her. The message was from someone with an Internet 'nick' called *flowerf*. He knew of no one by that nickname but he often gave his private email address to women he met on his travels and could easily have forgotten her name. He noticed the recipient was

Francine, printed it out and stuffed it in his jacket pocket to give her later that night.

"Excuse me a moment, uh sorry, I don't know your name." He said

"Its Rebecca, Rebecca Saunders." She replied.

"Hi Rebecca, nice to meet you." He laughed awkwardly and extended his hand. "I'm David."

"A pleasure David, nice to meet you too." She grinned impishly and shifted to the stool next to his. "Do you mind?

"Not at all, what can I get you?" He asked while he scanned the email message.

"I'll have what you're having." She answered. Cliff was standing within earshot and immediately took a glass and poured her a double Johnny Walker.

As David reviewed the message he suddenly realized who had sent it. "Oh no, this is from Yasmine Faiz." He moaned. "She's in some kind of trouble." He added as if Rebecca and Cliff were supposed to know what he was talking about. He picked up his cell phone and pushed the speed dialer for his residence. It rang twice then Francine answered.

"Franny, Yasmine is in some kind of trouble. I just read an email she sent to my office for you."

David exclaimed.

At first Francine was jolted by the news since she had not heard from Yasmine for almost two years. She was excited to hear that Yasmine had contacted her but alarmed that she might be in danger. If David's interpretation of her dream the previous month was correct then maybe it had to do with Yasmine being pregnant.

"David, please read me what it says." She pleaded as her heart beat faster.

"Sure, sure Franny, here it is: *David, please forward this message to Francine right away…aunty Francine, I need your help desperately. Y is in serious danger. I can't explain now. Please be by your telephone tomorrow morning at 10:00 am your time and I will try to call. I will explain everything then. I love you both. Yasmine."* But Francine, I got this email last week and forgot it was in my pocket." He added in disgust.

"Oh God no! What can it mean?" She cried.

"Wait a minute, here's the return address. Write it down." He commanded. He spelled the address carefully then had her repeat it back to him. "Sorry about that, at least you're back in touch with her. Let me know what's going on if you can reach her. Listen I gotta go, I'm in a meeting. See you in a couple of days. Luv ya, Bye." He didn't wait for a reply.

Terror rippled through her body. She broke out in a cold sweat and feeling dizzy sat down on a stool beside the telephone table. She reached for a bottle on the shelf above the table and poured herself a stiff drink. As she placed the bottle down she glanced at the label - Johnny Walker. Francine shook her head and laughed cynically knowing David was probably lying about his business meeting. She took a long drink then slumped over the table, buried her head in her arms and began to cry.

Eight

July - 15 - 1983

"Push harder Yousef!" Yasmine yelled in glee. "I can almost see over the trees." She clutched the chain handles of the swing tightly and threw all the weight of her seven-year old body into each forward thrust. "Higher Yousef, higher!" Then the swing began to lose momentum. "Yousef, why did you stop pushing?" Yasmine dared not turn her head at the height she had reached - she was already pushing the limits of her fearlessness.

Jasmine whined. "Yousef where are you? You promised to push me over the trees." Yousef did not reply. A dark skinned man had his hand over the boy's mouth. When the terrified child had been subdued the man dragged him into the trees beside a knoll that surrounded the playground.

Yasmine's swing slowed enough for her to drag her feet in the sand bringing her to a full stop. She swung the chain link swing seat around so she could see what Yousef was up to but he was no where to be seen.

"Yousef." She called out. "Where did you go? You promised. Yousef!" She yelled indignantly. There was no answer. At that moment a gray van sped from behind a tall hedge of cedars, turned sharply missing Yasmine by inches, careened around the concrete border of the playground, squealed into the parking lot then headed for the exit to the motorway.

Yasmine sat paralyzed in fear as the wild frenzy unfolded. When the van raced by she saw the dark angry face of a man glaring at her. "Be sure hands are tied and mouth taped." Abdul barked at his brother Ahmed.

" Stop commanding me brother." Ahmed shouted back in anger.

"Allahu Akbar - praise Allah, for once he succeed." Abdul uttered. The van left the parking lot and entered the motorway heading out of Oxford toward Birmingham.

Moments after Yousef was abducted Francine returned with three bottles of soda. "Where is that little imp Yousef hiding Yasmine, my sweetpea?' She chirped. As she drew near to Yasmine she saw the look of terror on the child's face.

"What's wrong Yasmine? What happened?" Francine exclaimed? She crouched beside the shaking child, dropped the sodas on the ground and embraced her. Yasmine relaxed slightly as Francine stroked her hair. "Its okay sweetie, its okay. Tell me what happened Yasmine - just tell me what happened."

"I don't know auntie Fran. Yousef was pushing my swing and then he was gone. I didn't see where he went auntie." She whimpered throwing her arms around Francine's neck. "And then I got really scared when a mean man in a big lorry almost hit me." Yasmine cried. Francine hugged the Yasmine tight to her breast as the child's tension released in a squall otears.

From what Yasmine had told her, Francine was certain Yousef had been kidnaped. She swung her head from side to side fearing that whoever took him might still be in the area. "Yasmine honey, can you walk?" The child shook her head. "Come with auntie Franny to the car honey, we have to leave right now." She said while trying to conceal her growing fear. "What about Yousef auntie?" The child asked in concern.

"We need to get some help honey, okay?" Francine answered with as much calm as she could summon as terrifying scenes of the nightmare that brought the children into her care flashed before her inner eye.

Francine scooped the child up without another word and ran toward the parking lot. Yasmine suddenly realized Yousef was in serious trouble and began to cry again.

"Auntie Fran, is Yousef going to die?" She asked wiping her tears.

"Of course not honey. Don't be scared, he'll be okay." But Francine was not at all certain Yousef would be okay, or that they would find him. She began to shake, trying in vain to hold back her own tears as the nightmare scenes of seven years before played over and over again in her mind.

A few moments later she and Yasmine pulled out of the parking lot and headed toward downtown Oxford. Despite her growing panic something made her turn her head and glance at the entrance sign that read: *Ladymore Park*. The sign had just been painted pink and the first four black wooden letters - *Lady* - reattached, partially completing the park's name. For some unknown reason it occurred to Francine that the sign was saying something about a lady on pink or a lady in pink...then she heard an unfamiliar voice in her mind say, "*Pink lady.*"

Nine

In 1968 Donald Heathrow dropped out of Columbia University and traveled to the Far East determined to find and meet with a famous swami. Donald was an excellent student and his family hoped he would follow in his father's footsteps and become a psychiatrist. He loved studying the fascinating workings of the mind and saw in that path a fulfilling life. However, he became disillusioned with where it had taken his father. The majority of his father's clients were high profile actors, politicians and Wall Street business people and over time the family's status in society had became more important to him than the healing influence of his work.

"You've sold your integrity for a few pieces of silver." Donald hollered at his father during one of their frequent squabbles.

"You'll do well to focus more on the promising future your studies and our influence have in store for you rather than listen to the hallucinogenic babbling of your hippy friends." His father countered in his most intimidating voice. Dr. Ramsey Heathrow always spoke softly, as if it were a prerequisite of his profession, but his apathetic approach had the same power to wound as if he had shouted.

Donald felt that his father gave with one hand and took with the other. He may have helped pacify the confusion in the minds of his patients but there was little doubt he left them empty and cold in the heart. To Donald mind, the heart was where the true healing occurred.

When Alan Fremont, a high school buddy, returned from India bringing incredible stories of a famous holy man materializing objects out of thin air, Donald thought his friend had been smoking too much hash. But he couldn't get past the fact that when he'd last seen his friend the year before, he was being treated for; Post Traumatic Syndrome, by a colleague of his father's.

Now, miraculously Alan appeared almost serene. Alan's horrendous experience in Vietnam had apparently somehow been neutralized.

"Hey Al, what's up with you, you seem to have gotten rid of those demons you brought back from Nam? Donald inquired.

"It's Baba man, the swami smoothed me right out when I was ready to chuck the whole damn thing." Alan replied in a mellow voice. It was obvious he was high on something, but there was no doubt Alan had changed for the better. When he dropped out of his therapy sessions and headed for India he was on heavy doses of antidepressants and tranquillizers. Donald didn't even know he had gone until he received a distressing card from Alan that was post marked from Calcutta.

'Just the place for me man. People die in the streets here all the time. I might just as well join em. It was good knowing you Donny boy.' That was all he wrote. He signed it 'A. Lost cause!'

Donald remembered the feeling of utter helplessness he felt when he read the postcard. "What the hell good is therapy if it can't touch a good guy like Alan?" He felt angry, helpless and frustrated. His father actually showed signs of compassion and tried to comfort him by explaining that some people are just too far gone when they begin therapy. At the time it made sense, but it didn't help.

Then one day, six months later Alan showed up at Columbia after Donald's last class. "How about a cup a java man?" Alan said with a big grin.

"Alan. Its you." Donald took him in his arms and gave him a big hug. " I thought I'd never....I mean." Donald stammered as tears filled his eyes. Then Alan cut him off.

"Thought I was worm bait hunh? Not yet old pal, not just yet!" Donald stepped back and looked at his friend who, to him had been dead but now was vitally alive, more so than he could remember ever seeing him.

For the next several hours Alan brought Donald up to date on his yearlong adventure. He explained that one particularly depressing day he was standing beside the Ganges river about midnight - ready to jump, when a pretty little Indian girl with dark hair and blue eyes - maybe five years old, came up to him and put her hand in his as if they were related. "You know man, it was as if she was my baby sister or sumpthin." He told Donald that he looked down at the little girl and she was just staring out across the river as natural as if the two of them did that all the time.

"I didn't have a clue what to think. I can tell ya though that I lost my desire right away for the deep six. Man, I just stood there and started cryin, I couldn't help it, it was like the nightmare of Nam just slipped from my hands like yesterday's garbage. First time I cried since my entire company got whacked in Nam - everyone 'sept me that is. Then the kid says, *"Pink lady* got message." She hands me a picture of this guy with a wild Afro hairdo in an orange gown. I looked at the picture then turned it over and found an address had been hand written on it. Then I looked down to ask the kid what it meant but she was gone. I mean she was really gone man! Just vanished! I nearly freaked."

Donald figured that in his state of mind at the time Alan could easily be hallucinating, which could explain the strange meeting with the child. He decided to let that go and asked about the picture.

"It was Baba man. Like I said, the picture had his address on the back. I figured, what the hell, I got nothin to lose, why not check it out. So next mornin I'm off to Puttaparti in Southern India. I get there a week later - never forget it, it was July 6th and there was this festival called Guru Poornima happenin - thousands of people swamped the place and I just sorta got pulled along with the crowd." Alan glazed over for a moment as if he was reliving the experience. "It was beautiful man, I mean the sweetest thing I ever saw."

Donald spent the next half hour listening to the details of the event. He said if Nam was hell, the festival with Baba was heaven. "I never got near him but at one point I was sittin, buried in the middle of maybe two thousand people about a hundred feet away from him and he looks straight at me, as if I was right in front of him. It was like a lightning bolt shot straight through me man, I swear!"

Tears filled Alan's eyes and he buried his head in his hands. Donald was speechless. He'd never seen his friend like this and had no idea what to make of the strange story. It sounded like a good drug trip but definitely too far out to be real.

Donald was heading into exams and didn't see Alan again for several weeks. When he met him it was in a bookstore café where Alan was working. He still appeared totally mellow, not at all like the half crazed guy he knew the year before. Still intrigued by their last conversation and Alan's consistent state of serenity, Donald thought he would pursue the subject a little further.

"Say Alan, got anything on that Baba fellow you mentioned last time we talked?" He asked half seriously.

"You betcha! Be right back." Alan came back a few minutes later with three books and handed them to Donald. "Check em out man. Let me know what ya think. I gotta get back to work now. I luv ya man." Alan headed to the back of the store while Donald watched him in awe.

Donald went to the café portion of the store, ordered a Latte and opened one of the books. As he turned the pages he began to feel a sensation that had eluded him for some time. He had not read a single word, yet he felt a warm surge flood his body. Later he recalled it as a sense of hope. When the next semester began Donald was on his way to India without the slightest idea of what to expect.

Ten

May - 24 – 1991

"It's gonna cave Smokie, its gonna cave!" Smokie's dad yelled above the roar of the fire.

"We gotta try pop, we can't just leave him there." Smokie hollered back.

A little boy sat cowering in the far corner of the room - a blanket pulled up above his nose. The fire below had weakened the floor and Jack's experienced eye told him it couldn't hold the weight of a full-grown man.

"We hafta come through the window over there, son." Jack screamed through the sound of collapsing walls coming from somewhere behind them. He knew there wouldn't be enough time. Far too often in his thirty years with the department, Captain Seagram watched helplessly while fire victims, rendered unreachable by flames, perished right before his eyes. Every face was permanently displayed like a wall of shame in his mind. It didn't help that he'd saved far more than he'd lost, those terrified faces reappeared, reminding him of his failure to fulfill his sacred trust - saving lives.

The thought that his own son, who wasn't even supposed to be in the building, might succumb to the same fate was too much for him to bear. He pulled Smokie aside and with pick in hand, carefully put one foot in front of the other as he walked the perimeter of the smoke filled room.

"Smokie," He choked, "tell them below to get the ladder up to this window."

"Okay pop." Smokie pressed the call button on his two-way radio and yelled into it. "Hello somebody, anybody, we need the ladder on the third floor, back side window."

"Oh God, that sounds like Smokie on the walkie. How the hell did he get up there? One of the firefighters yelled.

"Never mind that, what does he need?" His commander demanded.

"The ladder, they need it on the third floor back side window!" He replied. Within minutes the ladder was at the window and a firefighter was on his way up.

"They're almost here!" Smokie yelled, as his dad got closer to the petrified child. With the fire raging behind Smokie, his dad knew if the three of them were going to make it out safely, they had to contain the fire.

"Smokie, get in here and shut the door tight." He yelled. "When I open the window we don't want the flames sucked into this room." He knew he had only one chance to do what he was planning. Once the door was shut they only had half a minute before the smoke overwhelmed them. Shaking in fear, Smokie took one step inside the door and slammed it shut.

In one smooth movement Captain Jack picked up the child in one arm, opened the window with his free hand and passed the boy to the waiting firefighter. Smoke poured out the open window and a moment later the two men took their first breath of fresh air since entering the building.

"Now us Smokie." His dad said under his breath. " You saw how I made it over here son, you do the same." His dad said waving him on. "Com'on son, com'on!"

"Okay pop. I'm comin pop!" Smokie yelled.

"Just take it easy son, be careful please." His dad pleaded, sweat and smoke smearing his face.

The firefighters had managed to get the fire out on the floor just below them but the third floor, where Smokie and his dad were located, was a blazing inferno. Smokie inched his way around the edge of the room. He was about ten feet from his dad and a bit more from the window when his safety shoe punched through the floor. Captain Seagram's instinct to protect his only son was greater than his firefighting experience and he jumped forward. His bravest moment as a firefighter met the weakness point in the floor. His foot found nothing but air as the entire floor collapsed and he fell into the flooded apartment below with Smokie right behind him.

A moment later Smokie crumpled onto his dad as they hit a kitchen counter then tumbling to the floor in a heap. The next thing Smokie knew he was sitting on a chair in the gutted apartment opposite his dad who was relaxing on a burned out sofa.

"Well Smokie my boy, we saved the kids. Right now the little one is with his mom and dad in back of an ambulance. He's gonna be just fine." Jack said with a satisfying look on his face.

Smokie wondered how his dad knew that. "Must be a professional guess." He thought. Then suddenly he realized where they were. "Say pop, what are we doing here. Shouldn't we be gettin outta the building?" Smokie had absolute faith in his dad and would never question his authority or experience, but then he'd never been in a real firefight with him either.

He loved and respected his father dearly. Ever since he first tried on his dad's fire hat - his head disappearing inside - he spoke of nothing else but joining his dad one day in the department. "I'm gonna fight fires with you pop!" He said.

"Okay Billy boy. Let's see now. A real firefighter needs a special name, hem...I know from now on we'll call you Smokie." Captain Seagram laughed, hugging his son beneath the hat. From that moment on the name stuck and everyone, even schoolmates called him Smokie.

Smokie was visiting his dad at East 29th Fire Station when the alarm sounded. "Time to get some first hand experience Smokie. Suit up and we'll follow our boys from Ladder #7 to the fire." Captain Seagram said with a big grin.

It was a single alarm fire, the second floor kitchen in a Manhattan brownstone. It was 1991 and Billy was seventeen, 5' 7", rugged and handsome with short sandy hair and blue eyes. He had just finished high school and told his father on graduation day that he'd decided to join the department after the summer on his eighteenth birthday. As the Captain, his dad decided it would be okay to initiate him a few weeks early. It was definitely not procedure but what was rank for anyway. Besides, Smokie was only supposed to observe at the scene.

Jack had no idea how his son ended up in the building. By the time he and Smokie arrived at the fire the second floor was already ablaze. Jack jumped out of his car and began giving orders. Everything happened so fast, as it usually did in these situations, and when he said, "You two come with me." Smokie was standing with a group of firefighters and thought his dad meant him. Whatever happened, here he was now with his dad, cooling his heels in the burned out brownstone.

'Wait a minute.' Smokie thought. 'Did pop say, "kids"? There was only one little boy.' He looked at his dad who was lounging on the sofa as if it were their backyard hammock and they had all the time in the world. "Pop! What's goin on? Something strange is happenin. This doesn't add up."

"Smokie." His dad said solemnly. "I want you to know son I've always loved you, and I always will! I'm gonna be with you through thick and thin son, and even though you won't get to be the fireman you hoped to be, you got real important things to do later on. It had to be this way I guess, anyway that's what they're telling me. I'm proud of the choices you made for your future Smokie. Please tell your mom I love her and I sure am sorry I have to leave her so soon. I'll be seein you again on your birthday."

As his dad spoke these last words Smokie's attention was drawn to the smashed kitchen window where two firefighters had just crawled into the apartment. When he glanced back toward where his dad had been lying, he was gone.

The firefighters walked right past him toward the kitchen counter where Smokie watched them stoop down and gently lift up the lifeless form of another firefighter. Under him was his dad, Captain Seagram.

"Smokie's got a hell of a gash on his forehead but he's got a pulse." One of the men said. He felt for life in the Captain but found none. "Ah Geez, not you Jack." Tears filled the firefighter's eyes as he pulled off his glove and tenderly brushed ash from the side of his Captain's face.

Three days later Smokie woke up in a hospital bed with his mother sitting beside him holding his hand and crying.

Eleven

2001 & 1968

Someone had tracked in an October leaf and it lay at the foot of the wooden angel. Meereka ignored Benny's question, she looked down from her drawing and pointed to the leaf.

"Not die yet...*Pink lady* say, 'soon.'"

"*Pink lady* says, 'not die yet' - Meereka means the flowers." All eyes shifted to Smokie who had knelt down beside Benny. Benny nodded his head in agreement.

Francine gently tugged Dr. Heathrow's sleeve and whispered. "Did you hear anything?" Donald turned his eyes from side to side so that only Francine saw his silent reply.

Something was definitely happening and the fact that he and Francine were not seeing it did not negate the possibility of its reality. It had been thirty years since he first witnessed phenomena that could not be rationally explained. The scene flashed before his inner eye.

Moments after retrieving his knapsack at the arrivals level in Bangalore, Donald was accosted by a tall muscular Indian man brandishing a switchblade. Donald grappled with the fellow for his bag while his assailant swung wildly with the deadly weapon. What seemed like only a minute later Donald watched the mugger run off with his bag and dissolve into the crowd.

He looked down at the spot where his bag had been a few minutes before. His passport, money and clothing were in the knapsack. He sat down on the edge of the circular carousel and heaved a deep sigh - not of resignation, since he had not yet come to grips with his situation, but a sigh of relief. Under the circumstances the feeling made no sense whatsoever. He imagined he might be feeling somewhat like his friend Alan had just before his enchanted encounter with the little girl - hopeless.

"I bet you left your travelers checks *and* receipts in the knapsack didn't you?" A coarse female voice asked cynically. The question originated from the far side of the carousel.

"Pardon me!" Donald said.

"Seen it before. People think, 'what are the odds it will happen to me?' Then, sure enough, it does." She laughed. A slender, heavily tanned woman, maybe sixty years old with long salt and pepper hair tied in a ponytail, came around the carousel and introduced herself. "Hi, my name's Chez Shift, what's yours?"

"What? Oh, uh, I'm Donald, Donald Heathrow." He replied a little taken back. The woman looked American to Donald but had a faint Indian accent, which rendered her boldness curiously appealing. Donald smirked, a picture of a short Indian Kathryn Hepburn popped into his mind. If Chez noticed his expression, she didn't betray it.

"You look like you could use a friend. Come with me young man." She said firmly. Chez headed toward a sign that said *Park* in English and Hindi. Without thinking, he obediently followed her. Five minutes later the two were motoring away from the airport complex. For reasons he couldn't fathom, Donald relaxed and enjoyed the moment.

"Uncertainty can be very freeing young fella." Chez said. "No past, no future, only now." He really didn't understand but for some reason it made a strange kind of sense to Donald. He decided to go with the flow of it and see where it took him. "That's the spirit." She said as if sensing his mood. "Surrender invites a person to their destiny and brings along the power to achieve it." Her manner was confident and certain with no frayed edges of doubt.

Donald's mid section was dancing. His bohemian spirit was reborn. "This is living!" He whispered unconsciously. Chez grinned.

Twelve

June - 2 - 2001

"I'm off to Capacelli's chief." Benny hollered over the din of the afternoon crowd in Precinct #1. He negotiated his way down the congested stairs and called out to the desk sergeant again. "What can I get cha?"

Sergeant Steven Savino looked nothing like his Italian father. "All Irish genes." His dad used to kid him. "Not a single wop hair on your body." Nevertheless, the sergeant was a bit short for a cop. Like his dad, he was only 5'- 6" but his hair was the color of beach sand and his eyes as green as a Leprechaun's fedora.

"Get me a grande cappuccino Benny, and its sergeant not chief." He laughed.

"Well, that's the department's mistake isn't it?" He joked. "Be back in twenty." Benny yelled, exiting the precinct with a backward wave.

'I love that kid.' The sergeant thought smiling. 'He's about the brightest thing in this place.'

"Hey-a Angelo, I gotta three order-a for a you-a." Benny said as he burst through the door of Capacelli's fine Italian Bistro.

"Anything-a for you-a, senor Benito. What-a can-a I get-a for you-a?" The corpulent proprietor asked. Angelo Capecelli wore his work tux like a straight jacket. His every move was a monumental achievement. Benny felt weary just watching him. Capecelli's had the best specialty coffee near the precinct so he was a regular at the Bistro a least twice a day keeping the boys in blue, who had a taste for high octane caffeine, satisfied.

"Two grande cappuccinos for the chief and Mac, and a tall iced coffee for our man Leroy. Oh, and a dozen of your best donuts to go." Benny added with a snicker.

"Senor Benito!" Angelo whined. "You-a know we don't gotta no donuts. Dis ees-a classy place-a."

"Okay." Benny said. "I forgot. Then give me a dozen of your best Italian pastries."

45

Whenever the two kibitzed with each other they played a little game of *straight face*. Who broke into a smile the first was the loser. This time it was a tie as a pair of belly laughs filled the almost empty restaurant.

"I get-a you nex-a time-a Senor Benito!" Angelo laughed.

"Not! Benny replied. "Not!"

After the incident with the street gangs and his dogs, Angus Macdonald took a special interest in Benny. Within two weeks he, Meereka and his mother were relocated to a small but comfortable coach house above the Macdonald's estate garage. Angus and his nephew, constable Larry MacDonald made an arrangement to have Benny do goffer work around the precinct to pay the rent. With his new job Benny earned enough to cover the family's expenses that provided him with the freedom and opportunity to pursue his growing interest in detective work.

Thirteen

1946 - 1951

After Nadira's funeral Ibrahim left Jordan for the holy city of Mecca in Saudi Arabia to seek understanding and spiritual solace. He did not return for five years. He left the day-to-day operation of the *House of Faiz* with his assistant Abdullah Al Ammad who he had made a partner. The two young men had been close friends since childhood and Ibrahim trusted and loved Abdullah like a brother.

Abdullah also had deep love and respect for his friend and considered him his spiritual mentor. He would often say to friends and men of business, "No better servant does Allah have on this earth then Ibrahim." Many believed that the favor of Allah was the great gift bestowed upon those who honored one of his devout servants. For that reason, many chose to do business with Ibrahim and his company.

But Ibrahim's heart was true, he believed the success of his business was an instrument Allah had given him to share with all he found who were in need. He would not allow it to rule his life nor would he allow his personal loss to poison his mind or harden his heart. His sabbatical to Mecca was made in search of a deeper understanding into the changing tides of fortunes in life and to consecrate his devotion to his God.

When, in 1950 Ibrahim's heart led him back to his homeland, he returned via England to negotiate a trade agreement for the *House of Faiz* with wealthy merchants that Abdullah had been cultivating for a year. Ibrahim respected the engineering accomplishments of the ancient Romans, and when his business was complete, he decided to visit the spa's they had constructed in Bath before he returned to Jordan. It was there that he met Jacqueline Buchannan.

His new business associates gave him letters of introduction to business connections in the area. They were wealthy landowners and gave Ibrahim the royal treatment when he arrived. While he was taking a tour of the ancient city of Bath by the head of the family business, Ibrahim was introduced to the patriarch's daughter.

Jacqueline Buchanan was a stunning twenty nine year old widow. She now lived most of the year in the country. During the war she had spent a good deal of time at the family's residence in London as a hospital volunteer.

Her philosophical bearing suggested much more experience than her twenty-nine years. Despite her obvious worldly wisdom, an unearthly beauty lay close beneath the surface. Her ancestry was Scottish and much of the family land was devoted to the growth of industrial rapeseed that was mainly used to produce lubricants. Since Ibrahim's parents had been farmers he possessed a little knowledge about this particular crop. Many of his business associates dealt in olive oil and he had heard of the development of a certain form of rapeseed that produced an edible vegetable oil called Canola.

Ibrahim discussed this with Jacqueline and in good humor commented that her parents had probably disposed of more inferior harvests than *his* parents had produced in total in the many years they had farmed before moving to Aqaba. Jacqueline complimented Ibrahim on the significant accomplishments he had made in his life from such humble beginnings, then added, "Allah has seen fit to shine his light upon you."

Ibrahim admired the deep insight Jacqueline possessed and asked her what God she worshiped.

"With respect dear Ibrahim, there is but one God. He wears many masks and bears many names with which to attract the devotional eye and ear of the beholder." Ibrahim was enchanted with Jacqueline's depth of spiritual insight and invited her to join him for tea at his temporary home in Ealing that he was sharing with his son Mika'ill and their servant. Mika'ill took an instant liking to his father's new friend. Few women had graced their home while he and his father lived in Mecca and the boy, having no recollection of a mother, was drawn to her genuine maternal warmth.

Ibrahim quickly learned Jacqueline's spiritual interests extended well beyond his simple devotion. He was surprised at the tolerance he allowed himself as she gently eased him into a far more elaborate and deeper definition of God's universal embrace.

"Dear Miss Buchanan, since birth the name of Allah has sweetened my every thought and been food for my hungry spirit. Allah has laid the fruit of many trees at my table. Alas, sour has been the taste of its most heavenly gifts. Yet my heart remains steadfast and devoted to Him."

Prior to his visit, Jacqueline had learned from their mutual friends of the untimely passing of Ibrahim's wife and of the tragic death of his family before that. "Each of us has a life path dear Ibrahim, what the Eastern teachings refer to as *dharma*. It is our chosen vehicle to serve and love our fellow-man and the surest road back to our true home in God." She explained her philosophy without a trace of sympathy. Jacqueline knew that to enable one's sorrow was to expand it. She spoke as one who sees her fellow pilgrim on the path of life as one with herself, to be supported, encouraged, and inspired but never pitied.

From that day on Ibrahim and Jacqueline became steadfast friends. He extended his stay indefinitely in England and Jacqueline moved to her family's residence in Mayfair to be near him. Then, on one of Ibrahim's visits into London to discuss the possibilities of entering the American market with his new British business associates, he met Jacqueline at her flat for the first time.

While Jacqueline went for her wrap, Ibrahim studied a wall decorated with child-like paintings. Each had been carefully framed and arranged with love. Beneath the gallery was a small round circular table covered with an embroidered cloth that hung to the floor. On it stood a small gold-framed picture of a little girl. Etched on the frame were the words, '*Pink lady* - a gift from God.'

Jacqueline quietly entered the room and stood in silence behind Ibrahim while he read the inscription. As he turned and looked at her face, she smiled sadly. A single tear trickled down her face and she whispered, "My daughter was autistic. *Pink lady* was the nickname she called herself. The day the war ended she passed to spirit in my arms. It was her fifth birthday. Her last words were, '*pink lady* see you again, when you ready to come home.'"

Fourteen

October - 5 - 2001

When confronted with images that are beyond belief, for some people an invisible safety valve suddenly shuts down their emotional sensors. Their world becomes surreal, a holographic movie that swirls around them, wild and palpable, yet unable to touch them. It's like a nightmare with bizarre entertainment value, similar to a horror film that builds fearful anticipation to a crescendo. Then in a flash, the images overwhelm the senses with terror. It's a weird dichotomy, like feeling feel vitally alive in the face of death.

Francine was still standing on that island of disbelief, remote and insulated, unable to accept her part in the nightmare. The dream had absolutely no value yet it was familiar. She wondered why familiar felt safe. Donald explained that fear of the unknown was an unacceptable alternative to walking through fear, a condition that kept millions of people stuck in a dysfunctional life. Now that the spell was broken, Francine should have been able to shake the images from her mind, but they remained. She clung to them like a drowning person grasps whatever is nearest, even when they realize the shore is near.

The holograph replayed in her mind as the strange scene unfolded with Benny, Smokie and the wooden statue. She wondered, " How often have I heard the name *pink lady* since that terrible day?" She was glad Jacqueline and Ibrahim had not been there to experience what she and so many others had to live through. Would mummy have believed it? "Probably." She considered. "She believed anything was possible."

Francine wondered if the prophet saw Gabriel like this wooden statue when he was given the verses to the Qur'an. 'Perhaps he was transported to another world, some place of incredible beauty. That seemed appropriate. Or perhaps it was as simple as this little scene in which a voice seemed to be speaking only to her two friends." She wanted to know why she couldn't hear or see as they could. Why could some see and hear these things while others were left to wonder. Why was she left out? Her heart was aching. But still, she could not touch the images she had not been able to allow in for all these years.

Donald slipped his hand in hers and squeezed it. 'Had he heard her thoughts?' She wondered. She knew he was highly perceptive, even intuitive. Right now she didn't care. Benny turned and looked up at her with compassion. God how she loved this kid, so many people had been changed forever these last few weeks and Benny was right in the heart of it all. 'Is he lost too?' She asked herself. 'God knows he too has suffered great loss.'

Benny looked up at Francine and nodded as if agreeing with the voice in his head. "Meereka says, '*pink lady* was there, and, it's okay to cry now.'

Donald squeezed Francine's hand again. Tears began to fill her eyes as a great swell of emotion rippled through her body. "Oh my dear God it hurts so much!" She cried. She doubled over as the ache in her heart grew. Francine's body shook violently as Donald helped her to take a seat in the front pew a few feet from where the wooden angel lay. Smokie and Benny immediately drew near enough to offer their unspoken support. Smokie gently laid his hand on Francine's shoulder. Then the two watched as Meereka walked over beside her, reached up and placed her little hand on Francine's forehead. The shaking immediately ceased and Francine calmed, continuing to weep softly.

Donald glanced at the two men as if to ask, "Did *pink lady* do that?" Smokie nodded.

"What is she doing now?" Donald whispered.

"She's looking up at you and holding your hand." Benny replied. "Wait a minute...she says 'close eyes.'"

Dr. Heathrow immediately complied. He gasped as a brilliant pink light blazed before his inner vision. In the center was little Meereka. She held out two flowers just like those in the drawings Benny had shown them earlier.

"Must help save flowers." She said. "Auntie Franny knows." The vision faded and she was gone. For a moment Donald held his eyes shut. 'Something else about the two flowers, but what?' He thought.

From deep within Donald sighed then sat down beside Francine. He put his arm around her shoulder and waited for the right moment to speak. Finally she sat up and leaned her head against his shoulder. Then he drew her closer.

51

Donald knew the answer to the question he was going to ask but also knew that Francine had buried it. He also knew now was the time for her to release the wound. "Fran, we need to ask you something? Is that okay?" She nodded once. "Does 'auntie Franny' mean anything to you?" Francine was stunned for a moment then sat bolt upright and turned toward Donald.

"Where did you here that name?" Donald could see the urgency in her tear stained face.

"Meereka just used it. She also said, 'Must help save flowers.' Does it mean anything to you?"

Despite the significance of what Donald had just said to her she felt herself giving in to a cynical notion. "Now *he's* hearing from her too!" A moment later she remembered the last time she had heard the phrase 'auntie Franny' spoken to her was over two years ago. 'Auntie Franny, I am sorry I can't help it. Finding Yousef is more important to me than anything else.' That was the last time she heard from Yasmine.

Francine buried that heartache along with the lie she had been living with David. Little did she know the depth of agony that was yet to be laid upon her heart. Then, on the eve of that wretched day there was David's call and his reference to Yasmine's email. Naturally she wrote to Yasmine immediately, but the email message bounced back. She researched it with her Internet server, but the address had been blocked.

She knew there was something more, something vitally important, but it was just an echo. Donald studied her face. He could feel her struggle. "What is it Franny? What are you feeling?" Francine shook her head then whispered.

"Its locked up Donald...I don't know what it is. I want to remember but it just won't come."

Fifteen

August -11 - 2001

"Hey Captain Fox, how come we don't have a dalmatian doggy in the station?" Smokie asked with a childish grin. Smokie hid something behind his back while he waited for the Captain to reply. Roger Fox knew the boy standing beside fire engine #47 all too well. Smokie had become like a son to him since his predecessor Captain Seagram, Smokie's dad, died ten years before. That was the dark day of Smokie's departure into another world.

"Okay, I'll bite, I'll bite, I know you Smokie, you got something up your sleeve. C'mon, tell me what's up." He was playing Smokie's game, enjoying it and struggling to keep a straight face. He thought, 'Twenty five years with the department and I still wonder why bad things happen to good people.' It took him back to a strange experience.

Two summers ago at the department's annual picnic while everyone was eating, the Captain stepped away from the table for a quiet moment when he noticed Smokie sitting by himself. The air was still and warm and he was dangling his bare feet over the edge of a dock, gazing peacefully out across a placid lake. He felt drawn to the lad and quietly took a seat beside him.

"Its just a dream Captain Fox." Smokie uttered in a monotone voice. Smokie nailed the captain's unspoken question. 'How did he do that?' He wondered. The Captain looked at Smokie who was staring straight ahead in a daze.

"Is that where you are Smokie?" He asked. Smokie turned his head and smiled sadly. For just an instant it was not the face the Captain knew, but the look of one who understood his deep sorrow.

It was not the only time the boy had shaken the Captain's concept of reality. There was also that old woman. 'God, what was that all about?' He wondered.

He and Smokie were in the lunchroom playing dominoes six month before when the alarm sounded. As usual the department swung into action and the Captain watched to see that everything went smoothly. Smokie glanced up from the game, much the same as he had just done a moment before. His eyes glazed over and he said, "The old woman is in the basement."

Captain Fox asked Smokie what he meant but Smokie just grinned and pointed to the dominoes and said, "It your turn Captain Fox."

The Captain didn't know what to think but suddenly had an impulse to find out who called in the alarm. He went to the intercom, called down to dispatch and asked about the call-in. "One of the relatives lives next door and saw the flames Captain." The girl replied.

"Is there, that is... did they say anything about an old lady?" He asked feeling awkward.

"How did you know Captain? The caller was terrified she may have already succumbed to the smoke because she sleeps during the day on the second floor." The dispatcher replied.

"This is going to sound crazy but, uh, get the engine on the horn and tell them to check the basement as soon as they arrive!" The captain ordered.

"Ya, sure, sure Captain." She replied.

Twenty minutes later dispatch called and confirmed that the firefighters located the woman safe in the basement. Captain Fox sat down again and asked, "Smokie, you were right. The old woman was in the basement. But how..."

Looking up at the captain with a clueless expression Smokie asked, "What old woman Captain?" Then he placed the winning domino on the table, threw up his arms and yelled, "Hurrah! I beat you Captain Fox."

The blow that Smokie received to his head when he fell through the floor of the burning brownstone onto his dad's body stole his life. That's what everyone in the department thought but Captain Fox was no longer certain that was true.

For ten years Smokie did odd jobs around the station. He swabbed floors, cleaned toilets, polished the firefighter's dress shoes and buckles - 'anything to keep him out of harm's way,' that's what the Captain thought. Smokie was Twenty Seven, but acted more like Seven, a wonderful Seven Year old - an angel.

Captain Fox tapped his feet and tried to look stern but the corners of his mouth kept tweaking, betraying the grin he struggled to control.

"We've got one, we've got one Captain Fox!" Smokie yelled in glee. He held up a DVD of '101 Dalmatians' and giggled. The Captain welled up and shook his head in wonder.

'If that poor kid is lost and the rest of us are normal I wonder whose better off?' He thought. The Captain took the DVD from Smokie just as a cute idea came to him. "But Smokie, we've only got room for one doggy here. "You've brought in 101 of them."

Smokie immediately stopped laughing and appeared very concerned. He took the DVD back, studied the title and frowned. Then his face lit up and he grabbed the Captain tight around the shoulder. "Oh Captain Fox, I bet you're making a joke. Jokes are a good thing Captain Fox, they make people happy inside." He turned and headed for the stairs leading toward the second floor. Without turning he added in a monotone voice, "Now we have a fox and a dog in the station."

The Captain stared at Smokie and thought, 'There's just no way he could have been faking all these years.'

Sixteen

October - 5 - 2001

The door at the back of the chapel opened and an old man trudged into the sanctuary with a coffee wagon. "Hi there Misser Donald." The man said with an enormous grin that displayed a perfect checkerboard of white teeth in stark contrast to his black leathery skin. Dressed in neat khaki work pants and a tee shirt he lumbered down the aisle between the pews, limping with one foot in a cast.

"Hello there, Linc." Dr. Heathrow responded. How's the family?"

""No complaints Misser Donald, no complaints. The good Lord see fit to let me an mine have another day and I thanks him fer the blessin - sure enuf!" Linc chuckled.

"Folks," Donald bellowed, "this here is the oldest living fixture in St. Paul's, Mr. Luke Lincoln Saunders."

"Jus calls me Linc folks, like the big flashy car. But you all could likely tell that by my looks?" He chuckled. "Got no use fer cars no more, no sir! The Lord saved me the cost a wonna them contraptions when he give me this here draggin leg, and I thanks him fer the blessin - sure enuf. The fact that Linc had never owned a car was beside the point. Everyone took an instant liking to the old fellow and each in turn offered a hand in greeting.

"No need to introduce these two." He said as he shook Smokie and Benny's hand in turn. "Seen you two fellas on the TV enuf times to know ya by now. Don't know how ya done it but the Lord musta had a hand in it."

"Linc got hit by some falling rubble, that's how he got the injury to his foot." Dr. Heathrow explained.

"Was headin over here to St. Paul's when the sky fell in, I was. Bin commin here mos every day now fer 10 years since I retired, to help out much as I can. Lot busier here since that day, it is, a whole lot busier. Lots a folk like you, all commin in for healin is my guess. Ol Linc does his part tho, same as always."

Linc poured coffee for the three men, keeping one eye on Francine who had her head buried in her hands. "Got some hot water here lady and some a my Abigal's special herb tea. My dear ol lady's been makin her special herb tea for nigh on to forty years. Lotta folk here seems ta like it. Fix ya some if ya likes?" He started preparing the tea without waiting for a reply.

Francine slowly raised her head attempting a smile. Her eyes were almost completely swollen shut from crying. Linc grimaced.

"Jus be a minute lady, make ya feel a whole lot better." He turned toward the coffee wagon to prepare the tea and immediately Francine's expression changed to one of surprise. Dr. Heathrow noticed her expression and hesitated for a moment. He'd seen the look on many of his patients. It was the look of sudden recall.

On the back of Linc's tee shirt were large red letters that read, "WWJD." Donald looked at the letters that he knew meant 'What Would Jesus Do?' He could see it had twigged Francine's memory, and that she was still struggling to bring the lost picture into focus.

"What do the letters remind you of Francine?" Donald asked gently.

Linc turned and noticed everyone was staring at his tee shirt. "I always asks the Lord what ta do when I is in trouble. Best medicine there is." He handed the steaming tea to Francine and waited until she had a good grip on the cup before letting go. "Best thang ta do is jus let go lady, jus let all them dark thoughts float down the drain, leaves room for the good stuff. Works fer me, an always did sure enuf."

Francine's face brightened once again as tears streamed down the corners of her eyes. "The last time I spoke with David he gave me an email he'd received from Yasmine. He'd forgotten he had it. Naturally I tried to reach her but my email message to her bounced back. That night I had a vivid dream. It's just coming back to me now. In it, David was with Yousef. They were in some kind of terrible conflict and David was speaking to me on his cell phone. His last word to me was, 'Francine, I'm so sorry, so sorry. Oh God, please be with us...' then the line went dead."

She looked up at Donald and an expression of silent panic slowly masked her face. "Oh God Donald, the next day David's airplane crashed into the...the dream, it must have been a preview of what was going to happen." She paused for a moment as if trying to grasp another thread from her vision. There's more. Yasmine is in terrible danger, and she's pregnant. It's Yousef's baby. We've got to help her. I must remember all he told me." Again she buried her head in her hands and wept.

"Jus asks the Lord dear lady, jus asks the Lord." Linc urged.

Francine took a deep breath and released it. "Please God show us how to help my dear Yasmine and her unborn baby. Please help us." She prayed. At that precise moment Francine felt a small hand press into her own. Then the voice of a little girl said,

"*Pink lady* help you now." Francine gasped and sat up abruptly. She shot an anxious look first to Donald, then to Smokie, then to Benny. Although she could not see the little girl she had definitely heard her speak and felt her touch. It was obvious everyone else in the room had also heard her speak.

"Ya jus has ta ask is all, opens the door fer help to come." Linc said with child-like innocence. "I bes be on my way folks, thangs ul jus take care a thimselves now is my guess. Jus need to be thankin the Lord for the blessin." He took the handles of his coffee wagon and limped toward the door. "Nice meetin you folks, specially you little girl." He glanced sideways as he reached the door and waved at an empty spot beside the wooden angel.

Seventeen

October - 5 – 2001

&

August 1968

Since Donald's experience in India in 1968, he had been open-minded and receptive to unexplainable phenomena - perhaps too receptive. On more than one occasion the university advised him to restrain his metaphysical tendencies. Donald essentially had no problem with their request since he was content to focus on the *essence* of alternative belief systems, which he believed was love in action. Since Meereka came into his life, that belief became a certainty.

No intellectual formula or tested theory of clinical psychology ever achieved for him the effectiveness that simple compassion and genuine loving concern had illustrated. He had also discovered that the more academic knowledge he acquired the less he actually used it. He found that by allowing his heart to remain open, he would be shown exactly what he needed to know in any given moment to best treat his patients. He called the technique *The Psychology of Letting Go.* Unlike his dad Ramsey who preferred to work primarily by the book, Donald used love and compassion as his primary method of treating patients.

Now that the simple, angelic influence of Meereka had come into his life, he could no longer sit on the fence. Donald was forced to choose between the 3-D world of concrete facts and the ephemeral world of intuitive knowing. It brought him full circle to the surreal experience he had with Chez Shift in India and he was compelled to re-evaluate what had really occurred.

"I don't believe I have ever heard a name like Chez Shift." Donald said.

"You must believe it or I wouldn't have the name." Chez replied.

"Huh? I must believe it or you wouldn't be called Chez Shift! What in God's name does that mean?" He asked confused.

Chez ignored the question. "Which name of God are you referring to?"

'This is getting weirder and weirder.' He thought. Chez turned her face toward Donald and grinned. He smirked as it occurred to him that he was being taken for a ride in more ways than one.

"Ha!" Chez laughed.

"Say, are you one of those...that is, can you..." Chez interrupted him.

"Minds? Can I read minds?"

"Yah! Can you?" Donald asked a little embarrassed.

"Can't you?" She asked. Donald was again surprised by the matter-of-fact manner she spoke about supernatural things.

"Everything's possible Donny boy. Have you forgotten that as well?" She laughed.

As they drove Donald stared straight ahead down the highway. He came to India hoping to experience the unexplainable then have it explained. Now that he was in the midst of an unexplainable experience he found it very unsettling.

"Not what you expected is it Dr. Heathrow?" She laughed.

"What did you call me?" Donald asked in surprise. "You called me Dr. Heathrow!" He was becoming extremely agitated while excited in the same time. "You're a very frustrating person." He added, shaking his head.

"I am exactly what you have created me to be." She said.

"But I don't even know you. How could I *create* you to be anything?" Donald was completely exasperated. He felt like opening the window and yelling at the top of his lungs.

"Go ahead. It'll do you good. You've got a lot of pent up frustration buried inside you. Go ahead and let er rip, no one will hear you." She urged.

At that point Donald didn't care if anyone heard him. He rolled down the window of the jeep and screamed. "Help! I want out!"

"Good request." She said. Donald noticed her manner had become softer gentler. "See how peaceful your world becomes when you get rid of all the unwanted stress." Chez whispered.

"It sounds like you're telling me that you are acting out what I am feeling. Is that what I'm supposed to believe?" He exclaimed.

"You must believe it otherwise it wouldn't be happening." Chez replied with a laugh.

"This can't be real." Donald muttered in frustration.

"It is and it isn't." She commented. "Well, here we are. I would say go ahead and get your stuff, but then again you don't have any stuff, do you?" She giggled. Donald just frowned and shook his head. The jeep pulled up in front of a cozy little adobe homestead, seemingly in the middle of nowhere. Donald felt lost. It felt like no time had passed at all and yet it seemed like he had been talking with Chez for hours.

"Follow me." Chez said curtly. Donald felt like he was checking into a remote villa on some adventure tour.

"It *is* exactly what you want it to be Dr. Heathrow." Chez said.

"There she goes with the Dr. Heathrow thing again." Donald muttered.

When they walked through the front door of the adobe the space inside felt much larger than the building appeared outside.

"What you see with your eyes is not always true...is it Dr.. Heathrow?" Chez commented.

Donald silently agreed with her then realized he was exhausted.

"Park yourself in the far room Doctor. We'll eat when you've rested." Chez pointed down a long ceramic tiled hallway that radiated welcome.

Donald awoke feeling he had never experienced such a refreshing sleep. A moment after opening his eyes there was a knock at the door. His stomach growled as he answered the knock with a yawn. "Come in."

A beautiful young woman with unnerving stiffness entered the room. She was tall and slender, had piercing blue eyes and auburn hair that hung to her shoulders. Despite her severity she had a delicate, fragile essence. Donald found the contradiction unsettling.

"Hello. I am Eagle Feather. "Your meal is ready!" She had the same confident manner as Chez but without the humor. She turned abruptly and walked down the hall out of sight. Donald shook his head in bewilderment, then roused himself and headed down the hall turning in the direction in which she had vanished.

The room he entered was a large octagonal, amply windowed kitchen. It had a vaulted ceiling with a center island combination eating cooking area. It was dark outside. Two blood red candles provided an eerie dim light. There was a single setting with a simple vegetarian meal of fruit, nuts and steamed vegetables laid beside a tall pitcher of water. The kitchen was perfectly still. It felt two dimensional like a still picture from a magazine. He waited for several minutes. When no one arrived to join him, he decided the meal must have been laid out for him. He sat down, looked around once more, and hollered. "Thank you Chez or Eagle Feather or whoever made this for me. It looks delicious." There was no reply.

Just as he was finishing his meal a little girl walked into the room and scrambled up onto the stool beside him. She had the same piercing blue eyes and long auburn hair as Eagle Feather. She acted as if Donald was just one of the family and calmly asked him for a glass of water.

Donald took an empty glass from a row in front of him. The glasses were the same blood red color as the candles. He poured a glass for her and gave it to her.

"Thank you Mr. Donald." She said.

Donald looked at the little girl in surprise. 'Someone else used to call me Mr. Donald, I just can't remember who it was.' He thought.

"Not now, later!" The little girl said.

"Another mind reader. Does everybody in this house read minds?" Donald asked.

"Nobody here but you Mr. Donald." She replied.

62

"And you." Donald said correcting the little girl as gently as he could. She placed her glass on the counter, turned and looked straight into his eyes and smiled.

"If you say so Mr. Donald."

"This is really a spooky family. Doesn't anyone act normal?" Donald asked. He didn't actually expect the little girl to reply.

"What do you consider to be normal Dr. Heathrow?" A voice behind him asked.

Donald turned to find Chez casually leaning against the entrance way to the kitchen. He stood up and smiled wanting to express his appreciation for the meal but was he interrupted.

"Don't tire yourself. You've been through a lot. You still need rest." She said.

Although he had awoken from a deep revitalizing sleep just before eating, he suddenly realized she was correct, he still felt extremely weary.

'Must be jet lag. I think I'll go back and lay down for awhile.' He thought.

Chez moved away from the door and allowed him to pass. He turned to say good night to the little girl but she was gone. Since there were no other exits from the kitchen he wondered where she had gone. 'Maybe she's playing on the floor behind the island.' He figured. "Good night little girl."

There was no reply.

Eighteen

1951 - 1952

It was 1951 and Jacqueline had agreed to marry Ibrahim. Arrangements were made to hold a grand ceremony in Bath where most of Jacqueline's extended family resided. Ibrahim's devotion to the strict Islamic interpretation of the Qur'an had, until then prompted him to underplay anything that might suggest an attitude of materialism. However, in the year since he and Jacqueline met he gradually acquired a less rigid religious perspective.

Ibrahim had been studying the works of the Sufi poet Jalaluddin Rumi who lived during the thirteenth century. As the innermost quality of Islam, he found Sufiism guided him to the true essence of the Qur'an. Jacqueline suggested this course of study hoping Ibrahim would begin to embrace a broader focus of the God he called Allah. As was his practice with anything to which he gave his attention, Ibrahim immersed himself in the deeper reflection of self-knowledge he found there. The result was predictable, as Jacqueline had hoped. Ibrahim opened to many other philosophies that dealt with the goal of mankind's perfect union with God.

With the wedding arrangements complete, many of Ibrahim's friends and business associates in the Middle East who he had not seen for almost six years, accepted his invitation to attend. In the process, Ibrahim was delighted to learn that his business partner Abdullah was also engaged to be married.

"Allah has seen fit to shine his light upon the *House of Faiz*. His faithful servants have been singled out to receive his favor." Abdullah told him by telephone.

"Yes, dear friend, we have been greatly blessed, but favored, no." Ibrahim explained. "I have learned that all are honored as one in his kingdom, and that no one is favored above another. All are God's children, destined to reunite one day in the glory of his love."

"Dear Ibrahim, I am not your equal in devotion or understanding of Allah. You have been so much more than my business partner. You have been my dear teacher and my inspiration for these many years. I would never seek to disagree with one so learned as you, such a dear servant of our Lord...but," Abdullah hesitated nervously. He had never before questioned his beloved friend and mentor. "What of the many who fail to follow the strict tenets of the Qur'an, are they not doomed to suffer greatly?"

"Dear friend of old, I have no desire to disillusion you or give you cause to lose faith in your partner, but I have come to a deeper awareness of our purpose here on earth. I now believe that no man is doomed forever, no matter how scarlet may be his current sins." Ibrahim replied. "Let us not speak of this now dear friend, let us prepare to feast at the table that has been laid before us.

As suggested, Abdullah refrained from further discussion, however he was very disturbed by Ibrahim's comments. He was certain that his self-imposed exile in Mecca had not been the cause of Ibrahim's radical interpretation of Allah's strict code for living. That could only mean that Ibrahim had been influenced by his year in England. Now that he was to marry foreign blood, Abdullah had considerable apprehension that Ibrahim was drifting into very dangerous waters.

In the early summer of 1952 Ibrahim and Jacqueline were joined in marriage, not once but twice. Ibrahim respected Jacqueline's desire to honor the religious heritage of her family and a traditional Islamic ceremony followed immediately after a Christian marriage.

While Ibrahim's guests were pleased to see that his spiritual roots were observed, many were disturbed that his new wife had not converted to Islam, nor did she appear to have any particular interest in religion of any kind. When questioned about her beliefs she simply said *God* was her only belief and that the truth behind God, which she explained was love, did not need elaborate explanation, it needed only demonstration in one's daily life.

This radical free spirited attitude would have been simply ignored were it not for the highly visible stature Ibrahim held in the Islamic community. His reputation reached through most of the Middle East. Ibrahim's devotion to Allah had been a spiritual light in the lives of thousands of devout Muslims and now, apparently he was under the influence of an infidel.

"Our brother seems to have forgotten how the abundant fruits of Allah came to his table." One important political guest from Amman whispered to Abdullah at the wedding reception.

"No greater servant does Allah have." The statement had almost become an appellation and Abdullah quoted it without thinking.

"Yes, yes I know the great works our brother has performed in the name of Allah, but I wonder, does he still hold the same devotion he once did." The politician added. Abdullah concealed his own misgivings but knew in his heart that once they learned of Ibrahim's relaxed spiritual attitude, many men of business and government who had favored the *House of Faiz*, would seek others to replace the business affairs they conducted with he and his partner.

A month following their wedding Ibrahim took Jacqueline to his ancestral home in Ma'an. Then, he showed her where he began his trade empire in Aqaba. From Aqaba they traveled to Amman for Abdullah's marriage to Shahira, whose family had traveled from Afghanistan to attend. Jacqueline quickly fell in love with the rich culture of the Middle East that she had been studying with a penchant since she first met Ibrahim. She knew that he would remain in England with her and his son Mikha'ill if that was her wish, but when she saw the depth of his love for his homeland she urged him to make a new home in Jordan for his new family.

Ibrahim was overjoyed, however he agreed on the condition that the Faiz family would spend a good deal of each year in England so that Jacqueline could be near her family.

"My dear husband, I have a vision of the entire world waiting the gifts you have to offer. The planet is evolving quickly now that the great conflict of the last decade is well behind it. Many will be tempted to make money and power their idol. They will need the wise counsel of those who have attained a balance of wealth and spiritual devotion to show them the path to true happiness.

Ibrahim's heart overflowed as his union with Jacqueline grew deeper. He believed that Allah had sent to him an angel as an emissary to love and guide him in the wise use of his power and influence. However, as Ibrahim's heart grew warmer many old friends grew colder toward him. For many, the feeling of betrayal had poisoned their minds and with this a bitter taste of resentment. Ibrahim said nothing to his wife about it but Jacqueline heard persistent rumors that Ibrahim had fallen out of favor with many in the orthodox Muslim community.

A year passed and Jacqueline presented Ibrahim with a baby girl. They named the girl Francine. Within a week Abdullah's wife Shahira also gave birth to their first son, whom they named Abdul bin Abdullah. Michai'ill, who had just turned eight, was delighted to have a new sister. And with the birth of Abdul, he felt he also had a brother. For the moment, the sun broke through the gathering storm clouds over the *House of Faiz*.

Nineteen

September - 5 - 2001

"Hey Dick Tracey, c'mere." Detective Thompson yelled from across the motor pool. Benny had his head under the hood of a bright red Ferrari that had been impounded in a drug bust earlier that day. He stood up and saw Detective Leroy Thompson waving a large Envelop at him. Leroy was probably the best looking black man on the entire New York City police force. With his head clean-shaven, he was just over six feet. Although Leroy worked out, he was more toned than muscular as a result of jogging every day in Central Park. Detective Thompson was the picture of fitness and could easily be mistaken for a movie star. When he walked into a room, all heads turned.

"Thanks for letting me check her out fellas." Benny said to the officers giving the vehicle the once over for evidence.

"*Thank you* Benny for those Yankee tickets." As Angus MacDonald came to know Benny's family he supported them in any way he could. Ballpark tickets was just one of the ways he lent that support. Benny was delighted to be in a position to mirror that generosity when the time was right. "My kids said they'd be happy to trade in their old man for the guy that could get them cool seats right beside the dugout. One of the officers laughed.

"My pleasure officer Wychoski, anytime." He laughed.

"You boys find anything in that beast yet?" Detective Thompson asked.

"Oh you know, the usual. A package of Benjamin Franklin's, maybe *50 large*." Benny replied with a smirk.

"Huh, chump change for those slugs. It was probably a small payoff to have the right person look the other way." The detective said. "All I get for turning my head is a pain in the neck." The detective twisted his neck from side to side and rubbed his neck. Benny immediately stepped behind the officer, gently applied his hand to the back of his neck and held it there for a minute.

"Why don't you try some T'ai Chi detective, its supposed to really smooth out the nervous system. Benny suggested.

"Maybe I will, I've seen a lota people doin it when I run in the park. Its kinna eerie, like watching a slow motion movie. A real cross section of people too, not just Orientals. Just last week MacDonald and I questioned this Wall Street tycoon, David Bryan, maybe you've heard of him." Benny nodded his head. "Looks like he got caught with his fingers in the cookie jar. The DA wanted to see if he could make a strong enough case to have him indicted. That guy's really connected. Why does a hot shot like Bryan steal pennies when he owns the mint. Go figure?"

"Maybe to see if he could get away with it? Maybe the money gets boring after a while." Benny suggested. The detective just shook his head as if he would like to be in the position to be bored having *too* much money.

"Hey! That feels a lot better. What did ya do kid?" He asked.

"Meereka taught me the technique." Benny answered.

"I swear that kid's an angel. For a little girl that doesn't say much, she sure seems to know a lot about things that count. Ya gotta wonder where it comes from."

Benny nodded his head and smiled. "Everyone's got a lot of theories, mostly about God and stuff, but I don't know. All I can say is she's special and I love her so much. Soooo, anyway, tell me what happened with the tycoon Leroy."

"Take a ride with me kid, I gotta go get a search warrant on that very case. The detective headed for his car and a few minutes later the two pulled into the afternoon traffic. "Strange." He said finally.

"What's strange?" Benny asked.

"That we'd be talkin about this guy just as I was headed out for the warrant on his office. The detective replied.

"Happens to Meereka all the time, something called synchronicity. Benny commented.

"I'll bet it does. I'd believe just about anything about that kid." The detective said. He went silent for a moment then all of a sudden it came to him why he brought up David Bryan in the first place. "As I was sayin, I question this big shot Bryan and the next morning I see him out doin the

Tied Chi thing in the park with a lotta other tight suits. He coulda fooled me. He looked like a handball and martini type. "Weird."

"If I've learned anything working with you these last few years Leroy its that people live in many different worlds at the same time. Maybe Bryan was just tapping into his better angels." Benny speculated.

"What's that? Better angels?" When I met the pompous ass he didn't have any wings that I could see. The detective exclaimed.

"Well, maybe they're just hidden under a shell." Benny suggested.

The detective gave Benny a curious look then remembered why he originally wanted to see him. "I almost forgot." He slid a large Envelop across the front seat to Benny. "Have a look at what's in there and tell me what cha think. All this stuff came in ta the precinct the day after Labor Day. The captain and I thought you'd be the perfect one to figure out what it all means."

Benny opened the large manila Envelop and pulled out a package of drawings and a bundle of notes and letters clipped together. The pictures appeared to be drawn by children. Benny began to scan them. When he got to the third drawing his heart skipped a beat. *Pink lady* was written in large block letters at the top of the page. Below it there were two burning sticks. "This looks like a couple of burning incense sticks."

"We thought that would get your attention. Wait till ya see the rest of them. The letters are the same, all about dreams kids are havin - all similar. That one yer holdin is the only one with *pink lady* written on it. I remembered you said there was somethin about that name comin up right after Meereka got well." The detective said.

"Yes, that's right. For the first few days after Meereka was healed she kept mentioning *pink lady*. She said, "*Pink lady* want Meereka to stay here."" Benny explained.

"Spooky! Anyway, that's why we thought you aughta look at this stuff." The detective said.

"But, I don't understand Leroy, why would parents send their kids drawings into the police department?" Benny asked.

"Benny, that's why we want you to get involved, we don't have a clue. It gets even better though. There isn't even a single return address, and, if you can believe it, the mail came from all over the world. Some of the mail was post marked weeks before it arrived, but like I said, all of em arrived on the same day, the day after Labor Day. The chances of it bein a prank is pretty slim, besides how could all this mail arrive on the same day?"

Benny stared at the pictures in disbelief.

Twenty

September -10 -2001

David slammed the lid on his cell phone shut, annoyed that his budding tryst with Rebecca had been interrupted. Still, he couldn't deny Yasmine had been one of the few pockets of light in his otherwise gray relationship with Francine.

It was almost two years since Francine received any word from Yasmine. A cold wind blew through her life on that day back in1999, a day that confirmed his marriage to Francine was definitely over. Francine received a letter that was post marked from Amman, Jordan but without a return address. As David recalled, the letter appeared to have been written in a rush, like a choppy like a telegram. It was not at all Yasmine's style, she could easily spend an hour chatting enthusiastically with her aunt, and her letters were invariably like short stories.

This letter was very emotional in content. Yasmine wrote that her brother Yousef, whom she had not seen or heard from since his kidnapping in 1983, had contacted her. She went on to say she did not know when she would be able to communicate with Francine again. The letter added that she was very sorry and wished she could provide more details but for the time being it was impossible. It was signed, 'My love forever, Yasmine.' Francine was in shock. The good news was that Yousef was alive. The bad news was that Yasmine had disappeared from her life as abruptly as Yousef had all those years before.

"Why can't she communicate with me? What can this mean?" She moaned, the puzzling letter dangling from her hand. She cried herself to sleep that night. From that day forward Francine immersed herself in her social work at Columbia University. Before that, the marriage may not have been on solid ground, but now it was dead and buried. A marriage document and the address they shared was their only link with one another.

David was very fond of Yasmine and at the beginning of his marriage to Francine he met her for a meal whenever business took him to the UK. On two separate occasions he and Francine joined Jacqueline and Ibrahim in Bath, then together Yasmine joined them for a vacation in Europe. They spent a week at the family estate in Bath then the five of them motored around the continent for ten days.

At first he enjoyed Francine's parents company but soon found them too stiff for his liking. Their conversations usually headed into spiritual territory, a topic that held little interest for David. He knew Ibrahim's extensive business dealings were often influenced by his deeply spiritual inclinations. This later convinced David that his own disinterest disqualified he and his company from winning a huge contract to supply computer technology to the worldwide operations of the *House of Faiz*.

Failure to obtain the deal was a major embarrassment for David and came at a critical time when he was making a power play for the top seat as CEO of his company. After that incident he spoke with Ibrahim only once more, in 1996 when Jacqueline passed away. In Francine's view David's behavior was childish and selfish.

"David, this is family! Isn't it enough that we have no children of our own and that Yasmine is so far away?" She complained. But the perceived blemish on David's credibility was too much for David's colossal ego to bear. Over time the wound festered and David's bitterness manifested as a growing indifference toward Francine.

A tiny pang of remorse shot through David's solar plexus, as he thought about their life together. 'Perhaps I should have been a little more supportive on the phone, maybe our marriage *is* in the toilet but I do have *some* feelings for her - she must be hurting like hell right now.'

David fiddled with his cell phone, contemplating whether to call her back. It was not his way to apologize for anything but in this case he might make an exception. He was about to press the speed dialer when he glanced down the bar past Rebecca. As he looked to the end of the bar he was surprised to see a little girl sitting by herself drawing a picture with crayons. At that moment the little girl looked up and smiled at him. A shiver ran up his spine. The experience held his attention for several seconds then he broke from it, turned toward the other end of the bar where Clifford was serving another customer and hollered,

"Hey, Cliff! Since when do you serve kids in this joint? Cliff turned and looked down the bar.

"What kids Mr. Bryan?" He asked with genuine concern. David looked back at the empty space where he had just seen the little girl a moment before.

David looked around. "What the? Hmmm, where did she go?" David looked around the bar. Rebecca, you saw the little girl sitting at the end of the bar drawing didn't you?"

"Sorry David, no I didn't." She gave David a weird look as if she was trying to see if he was joking with her. David looked back at her in a way that suggested he was almost pleading she confirm what he saw. Rebecca looked at him again. "Uh sure David, whatever you say." She was anxious to take their meeting to the next level and didn't want to aggravate him more than he appeared to be. Rebecca's obsequious reply had just the opposite effect she hoped for. David glared at her, then at Cliff, then back at Rebecca.

"I'm sorry Mr. Bryan. I really didn't see her." Cliff pleaded. He knew David had a hot temper and could explode in a minute. "Please, let me get you another drink Mr. Bryan, its on the house."

"What? Are you kidding me? He fumed. "Are you two telling me you didn't see the kid? Rebecca, you were looking right at her when I saw her." Rebecca recoiled in fright. "I don't know what's up, but I'm not playing this game. David threw a Fifty-Dollar bill on the bar and stormed out.

The private elevator that led directly to his penthouse suite was just outside the bar. David stomped across the corridor and pressed the elevator button. He tapped his foot impatiently while he waited for the elevator to arrive.

"What's holding this thing up? I'm the only one that's supposed to be using this elevator?" He grumbled.

A gentle female voice whispered from behind him as the elevator doors opened. "Time expands and exaggerates your senses when you make pain your master." David stepped into the elevator, turned and looked to see who had just spoken to him. Instead of the adult woman he expected to see, the little girl who had been drawing at the end of the bar looked up at him, smiled and handed him her drawing.

"This is for you mister David." She said. Stunned, David took the paper and watched the little girl scurry away as the elevator doors closed.

"What in God's name is going on?" He yelled. The elevator seemed to crawl toward the summit of the hotel. David felt trapped and confusion inside his anger. He wanted to scream at someone. Then he realized he

74

was still holding the little girl's drawing. He was about to tear it to shreds when he caught sight of his first name at the top of the page. Below the words "Mr. David" there were two faces drawn. With a few simple childish crayon strokes one face had a sad expression in blue and the other an angry expression in red. Below the two faces were the words, "Help him."

David was shocked and again about to rip the drawing apart. He held it with both hands shaking, but something inside him kept him from destroying it.

Twenty-One

October - 5 - 2001

Silence filled the sanctuary for several minutes after Linc departed. A heavenly essence emanated throughout the room. No one spoke for several minutes. Finally, Donald whispered,

"The better angels of our nature...the simple goodness within each of us...like the divine message of an angel...the message of love in one of its many disguises."

"Meereka *is* an angel." Smokie said innocently. Benny gave him a warm smile.

"Meereka has been the blessing of an angel in my life and everyone that knew her since she was born." He said.

"She is a *real* angel Benny." Smokie repeated more firmly.

Francine and Dr. Heathrow had a look of concern on their faces for Benny as he realized what Smokie was saying. It was certain now that Benny had some form of direct contact with Meereka. Each one in the group, including Linc, had experienced contact with Meereka and could not deny she was somehow making herself known beyond the veil of death. But what was not apparent was how Benny registered that contact in his own mind. When he joined the group it seemed evident he had not yet accepted the fact that Meereka had passed away.

Benny was deep in thought. Donald's experience as a psychologist told him what theoretically was going on in Benny's mind as he denied that little Meereka was gone. But that was not what was happening. The last few weeks convinced Benny there was no difference between life as the world knows it, and the other side. He had personally witnessed too much in his life to ever believe a cut and dried version of life and death.

There was no way of telling what was going on in Smokie's child-like mind. Perhaps it was his very innocence that opened the veil and allowed him to see and communicate with Meereka. Donald wondered if that were true, how many other people, considered by the world to be handicapped by their inability to communicate normally in the world, were in reality living most of their lives in another world, one rich in the expression of the *better angels* Lincoln referred to. He prayed it was true.

Benny sat down in the front pew opposite Francine. He seemed to be staring into space but since Francine was sitting with him at eye level she noticed he was focusing, as one would do when they are looking at something in particular.

She glanced at Smokie and saw that he too was focused on the same spot. They appeared to be listening. Francine wondered why she couldn't hear what they were hearing. She looked up at Donald who was also watching the two commune it seemed, with empty space.

"*Pink lady* say; 'not empty space.' " Smokie whispered without taking his eyes from the spot where presumably the voice was originating. " 'All filled with light,' she says, 'but people like to look at dark.'"

Smokie stood up and Francine was certain a faint light was actually shining from his face. "Lots of angels came to this city last month." He said. Francine's heart skipped a beat. She hoped one had been with David.

"*Pink lady* says, 'he help her save flowers.' " Benny whispered. "She says, 'Franny needs to remember what he said,' and, she says, 'ask him.'"

Donald was certain that *pink lady* was somehow involved in the prophetic drawings and notes that Precinct #1 received from all over the globe. Now Meereka's drawings had shown up along with her warnings about saving the flowers.

"Francine, I think you should try." Donald said feeling the atmosphere was rich with possibilities.

'Could it really be possible to reach David?' She wondered?

"Okay Donald, I'll try. How do you think I should proceed? I mean, I've never done anything like this before."

"Its just like praying, Franny." Benny said, "Just speak to David, in your mind." Francine nodded, took a deep breath then closed her eyes.

'David, if you can hear me, please tell us how we can help Yasmine.' She opened her eyes and looked around hoping for some sign that she had connected with him. The chapel was absolutely silent. Suddenly everyone recoiled as Donald's message beeper went off.

"That's odd, I turned this off before we began our session today." Donald checked the message which said, 'call office.' "But there should not be anyone in the office right now." He murmured.

"Maybe it's a sign." Benny whispered, as if everything should be treated with special reverence after what had happened earlier. "Call and see Dr. Heathrow, call!"

Donald nodded and reached around the side of the pew for his briefcase. He opened it, took out his cell phone and dialed his office. It rang three times then his answering machine picked up. He was about to hang up but thought perhaps there was something in his generic message that might suggest a symbol or a sign. He listened carefully, as if for the first time, but noticed nothing unusual.

"Just my answering service." Donald said shaking his head. Francine looked disappointed.

"Answering machine doctor?" Smokie said.

Everyone turned and stared at him. "Of course." Benny said. Francine beamed.

"Francine, if David left a message at his office, wouldn't his secretary have picked it up by now?" Donald asked.

"Yes probably. Come to think of it, he had a special answering service he used like a Dictaphone. He used it as a back up. You know, in case he had an idea and the batteries had run out on his pocket recorder. He could call it from anywhere in the world when he wanted to retrieve his own messages." She explained.

"That's it! It has to be. Do you have the number?" Donald asked.

"Not here, but his secretary likely has it." She said with growing excitement. "But the office will be closed by now."

" Do you know his secretary's personal number?" He urged.

"Yes, yes." Francine said with excitement. "I have it right here in my phone directory." Francine picked up her purse, flipped through the directory and stopped at the M's. "Here it is, Janice Miller's cell phone number."

"Here, use my cell phone, maybe we can hear if there was a message on it right now." Donald exclaimed. She dialed the number. It rang three times then went into a voice message. Francine was about to hang up when Janice picked up.

"Janice Miller speaking. Who is this please?"

"Its me Janice. Francine." Donald handed Francine a notepad and pen.

"Hello Mrs. Bryan. How are you getting on dear?" She asked gently. Janice was in her late sixties, a seasoned executive secretary who had lost her own husband to a heart attack the previous year. He was only Sixty-Three and was just about to take an early retirement from one of David's subsidiary companies in Long Island. They found him slumped over his desk at the office. It hit Janice pretty hard and David took care of her as if he was a devoted, loving son. Despite David's obvious dark shell, Francine knew there had been an angel trying to escape, too little, too late as it turned out.

"I'm pretty fair under the circumstances Janice. Thanks for asking. Janice, I have a big favor to ask of you. Its very important." Francine said.

"Certainly, anything dear. What is it?" She asked.

"David's special answering service...do you have the number?" Francine asked anxiously.

"Just a minute dear, I believe I do. Hold on please." Francine could hear Janice unzip her briefcase in the background. A moment later she came back on the phone. "Here it is Mrs. Bryan." She gave her the number then asked her if something was wrong. But Francine already knew that David had not spoken to his office that morning and felt there was no need to bring her into the situation.

"Thank you Janice. I'm not certain. I'll tell you when I learn more. Thanks very much. I'll keep in touch." Francine rang off the line, grinned and waved the number back and forth like a trophy. "Okay, here goes." Her heart was racing as she carefully dialed the number. It rang once then the automatic message service picked up. Francine listened for a moment then hung up. She looked disheartened.

"Oh no!" She cried.

"What's wrong?" Benny asked.

"We need a password." She replied.

Twenty-Two

1950's & 1960's

Business flourished during the 50's and 60's for the *House of Faiz* despite pockets of suspicion concerning Ibrahim's newly acquired, open-minded attitude toward the strict interpretation of the Qur'an. New ventures presented themselves through Jacqueline's family interests that extended into food products. By the mid 1960's Ibrahim and Jacqueline together shared equally in the ownership of Brarab Industries with the *House of Faiz*. Based in London, their new corporation supplied edible oil based ingredients to the food industry. By the end of the decade the company had manufacturing plants throughout Europe, the UK, the Americas and Australia.

Ibrahim and Jacqueline traveled extensively during the first twelve years of the corporation's rapid growth and the original *House of Faiz*, still based in Amman, Jordan continued to be managed by Ibrahim's trusted partner and friend Abdullah.

Mika'ill and Francine traveled extensively with their parents, accompanied by a tutor and nanny. Their true education however came from Ibrahim and Jacqueline, whose primary interest in life was the pursuit of self-realization through research and dedication toward spiritual wisdom.

In 1966, by the time Brarab Industries was solidly entrenched in its primary target markets, Ibrahim was spending a considerable portion of his time writing. Jacqueline encouraged him to chronicle the evolution of his philosophical and spiritual perspective which she believed would one day serve as a bridge to harmonize the deep seated differences in conflicting world religions, particularly between Islamic, Judao and Christian beliefs.

"Perhaps not in our lifetime dear husband, nor in that of our children, but one day the solid foundation of honor and integrity, which you have laid with God's guidance, will provide a channel through which your understanding of truth may contribute to the unification of spiritual harmony around the world."

With an open mind and heart Ibrahim listened with his heart to Jacqueline's mystical wisdom, certain that Allah's divine counsel spoke through her.

With Ibrahim away from the Middle East much of the time and Abdullah left in charge, the *House of Faiz* with its extensive philanthropic outreach, remained a shining light in the Islamic community. As long as Ibrahim's unrestrained spiritual aspirations remained his own and did not spill over onto his Muslim countrymen, the support system of friends, politicians and businessmen, who had helped build the *House of Faiz,* remained loyal.

Meanwhile, Abdullah's son Abdul had arrived at the manly age of thirteen and had an Eight-Year old brother, whom the family had named Ahmed. Most of Abdullah's family were of Lebanese descent and during the 50's and 60's, when business permitted it, he and his wife Shahira spent a good deal of time in that region with their two

It was not until the late 1960's that the gathering storm clouds, seeded in 1953 with the marriage of Ibrahim to Jacqueline, began to show signs of lightning.

Jacqueline sat on the patio of their midtown Manhattan Hotel suite enjoying a flawlessly beautiful summer morning. She had a penchant for strong Arabic coffee. Ibrahim inspired her to sample it many years before and she sipped a cup with delight while reading the New York Times.

Ibrahim was in his library studying a text on North American shamanism in preparation for a visit later that week from well-known ex-Rabbi, Benjamin Pearlman. The little he knew on the subject fascinated Ibrahim. He was doubly anxious to learn how a man who had been an orthodox Jew for almost forty years of his adult life had been inspired to leave his faith for what many would consider a totally incompatible spiritual practice.

Mika'ill and Francine were across the street in Central Park listening to a *Mainly Mozart* concert. Mika'ill had become a competent violinist and was anxious to hear how a local university ensemble would interpret his favorite classical composer. Francine was quickly acquiring a taste for the classics but for the moment, at thirteen, she leaned more in the direction of Rock n Roll. Mika'ill tolerated his baby sister's *infidel* tendencies, as he jokingly put it, but allowed for the tainted influence of her English blood.

Francine, who was as close to a brother as a growing teenage girl could be, accepted Mika'ill's frequent ribbing as a sign of his love for to her. No one could move her brother out of his somber self-importance quicker than she.

82

"Mika'ill, my some-day big shot brother, come down from your high horse, or should I say pony. I think Brarab Industries and the *House of Faiz* can survive a while longer without the benefit of your genius." She would giggle. Mika'ill melted at the sound of her laughter, feeling safe to drop his austere masks where she was concerned.

Jacqueline was scanning the international news for anything related to Brarab Industries' recent takeover of a large farming conglomerate in Mid Western Canada when she spotted an ominous article concerning Lebanon. It outlined how large numbers of armed Palestinian guerillas were pouring across the border into Lebanon and establishing militant training camps.

A cold shiver penetrated her heart as she experienced a foreboding vision. It was a feeling all too familiar to her in the early days of the last Great War. She knew this type of vision always foreshadowed a dark cloud in the future of someone or something close to her. This time she knew it would fall upon the *House of Faiz*.

Twenty-Three

September - 2 - 1968

When Donald awoke for the second time in the remote adobe home of Chez Shift, he had just experienced a fascinating lucid dream.

He was sitting with a small group of Indian men and women, perhaps eleven or twelve in number, listening to a man, the one he had come to the region to meet. The man sat before the group on a small square mat and emanated a loving child-like innocence. However, when he spoke it was as one with great charismatic knowing. Confident certainty wrapped around his simple words.

Each of the men and women gathered, including David, were dressed in simple white linen robes, while their teacher wore an orange one-piece robe. His black hair was like a wild Afro. Donald thought if his hair had been yellow it would have resembled a halo.

"All in this world is an effect of your mind, changing more quickly than the breath you breathe. Life and death are dances of the sleeping dreamer. To the one who awakens, a world of changeless beauty awaits. Perpetual bliss is the natural state of the one who walks the conscious path of life. Seek therefore the changeless and find joy that never ends."

Donald knew more was said, but he could not recall much of it, only the swami's final words, which were directed to him.

"What I have shared will for a time simmer beneath the surface of your conscious mind inspiring your thoughts, your words and your deeds. The day will come when my words will return to your awareness. On that day, your life will be transformed." In that moment the swami's appearance changed to that of a little girl, with the same loving innocent smile as his. She held out her hand, which contained two flowers, "Help *pink lady*." That was all he could recall of the dream but he knew something indescribably beautiful had enraptured his soul.

What immediately came to mind was his father's psychiatric practice. It suddenly became clear to him that in order for his dad's patients to identify and trust him, they must have sensed something in him that gave them a feeling of affinity. He could only create *who he was*, his patients, his practice, his friends, his world. His world must reflect that back to him validating that what he thought, at least to him, was true.

He could change *his* world only by changing his mind about himself. That would not occur until he became sufficiently dissatisfied with his world to search beyond what is changeable. This new perception helped Donald realize that when he argued and criticized his father he was judging an aspect of his own world, which also had to be an aspect of *him self.* He needed to cease judging his father and his own world would become better. It all made such simple sense. At that moment there was a knock at his bedroom door.

"Come in. He said. Eagle Feather opened the door and calmly announced the arrival of Donald's parents.

"My parents? What are they doing here? How did they find me here? Why are they here?" Donald seemed agitated and looked perplexed.

Eagle Feather put her finger to her lips. "Shhhh."

"Ooooh Donald, we were so worried dear!" His mother lamented. "How are you feeling now?" Her eyes were puffy and red as if she had been crying for hours. Dr. Heathrow stood by embracing her tightly around her waist. Donald had never before seen his father look so pale and worried.

"Hey, what's going on your two? How did you find me here anyway? Where ever here is." He added under his breath.

"Oh Ramsey, he's lost his memory!" His mother wailed as she reached for a tissue from a box on Donald's side table.

"We've got our son back dear." He said gently. Calm down sweetheart, everything else takes a back seat to that."

"What are you guys talking about? You're acting very strange." Donald exclaimed while shaking his head. He slid his body sideways to get off the bed and felt a pull on his left arm. "Hey, what's this thing doing in my arm?"

"Lie back down Mr. Heathrow." The young nurse commanded. It was Eagle Feather. He looked at her nametag, which read, 'Heather Eagle.' "What the? He exclaimed.

"Hold still while I take care of that." Her manner was all business. She took hold of his arm, pulled away the bandage that was holding a needle immobile and pulled it out, all in one deft movement. Donald threw his legs over the side of the hospital bed just as a doctor entered the room.

"Hello Dr. and Mrs. Heathrow. Good to see you again. The nurse at the monitoring station informed me this lucky young man had finally come around." She said with a big smile

"Yes, thank God! And we have you to thank for it Dr. Shift." Donald's mother said as Dr. Heathrow wiped the tears from her face.

'What's got into my dad?" Donald wondered. 'This is not the Wall Street shrink I know.'

"If it had not been for the efficient and quick thinking actions of Dr. Shift three weeks ago, you would not be with us now." His father said.

Donald thought, "As far as I know, up until a minute ago, I *wasn't* with you.

"Dr. Shift just happened to be arriving on the same flight that you were on when that terrible man attacked you. You might have bled to death." His mother explained between sobs.

"Bled to death?" All of a sudden Donald realized what they were saying. The tall, knife wheeling Indian that stole his bag at the airport. 'I must have been stabbed during the attack.' Chez Shift was a doctor that miraculously was in the right place at the right time. The trip into the country, the adobe house, the...none of it had happened. I must have been hallucinating. Donald bowed his head. "Unnnbeeelievable!

Say, Dr. Shift. Is your first name Chez?" He asked. The doctor was silent. Donald turned slowly to see why the doctor was not answering. Her face turned pale as if she was about to faint.

"What is it Dr. Shift?" Donald's father asked. Her breathing was erratic and she sat down in a corner chair.

"Just give me a minute, I'll be fine." She whispered. When her tremor subsided she took a deep breath and shook her head. She appeared to be deciding whether to explain herself or not.

"Why not!" She whispered under her breath. "I don't know how you know that name Donald, I've never spoken of it to anyone. Years ago, when I was in medical school in France I had an intense love affair with another medical student. He came from a very influential family in Paris and lived in high society. I became pregnant and wanted to keep the baby however, much to my remorse I allowed the family to persuade me that it would not be in the best interests of their son's future if I followed through with the pregnancy. I still can't believe they talked me into an abortion. It was Paris where that sort of thing was thought of much different than in many other countries. At the time I was young, foolish and easily manipulated.

The guilt I carried around with me after the abortion was so great that when I obtained my medical degree I came down here to Bangalore to work with the poor in this free medical facility. There are lots of others with stories much like mine working here. Had I kept the baby I was going to name her Chez, after my boyfriend's family business *Chez D'Or.*

Twenty-Four

October - 6 - 2001

When Janice gave Francine David's answering service number she knew Francine would need a password. She held back that vital bit of information because she needed time to think. As soon as she rang off with Francine she turned off the power button to her cell phone so that she couldn't be reached until she decided what course of action to take.

It was two weeks after his death that the police finally finished questioning Janice about David's business affairs. Since virtually all his files, both paper copies and those on the corporate computers were destroyed on 911, the case against him looked slim. Few people knew about David's special answering service and Janice decided at the time to keep it that way. In any case, she had taken no chances and simply erased the entire file of messages without listening to them. That way if the answering service was discovered she would have no need to lie to the police.

David may have been selfish and thoughtless but he was there for Janice when she needed him the most. She owed him something for that. And there was also a second motive for her action. Now that David was gone she was determined to keep Francine in the dark about the skeletons in David's closet. Francine had suffered enough, 'What good could possibly be served by exposing her to more pain?' She thought. That was before Francine's call. Obviously Francine knew something was on the message service. Why else would she ask for the number?

Janice knew David's marriage with Francine was in name only, but she was certain Francine knew nothing about his relationship with Amy. She was doubly sure she knew nothing about any of his business dealings. After David's company lost the bid with the *House of Faiz*, Francine was shut out of everything concerning his business affairs.

'God, he could act like a child when he failed to get what he wanted. No one was immune to his wrath when he felt scorned.' She remembered. That side of David brought her close to giving her two weeks notice on more than one occasion. 'How could a man be so kind and so generous with his heart on one hand and so ruthless on the other?' She just couldn't understand it.

'What could Francine know that I don't?' Janice lamented. She was up most of the night agonizing over why Francine wanted what was on the answering service. Nothing came to mind that made sense. She decided to wait for the call she knew would come the next morning and see how it played out.

There was no group session planned for the next day so Donald suggested he and Francine meet for an early breakfast and call Janice together. She agreed and at 7:00 am they met at The Plaza for coffee and croissants.

"I'm too anxious to wait till we're finished Donald. Could you please order and I'll try Janice." Francine asked.

"Go ahead Franny." He replied.

Francine dialed the number and Donald waved the waitress to the table.

"Hello Janice, its Francine."

"I've been expecting your call dear." She answered. Janice tried not to reveal her anxiety.

"You have?" Francine asked.

"Yes dear. I know I didn't give you the password. I'm sorry about that but I needed time to think.

Francine held the cell phone to her side and whispered to Donald that Janice had admitted withholding the password. David raised an eyebrow and Francine placed the phone to her ear again.

"Francine, are you still there?" Janice asked.

"Yes, yes. I'm here Janice. Dr. Heathrow and I are at the Plaza having breakfast and the waitress just came to the table that's all." She replied. "Why did you need time to think Janice? Is there something you don't want me to know?" Donald could see Francine was becoming increasingly agitated and took her hand gently in his.

"Try to settle down and focus on why you called, Franny. He whispered.

"Well yes dear, there was. I just didn't want to upset you more than you have already been these last few weeks.

"Never mind that right now Janice. Please tell me, did you listen to David's last messages?" Francine pleaded.

"No dear, I erased them all without listening." She answered.

"What?" Why would you do that? Francine shouted.

"Because I didn't want to have to lie to the police if there was anything incriminating on the service. If I don't know anything, I can't lie. And with all of David's files destroyed I hoped the authorities would drop the investigation. I was trying to protect you dear."

"Protect me? From what?" She paused for a moment as Janice's words sank in. "What investigation are you talking about Janice?" Francine demanded.

"Try to be calm Franny." Donald whispered gently again.

"But Donald, she says David was under investigation for something. Francine whimpered while holding her hand over the cell phone.

"We can deal with that later Franny, for the time being let's just find out what she knows about the messages." Donald said. Francine took a moment to compose her thoughts before going back to the call.

"Francine, if you didn't know about the investigation then why did you want to hear his messages?" Janice asked. "Please dear, tell me what's going on." Janice was becoming concerned that she had made a serious error by erasing the messages.

"I don't want to go into detail right now, all I can tell you is I believe David left a very important message, probably his last one about a life and death situation." Francine explained firmly.

"I'm sure it could easily have been a life and death situation under the circumstances." Janice said.

"No, no, I don't mean his, it's my niece Yasmine." Francine said. The tension was too much for her and she began crying.

"Yasmine? Is she in trouble dear?" Janice was shaking as she realized how foolish she had been not to consider that there may have been some messages other than those that might incriminate David on the answering service 'God, I'm so stupid. I was only thinking of my obligations to him.' She thought.

"Yes! Terrible trouble, but we don't know where she is. She wrote an email to us but when I tried to reach her the message bounced back *undeliverable*. I believe David somehow got new information concerning Yasmine and left it on his answering service." Francine explained.

Something sounded wrong to Janice, 'why didn't David just call Francine on her cell phone?' She wondered. 'And why would Francine think he'd found something new on that day of all days?' "Francine, I'm a little confused." She said.

"I can't explain right now, it's complicated." Francine knew her explanation would send up a red flag and wanted to avoid anything that might delay helping Yasmine. "I lost my cell phone the day before and I was in transit to the university when the sky fell in. David may have tried to reach me on that phone and because he couldn't I believe there is a good chance he left me a message on his private service."

Her explanation made as much sense as it could without more details, but logical or not it was clear Janice knew she had acted hastily in erasing the messages. "Oh dear. If only I had just listened to those messages. I thought I was doing the right thing." She said almost in tears.

Francine relayed the conversation to Donald who went silent when he saw they seemed to be at a dead end. For many years when a problem presented itself, one that appeared to have no answer he became quiet and turned his focus inward. More often than not he would soon get an impression or a hint of a new direction to take, sometimes a full-blown inspiration would suddenly flash before his inner screen. He had no idea where the idea came from, it just did.

Later, in research on meditation, he discovered his little technique was similar to what many specialists in the field referred to as 'going into *the gap* between thoughts'. There were many similarities between his personal quest for understanding the inner universe behind the mind, and the insights he received from time to time. Until now it had been a mystery, however in the last several weeks since the *pink lady* phenomenal began to surface, he sensed the riddle was about to be solved.

91

Without thinking, Donald suggested to Francine that she ask if anyone else might have had access to the messages. She made a strange face, then a light went on and she realized what he was saying could be true. She relayed the question to Janice.

"Please don't spare my feelings, this is too important. You know my marriage to David was over long ago."

"I know dear." Janice said. "Yes, there is someone, but she may not be able to help us."

"Why not? Who is she? Francine demanded.

"Its not that she wouldn't dear, its because she's in the hospital in intensive care. She tried to kill herself after she heard what happened to David."

"Oh God!" Francine cried! Francine told Donald the bad news. Again her emotions reached the breaking point and she began to sob.

Donald took the phone, "This is Dr. Heathrow Janice. Please tell me the women's name and which hospital she is in."

"Yes, yes, of course. Her name is Amy Meadows and she's in St Vincent's hospital."

"Very good, I know the Chief of Staff there, that should help speed things up." He said.

"Dr. Heathrow, I think I should be there when you try to speak with her. In her condition meeting Francine for the first time might be difficult. Perhaps I can help, she knows me." Janice suggested.

"Good idea. I'll call you back as soon as I know when we can get in to see her." He said sincerely. 'Thanks for all your help."

Donald made the call and within an hour Donald and Francine met Janice in the lobby of the St. Vincent's hospital.

Twenty-Five

1970's

The profound influence of parental and spiritual love on growing children cannot be over estimated. The future of the child is significantly influenced in direct proportion to that love, or the lack of it. Whether the peer pressure to indulge in drugs, alcohol and self indulgence or the extreme religious coercion to join a fanatical group of terrorists, sacrificing their lives in the hope of reaching paradise, youth are vulnerable or immune to the degree they experience the guiding light of love during their formative years.

By the mid 1970's the theater of madness in the Middle East was in full swing. Political ambitions diluted the purity of The Prophet's original message for many in positions of power, while multitudes of well intentioned followers concluded violence against anyone who was not a believer was their spiritual duty, particularly if those disbelievers were occupying what was believed to be Islamic Holy land.

Abdullah and Shahira were faithful Muslims who followed the tenets of Islam as close as their understanding of it took them. However, understanding is nebulous at best and depends on who is interpreting. Theistic leaders in the region often thought one thing, said another and did a third. The ability to divest oneself from the collective influence of thousands of like-minded people, people who were following a path of madness, took a powerful will that few possessed.

Had Ibrahim been close at hand during those turbulent years of increasing malcontent, Abdullah would certainly have been able to remain more heart centered. Ironically, while Abdullah was swaying with the tide of Middle Eastern insanity, Ibrahim was embracing the compelling heart of spirituality wherever it pulled him. Essentially, he divested his attachment to the body and mind of the ephemeral world of business and invested his spirit in the eternal universe that lay within.

His son Mika'ill took the artists path. Playing a great instrument can make a profound difference in a musician's life. Rarely though, do students of the violin own instruments that complement their artistic development. Through an influential colleague who had a connection at the Smithsonian, a Stradivarius was acquired which Ibrahim proudly presented to Mika'ill's on his Twenty-First birthday. That gesture of love sealed his musical future. He applied and qualified for The Julliard School where he could master the violin among the giants.

He was accepted by the prestigious school at the age of Twenty Four and while in his second year met and fell in love with a beautiful young Egyptian girl named Hayfa who was studying the viola in the same year as he. The two courted during their final two years of study and in 1973, after graduating, Ibrahim and Jacqueline took them home to Jordan where an elaborate wedding ceremony took place in Amman.

Mika'ill's life choice also closed the door on The House of Faiz moving toward the end of the millennium with a first descendent of Ibrahim at the helm. The trade off was more than joyful for Ibrahim and Jacqueline who saw in Mika'ill's decision a rich life they knew would be inspired by a higher inner power.

This left the future of the House of Faiz to Abdullah's two sons. His first son Abdul, by then in his early twenties, was dull-witted and reckless. On the other hand his brother Ahmal, who was in his late teens, might have been an excellent candidate to take the reins of power when the time came. Unfortunately, Abdullah's interest in the escalating Middle Eastern hostilities swayed Ahmal away from business and toward religious extremism.

Although Abdul was the eldest brother it was Ahmal that guided both their paths. The blind leading the blind as it turned out. There was ample opportunity to engage in militant activities and by the end of the 1970's the hotheaded Ahmal and his submissive brother engaged in a variety of hostile activities that lead them finally to Afghanistan. Their mother's homeland had been invaded by the Soviets and the brothers decided to join the resistence in that region.

The fact that Afghanistan was vastly out gunned by an aggressive super power made the adventure all the more defendable as an act of Jihad, a holy war. It was there they first came under the influence of a wealthy Saudi named Omar bin Lotfi. His support of the Afghans had a significant effect on the outcome of the war and a powerful impact on the brothers.

Early on in the Middle Eastern hostilities Ibrahim counseled his friend and partner Abdullah. "The world is a product of what we think and each of us in turn is influenced by that world, which validates for us, just like a mirror, what we believe to be true. Ultimately it becomes a powerful vehicle for driving the soul toward its true home. However many disasters may occur in that vehicle before we use it to steer us toward truth and love."

As always, Abdullah was deeply moved by his wise and thoughtful mentor. Unfortunately, Abdullah's constant exposure to the Middle Eastern conflict eroded the positive effect of Ibrahim's wise counsel. As a result Abdullah failed to extend the same insightful guidance to his two sons who were on the road to destruction, both theirs, and many others who would cross their path.

Ibrahim's frequent periods of absence from the Middle East during the 60's and 70's also contributed to the steadily growing unrest of his partner. Abdullah believed that the material power and spiritual influence Ibrahim possessed could be of enormous benefit in helping to crush what he believed to be the aggressors in the region. Because Ibrahim would not take sides in the conflict Abdullah eventually came to believe that his partner had abandoned his original spiritual devotion.

Abdullah, in moments of despair and witnessing the acceleration of hostilities in the region lamented, "Why has Allah's great servant abandoned his culture, his people and his friends?" Abdullah's son's were incensed by their father's distress and agreed with their father that Ibrahim had abused his faith for the sake of worldly power. It was Ahmal who first suggested Ibrahim should one day pay for his depravity.

******

Mika'ill and Hayfa were invited to tour with the London Philharmonic Orchestra in 1974 and Jacqueline's family gave them their flat in Mayfair as a wedding present. Meanwhile, Francine had already moved to England to study psychology and sociology at the renowned Oxford University. When her brother and new sister-in-law moved to London she was ecstatic. Like her brother, Francine had been weaned on unconditional love and nurtured with the open -ended ideal that anything is possible. Ibrahim and Jacqueline had given both their children ample evidence to validate that belief through the living example of their own lives.

Altruism to Francine meant world philanthropy. If there was a cause worth pursuing she was determined to submerge herself in it. Ibrahim and Jacqueline refrained from deterring her from anything her heart led her to including the suffering in the Middle East. When Mika'ill and Hayfa moved to London, Francine had a year before graduation. From there Ibrahim and Jacqueline believed she would return to Jordan. They were

95

more than a little relieved when Francine decided to stay in England to be near her brother and sister-in-law.

She had obviously found within her desire to serve and her deep love for Mika'ill, a way to reconcile the two great passions in her life. "There are many opportunities to help the oppressed right here in England." Francine told her parents. For the moment at least, the Faiz family was joyfully navigating around the growing storm clouds in Middle Eastern.

Twenty-Six

1997 &

September - 6 - 2001

From the first moment Benny entered the precinct with constable Larry MacDonald, everyone took an instant liking to him. Later, Sergeant Sarvino told Larry, "It was like a breath of fresh air entered the station. I can't explain it. He just lit up the whole place."

"I know what you mean Sarge, that's how my uncle Angus feels about the kid too." Larry laughed remembering his uncle's surprise when he met Benny. "He told me,

'The dobs got loose one day when I was out walkin them. I'm terrified they're going to get hit by some crazy driver see. I shout across the street at them and that's when the kid comes walking round the corner. He takes one look at what's happenin, squats down and opens his arms, as if he's expectin a little kid to come runnin into them. "Unbelievable!" I says to myself. Next thing I know the dobs stop dead in their tracks, eye the kid, then trot over to him as if they knew him forever. A few seconds later they got their heads buried into his arm pits. Its as if the kid's charmed or something.'"

"Wow! That's unreal. How do ya think he did it?" Sarvino asked.

"Beats me. He's got a little sister that was dying of Aids. One night she has minutes to live and the next morning she's totally healed. Called Meereka I think. It's supposed to mean miracle child according to Benny."

Sarvino scratched his head. "I've heard of stuff like that. You know, the healing water place, what's it called?"

"Lourdes." Larry replied.

"Ya, that's it! Maybe the family's got some special powers like that." Sarvino said.

"I dunno. My uncle's puttin the kid and his family up in his Coach House. Its like a palace compared to where they lived before. I'm just glad we can help out."

"Maybe it's the precinct that's gonna get helped out the most Larry." Sarvino said.

"Maybe." Larry replied. "Wouldn't surprise me."

Within a month of doing odd jobs around the station several staff members noticed that Benny had a knack for organization and logic. Detective Thompson decided to ask Benny to help him organize an old case file on a lost child.

"Been missing three years now kid, Its a cold file, but I like to keep my eye on it. Its kinda close to home." The detective said.

"How that?" Benny asked.

"Its my sister's kid, my nephew." He said. Detective Thompson looked lost in thought for a few moments after he told Benny about the file.

"I know how I'd feel if my little sister Meereka were gone." Benny said. The detective's chin quivered and he nodded.

Benny dug into the file like a natural born investigator. Three days later he asked the detective if he had checked on one of his sister's old boyfriends. The detective told him the guy was clean.

"Besides, he was only on the scene for a month and was long gone before my nephew's disappearance."

"Yes, but the file says he was once engaged to a woman that lost a child to a kidnapper. I told Meereka and she said, 'Find sad lady.'"

"Meereka? How could she know anything?" Detective Thompson began to regret his decision to share the case with Benny, yet he had to admit that he hadn't checked that angle. "Okay kid, I'll look into it." Two days later the child was found across the state with the woman who was now married to the old boyfriend. Sarvino never doubted Benny or little Meereka again.

Benny left the drawings and letters in the manila Envelop Sarvino had given him until he could look at them with Meereka.

"Meereka, I have something I want to show you princess." Benny said.

"*Pink lady* pictures?" She asked.

"Yes princess, I think so." Benny answered. He opened the Envelop and handed Meereka the one drawing with *pink lady* written on it. She took it, closed her eyes and smiled while clutching the drawing to her chest. She was silent for several minutes, lost in a world Benny could not enter.

Her eyes were still closed when she finally spoke, "Meereka going home soon."

She had never said such a thing before. Benny could feel the truth of it. His body trembled as tears filled his eyes. He sat on the floor and began crying.

She hugged him about the shoulders, "Meereka still be with Benny." Minutes passed and Benny knew his little angel would soon be gone. His heart ached.

Finally Meereka spoke. "*Pink lady* children see sad day."

"Sad day? What sad day princess, what day? Is it...is it the day you will go home?" He asked through sobs.

"Not gone Benny - just home." She said. "See pictures? Four birds fall from sky." She shook her head. Many people cry." Meereka had not looked at any other picture except for the one Benny had given her. She picked up the drawings and laid them side-by-side across the floor then began shuffling the order. When she was finished it was obvious they formed a pattern, like reading a comic book.

The first one was a sand pile, the next what looked like a horse on a sand pile, then a man on a horse on a sand pile. The following picture showed the man with something resembling a long stick in his hand. After that there was a close up of a man's face. Simple though the drawing was the face looked sad and angry at the same time. The next picture showed four birds flying. Then another picture had two birds flying and two standing sticks burning. After that there was a dead bird beside a five pointed star. The second last picture showed a dead bird lying on the ground in a field. In the upper right hand corner was a large red X. The last drawing was the one with *pink lady* at the top and two upright burning sticks below it.

Meereka said, "Letters all same." She took the letters and without looking at them, placed one on the top of each drawing. Later, when Benny read

99

the letters, all described the very same drawing on which his little sister had placed each letter, and all were from totally different parts of the world. There was one extra letter. In it was written three words, "*Pink lady* sad." Under the words were nine X's and eleven O's that appeared to be kisses and hugs.

While Benny struggled to remain unemotional, he looked up from the drawings and letters and asked, "Princess, what does it mean?"

"Angry people bring fire." She said.

He urged her to explain further but she said nothing more. Benny knew from experience there would not be any added explanation.

"Its amazing Benny, like a warning. But of what?" Sarvino asked when Benny explained what Meereka had revealed. The detective looked at Benny and saw he was in pain. "What kid? What is it? Can I help?"

Benny sighed and wiped a tear away. "Meereka says she's going home. She's going to die Leroy. " He began sobbing.

"How can you be so certain Benny? I mean it could be something else." But detective Thompson knew it was true. If Meereka said she was going home and that meant she was going to die, he knew it would happen. She had never been wrong.

"There's nothing we can do Leroy, not a thing." Benny lowered his head and silently wept. The detective put his arm around Benny like a father and sat with him in silence. Several minutes passed before Benny whispered.

"There's more Leroy. Meereka said that after the sad day there would be more drawings."

"More drawings? More letters?" The detective asked.

"Yes. I don't know why, but I know we should expect them and that they will be very important to us."

"In what way Benny?"

"I'm not certain. Meereka said one more thing, "Pictures help find people". Its as if these drawings and letters are to tell us something sad is

100

going to happen that we can't stop, and the ones to come are to show us how we can help those who are sad."

Twenty-Seven

September - 1968

&

July - 10 - 1976

Donald's brush with death in India proved a greater benefit to him than he could have possibly imagined, because an incredible transformation occurred in his dad.

Dr. Ramsey Heathrow lived a life of controlled balance. He was certain that understanding the human mind made him the master of his universe. When Donald's belligerent attitude toward his lifestyle escalated into what Ramsey considered a reckless gamble with a guaranteed future - secure and full of opportunity, he was shaken.

Dr. Heathrow knew Donald was young and the collective consciousness of the 60's was rebellious and certain to have an influence on him. But tearing half way across the globe in the dubious search of a so-called holy man, enticed by the Post Traumatic rant of his Vietnam veteran buddy, was reckless.

Ramsey and his wife drove Donald to the airport they felt certain he would change his mind right up to the moment he handed his ticket to the boarding attendant. So it was that two weeks before his senior year at Columbia University was to begin, he was on his way to Bangalore. Late the next day, Ramsey got the call that Donald was in intensive care and hovering between life and death.

On that day the Dr. Ramsey Heathrow Donald knew, experienced his own death. In less than 48 hours, control was torn from his grasp and an unknown authority clutched his heart. He could not believe a person could be in so much pain and still be alive, yet at the same time his life was far more palpable than it had ever been. The sense of profound loss, as near as it was, ripped the veil of false power from his grasp. He felt naked while vitally alive and aware of his own vulnerability.

Of one thing Ramsey was certain, the life he'd been living was not life at all. Until now, he had somehow managed to harvest the wheat from the whirlwind of chaff that flew from the chaotic lives of his rich and famous patients. The vicarious taste of forbidden nectar held no withdrawal symptoms and until that day, no pain. It was like riding the most terrifying roller coaster, with all the exhilarating highs and lows, totally numbed out on tranquilizers. Suddenly, his feelings had been switched on. He was like a deer stunned by the headlights, seconds from annihilation - unable to move - in stark terror.

In the two weeks he spent in Bangalore he floated in a sea of helplessness. His training and his confidence were useless. He prayed the first real prayers of his life in those fourteen days of limbo - timeless days - days of deep self-discovery. When Donald returned to finish his senior year in late 1968, Ramsey made two new friends; himself and his son.

The next four and half years for Ramsey, while Donald studied for his doctorate, were transformative for both he and Donald. Rather than cast aside the practice he had built, Donald suggested his dad reinvent it. Donald submitted that power, guided by a sincere inner urge to truly alter world consciousness toward selfless service, while utopian, was an ideal worth pursuing.

Further, he had the inspired notion that the future of the film industry had a very real potential to become a powerful teaching instrument. He visualized it as a dynamic subliminal device that could, over time, plant millions of idealistic seeds in the global mind.

"After all dad, the industry spends half its time searching for investment capital, and the money-people spend a good deal of their efforts wooing politicians to help improve their bottom line. The majority of your patients fall into one of those three categories."

Professionally, Dr. Heathrow would need to follow certain rules of integrity but socially he could lobby for whatever he pleased.

Before Donald joined him in his practice in 1974, he helped his dad establish a free clinic for Vietnam Vets and create a film production company which they called *Inner Scape Productions* to fund and produce movies with themes that fostered self actualized life styles. In their second year with *Inner Scape*, they met Ibrahim Faiz.

Ramsey returned from lunch one day and said, "Donald, remember the Senator said he would try to arrange a meeting with Barry Feinstein from Galaxy Studios?"

"Yes. Was he able to set something up for us?" Donald asked.

"Well as a matter of fact when I dropped into Cappaletti's for lunch, there he was with Feinstein who just happened to be in town."

"Really? How about that for synchronicity?" Donald loved when events created themselves around dreams.

"And, he was with another gentleman, a fascinating fellow named Benjamin Pearlman." Ramsey said.

"Why's that dad?"

"He's a Shaman!" Ramsey said.

"Well that *is* interesting. Maybe Feinstein is on the same track as us." Donald said.

"It gets better." Dr. Heathrow grinned. He was a Rabbi for almost 40 years. He taught the Kabala exclusively for the last ten of those years." Ramsey said.

"Pardon me!" Donald exclaimed. "He certainly sounds like an interesting character. I'd love to meet him."

"As a matter of fact he's holding a reception for a powerful friend of his from Jordan tomorrow evening. His name is Ibrahim Faiz, have you ever hear of him? Ramsey whimsically.

"The author of the of the best selling book *'The Same God'*. I wouldn't be much of a student of the *inner mind* if I hadn't..." Ramsey was looking at Donald with a sarcastic smirk on his face.

"Alright, you got me!" Donald chuckled. Since Donald's near death experience Ramsey made up for the lost years of fatherhood whenever he could. Donald possessed an innocent naiveté and could easily be toyed with. This was one of those occasions when Ramsey could take advantage of that quality as a playful endearment.

"Benjamin invited us to attend, which of course I accepted. I figured you wouldn't mind." Ramsey said.

"Absolutely not! Sounds like it will be a really fascinating evening." Donald replied.

The following evening Dr. Ramsey Heathrow and Dr. Donald Heathrow attended a black tie reception for Ibrahim Faiz held at the Vivian Beaumont Theater. Following the formalities Benjamin took Ibrahim aside and introduced him to Ramsey and Donald.

"Ibrahim I want you to meet two new acquaintances of mine. I believe we all share many of the same interests. May I present Doctors Ramsey and Donald Heathrow?" Ramsey extended his hand and Ibrahim grasped it warmly with two hands. He bowed slightly then repeated the gesture with Donald.

"And may I present my love and my inspiration, my wife Jacqueline." Ibrahim said.

Jacqueline had been speaking with the executive producer of the theater and noticed Benjamin introducing Ibrahim to Ramsey and Donald. Feeling drawn to them, she excused herself and joined the men.

"A great pleasure Mrs. Faiz." The two said in unison.

"I imagine you two have many things *just fall into place* like that." She said.

Ibrahim withheld a smile waiting to see how his two new acquaintances would react to Jacqueline's straightforward intuitive behavior. Donald turned toward his dad and they smiled at each other.

"I see now what you meant Benjamin." Ibrahim said.

"What's that?" Jacqueline asked.

"I told Ibrahim these two fellows would have a lot in common with your interests." Benjamin replied.

"Ah yes, I see. And how do you feel about that Dr. Heathrow and Dr. Heathrow?" She giggled.

"Somehow I feel, on some level, we already know each other." Donald said.

105

Jacqueline studied Donald's face as if she was looking for something that would tell her where it might have been. "Ever been to India?" She asked.

This time Ramsey turned and looked at Donald, not in surprise but with that incredible realization that sometimes occurs when the universe again validates that it really does know what Its doing. "As a matter of fact, we both have." Ramsey said.

Jacqueline gave Ramsey a sideways glance then immediately returned her gaze to Donald's face. "You've met him haven't you?"

"Excuse me. Met who Mrs. Faiz? Donald asked

"Please, call me Jacqueline. After all, as you said, we already know each other."

Benjamin and Ibrahim were enjoying themselves. "Whenever two old souls meet again and one is not certain of how or when, the dance can be delightful." Benjamin laughed.

Donald looked perplexed. He looked to Ibrahim and Benjamin for an explanation, then back to Jacqueline. She stood grinning at him, and looking like the Cheshire cat.

"Another time, another life my young friend. Jacqueline and you obviously know each other from another lifetime Doctor." Benjamin laughed.

"We have met on this stage before my young friend. Don't you find it ironic and amusing that this time we should meet here, *and* in a theater?" Jacqueline laughed.

Twenty-Eight

Abdullah's travel schedule rarely took him outside the Islamic world as Ibrahim handled all the international business for the *House of Faiz*. Both men were content with the arrangement. In the summer of 1978 however Abdullah requested an urgent meeting to discuss the status of their partnership. Ibrahim found it impossible to alter his commitments and could not meet Abdullah in Jordan. As a result Abdullah was obliged to set his feet upon American soil for the first time.

Ibrahim's fervent desire was to make his friend feel as comfortable as the occasion permitted. He knew Abdullah's heart had been dragged deeply into the dark shadows that were sweeping across the Middle East and he hoped the brief time away from the toxic influence in the region would help balance Abdullah's troubled spirit.

However, Abdullah declined his partner's invitation to stay with he and Jacqueline in their Soho apartment. He wanted to keep a safe distance from the old feelings he once held for his long time friend and partner. He feared that if his visit was too intimate he may not have the stomach for what he intended. Ibrahim settled his friend into the most comfortable hotel available near his home and arranged to meet with him after he had time to rest.

The ambassador from Jordan, who knew both men well, arranged for a meeting with local Muslim clerics and despite Abdullah's reluctance to meet Ibrahim in a sociable manner he allowed himself the freedom to enjoy the event with his lifelong friend, a feeling he had greatly missed. However, the gesture fell far short of pacifying Abdullah's misgivings about Ibrahim's abandonment of the strict doctrine of Islam.

His suspicions were confirmed when at dinner Ibrahim arranged for Abdullah and his wife Shahira, to include Benjamin Pearlman and a politician mentioned in Ibrahim's book *'The Same God'*. When the evening was over he told himself, 'There can be no doubt, my one time mentor, friend and partner can no longer be considered a faithful servant to Allah.'

The following day Abdullah met with Ibrahim in his Soho brownstone. He and Jacqueline purchased the home two years before to accommodate their frequent business trips to New York, the North American headquarters for Brarab Industries. The two men retired to the library and while they waited for Jacqueline to bring them coffee, Abdullah scanned the bookshelves. He noted with disdain that most of the books were of philosophies and belief systems that did not comply with the tenets of the Qur'an.

When they were settled in, Ibrahim waited patiently for what he was certain his partner was there to tell him. He could sense his friend's inner torment. Abdullah's world reflected only conflict, confusion and hatred. "Allah must have a mysterious purpose for the intense suffering I see all around me." He told Ibrahim, struggling to broach the reason for their meeting.

"Dear Abdullah, how wonderful it has been to call you my friend these many years. You are to me as a beloved brother. My heart despairs to see you in such torment. Our world can only mirror our thoughts, both our purest ideals and our greatest fears. To change humanity's thoughts enough to free it from the poisonous images that now flood our homeland will take a mighty force of will." Ibrahim allowed his friend a moment to adjust to the gentle atmosphere he had created. Then he continued.

"Abdullah, you have been a true and honest partner. I could have chosen no one greater for the many difficult burdens you have taken upon your shoulders. Let this parting you have come to request be one between brothers who have together, served well and loved well. Let no angry corner, from what might have been, remain in your mind and wound your heart."

Abdullah was amazed at Ibrahim's insight. He felt relieved but ashamed. Yet the sting of his mentor's departure from Islam could not be soothed.

"My brother Ibrahim, for most of my life I believed Allah had no greater servant than Ibrahim Faiz. Yet I find can no longer hold my tormented thoughts a moment longer. I must ask you why have you turned your back on Allah?"

Ibrahim's heart felt pierced with the anguish he felt for Abdullah. He wanted to reach out and magically heal the aching spirit of his friend, yet he knew that only Abdullah could do that for himself. Abdullah's confusion deepened as he watched the light in Ibrahim's face. He saw the radiant depth of love in this man he had doubted, a man he felt had abandoned his faith. 'How can a man love so much and not be a servant of Allah?' He agonized.

108

"You marvel at the expanded vision I now hold of God dear friend. Yet without the growth of man's awareness he can never hope to obtain a lasting peace within himself or his world. The words of The Prophet are true and pure, but the glass through which those words have been magnified is clouded by impure thoughts. Such is the power of our union with God that whatever we place our most passionate thoughts upon becomes our reality. Without wisdom, a world of violence and hatred can appear to validate our belief that the ends justify the means."

Abdullah remembered how he loved to listen to his friend speak of Allah as a boy. As Ibrahim spoke, for just a moment, those wonder filled days of devotion came flooding back.

"Our God *is* God my brother. But I have learned that Allah speaks through the understanding of mankind in many ways. These ways have come to be known by a multitude of names. Like the facets of a diamond, each facing in different directions, the light that shines through them has the same single origin. God is One, One with all that is, one with all mankind, no matter the belief system a person adheres to, even if he has none."

Abdullah's agonized over Ibrahim's words, so foreign they were from what he had been taught. He could not accept that the Jew and the Christian and the myriad other followers of false gods could possibly be following the same God of the Prophet. In his heart he wanted to find a common thread that connected their two faiths, but he could not. The disappointment pressed upon his heart. He could listen no further.

"Enough, one time partner, I shall hear no more. I seek a division of our company and have prepared what I believe is a fair and just offer."

Ibrahim was not surprised that his attempt to reason with his friend had fallen on deaf ears. He knew the years of conditioned hatred that polluted the atmosphere in the Middle East blinded many from the possibility of seeing the light when it came.

"Dear friend, I have no doubt your offer is just. We shall not speak of these disheartening details again. My lawyers will review your proposition and have an answer for you before the week is over. Please let us now separate as friends for the sake of the love that has passed between us."

Abdullah remained detached and departed Ibrahim's home carrying the added burden of a cold heart. A week later the two men divided their business interests, essentially giving the House of Faiz to Abdullah and Brarab Industries to Ibrahim. Ibrahim declined the cash offer his ex-partner offered to balance the deal evenly. He knew that what was his could never be taken from him as he knew within his heart and soul that the *House of Faiz* would soon experience difficult times.

His friend was an open book to the inner eye of Ibrahim and he knew Abdullah could not resist bringing his son Ahmed into a senior role with the company. Ibrahim had followed the progress of his partner's family with love, as would a protective older brother. He had seen the insidious influence of prejudice and judgement that permeated the minds of young men corrupted by fanatical interpretations of the Prophets wisdom. Abdullah's son would bring that infection with him into the company and turn the sweetness it once held, sour.

Twenty-Nine

July - 10 - 1976

Reconciled in heart and soul, Ramsey and Donald Heathrow extended their psychiatric practice well beyond the boundaries of pure mind science into the metaphysics of *cause behind effect*. It was therefore natural the concept of reincarnation would be one of the many subjects they explored. The empirical evidence of allopathic medicine was guided largely by factual and verifiable science. Anything that could not be empirically proven was considered dubious at best by most western minds.

Additionally, most Western religious persuasions did not embrace the concept of reincarnation of the spirit. Nevertheless, Ramsey and Donald's research uncovered the fact that it was at the Second Council of Constantinople in the year 553 AD, that the definition of reincarnation was declared as heresy, the results of a plot against it by Emperor Justinian.

Rather than discourage Ramsey and Donald this information inspired the two men to seek out references in the bible that had not been erased by this edict. They found the account of Jesus telling his disciples that John the Baptist was Elijah come again. In the book of Malachi 4:1-5, a similar reference to Elijah returning was made: *'Lo, I will send you the prophet Elijah before the great and terrible day the Lord comes.'*

Ramsey and Donald were also impressed by the work of Dr. Ian Stevenson who had been head of the Department of Psychiatry at the University of Virginia School of Medicine. He published a number of books on the subject of reincarnation that were highly academic in nature and based on rigorous research.

Exploration into the history of India, where reincarnation is an accepted aspect of man's quest for spiritual attainment, led them to numerous well documented cases of children who remembered the locations and names of spouses they had been married to in a past life. Most of the accounts had similar descriptions of how memories of previous lives had been validated by relatives when the children were taken to the villages or towns where they claimed to have lived. They learned it was common for these children to take their parents directly to the home of their previous spouse. Further validation revealed the children knew things that only the couple in question could have known when the two were together.

Despite their interest in subject, beyond their research, Ramsey and Donald had no personal experience with the subject until they met Ibrahim and Jacqueline Faiz at the Vivian Beaumont Theater in New York.

"Ah!" She sighed. "There you are."

Donald glanced from his father to Ibrahim to Benjamin, perplexed. He felt slightly off balance waiting for the other shoe to drop. Ramsey gave him an expression that said, 'Don't ask me, I'm as much in the dark as you.'

Donald finally dared bring his eyes back to Jacqueline's. Immediately he felt a penetrating and slightly intrusive gaze.

"Where?" Donald asked. In contrast to a rush of exhilaration that shot through his body, he felt very uneasy. 'What will she tell me?' He wondered. 'Who have I been? What could our past together possibly have been?'

"No memory? Nothing coming up?" She asked.

"Just the feeling I mentioned before." He replied. I feel somehow we know each other."

"Actors." Ramsey suddenly blurted. "We were actors!" The look on his face was of pure astonishment. He couldn't believe he actually remembered part of another life experience. The moment his father made his surprising announcement something penetrated the ancient vaults of Donald's cellular memory and he too recalled the life.

"We were part of a company of Shakespearian actors. Not just actors but members of a sect that knew the Bard's plays were all metaphors for mankind's quest to reawaken to the God within." Donald exclaimed.

Jacqueline was grinning from ear to ear like a Cheshire cat. "And now gentlemen, the play continues!" She laughed loud enough for everyone in the theater reception hall to hear her. "I suspect you two have cooked up some way for us to take the play to the next level.

Ibrahim watched the reunion with a look of absolute serenity. Inwardly he was affirming that everything unfolds, as it should in God's universe, despite appearances. Benjamin shook his head, laughing in joy.

"Yes, I believe we have, haven't we dad?" Donald laughed in amazement. "As a matter of fact 18 months ago we created a company called *Inner Scape Productions*. Our intention is to produce films containing material that inspires and empowers people. We want to use this powerful medium to plant seeds that people to search for the big questions in the only place they can be found - within.

"That's right. Ramsey elaborated. "We want to go beyond Self Actualization or *the freedom from the good or bad opinions of others*, as my colleague Abraham Maslow has pointed out. We want to encourage humanity to reach to the depths of their spirit and find that everything they have ever sought has always been there, waiting for them to rediscover." Ramsey explained.

"That's it! I believe my dear husband will agree you have our support in your new venture. Where do we go from here?" Jacqueline asked as if they were simply picking up the threads of an age-old tapestry they had been weaving for centuries.

Over the next several days Benjamin joined the two couples, comparing notes as if they had been on a research field trip and had just returned to base to consolidate their findings.

It appears, despite our divergent paths, we have returned to ground zero ready to see how the great Spirit, would have us serve our world this time." Benjamin said. Jacqueline shuddered visibly when Benjamin said 'ground zero'.

"What is it my dear?" Ibrahim asked.

"I don't know. Something very dark just passed through my heart when Benjamin said 'ground zero'. It felt distant - a thought form crystallizing far away in time, yet right here in New York." She shook herself, took a few deep breaths and proclaimed, "Ok! I'm back."

Over the next two years *Inner Scape Productions* funded two projects Donald and Ramsey had been working on since the inception of the company and began discussing how the group could produce a television documentary on Ibrahim's book *The Same God*.

By late 1978, just after the *House of Faiz* separated from *Brarab Industries*, Donald and Ramsey agreed to sell a half interest in *Inner Scape* to *Brarab*. In December of that same year Abdullah had a massive heart attack and died.

Thirty

Francine introduced Donald to Janice Miller as the three walked to the hospital elevator.

"Sorry we couldn't explain all the details to you Mrs. Miller, but we didn't want to jeopardize the possibility of you helping us." Donald explained.

"Donald, please call me Janice. Can you tell me anything more now? I mean, why do you think David had some last minute information on your niece. On that day of all days?" Donald did not respond.

The elevator doors slid open and the three entered as an orderly exited with a patient in a wheelchair. This simple act immediately conjured up a thousand similar images in Donald's mind of that terrible day. 'Senseless loss!' He thought. He shook himself knowing God's gentle hand was behind everything, no matter the outward appearance.

In the twenty-three years *Inner Scape* had been producing spiritually oriented movies he had learned *nothing* was senseless, nothing was wasted. All things worked together for good. At the core of his being Donald knew the world was evolving ever faster toward the *'light that passeth understanding'*, toward *'the better angels of our nature'*, toward *'the God within'*. He knew that as the light shines ever brighter, shadows stand in stark contrast, appearing more ominous and powerful than they once did when they blended almost seamlessly with a fainter light.

'How else can we know the dark angels of our nature, the shadowy concepts and hidden programs of outrageous fortune, if we don't allow them to rise to the surface of our experience, to be swept away by the winds of change. It is a change wrought in heaven?' Donald argued with the momentary doubt that filled his mind. 'Still, the ravages that lay beneath the shadows seem so real, so tangible, so raw, like an open wound. How real the unreal can seem when the hunger of ancient nightmares open their ravenous jaws begging to be fed by our fear?'

"No! I will not yield!" Donald said out loud.

"Pardon me?" Janice said.

Francine knew that Donald had sensed her presence in his thoughts. Sharing thoughts was a happy gift the two once shared, long ago, before the shadows came and shrouded her heart-song; before Mika'ill and Hayfa, before Yousef, before David. Could Janice possibly comprehend the world in which Donald lived? The world she had forsaken for a *'far country'* of grief. It really didn't matter if she could, in a few minutes they would meet Amy and whether Janice was in sync with them or not mattered little. Somehow, she knew Donald would reach Amy.

"Sorry, I was just thinking out loud." Donald said. Janice gave him a weird look. The elevator doors opened at the 4th floor and they approached the I.C.U. reception desk a few steps away. A stone face nurse looked up and glared at the clock as if to indicate it was past visiting hours.

"Hello, my name is Dr. Heathrow. Dr. Fitzpatrick gave us permission to visit with Amy Meadows. Can you please tell us which room she's in?" Donald showed the woman his medical identification. The nurse said nothing, glanced at the I.D. indifferently and pointed down the hall.

"444." She said indifferently. The nurse said nothing more and went back to her duties.

"God!" She's an iceberg, isn't she?" Janice complained.

"Intensive Care is much like the Emergency Ward. It usually inclines the spirit one-way or the other. The cold mask of shell shock or the compassionate warmth of an open heart." Donald said.

"I suppose." Janice whispered cynically.

A minute later they found Amy's room. Donald gave Francine a sideways glance as she ran her fingers gently over the room number '444'. Janice noticed the inference and asked if it had some special significance.

"Some people believe it is the number of the angels." Francine answered.

"Well, for her sake, I hope so." Janice said.

As Donald entered the room he immediately sensed the light of Amy's spirit had almost left her body.

'It will not be long now.' He said to himself. He noticed how worried Francine looked. If she had picked up his thoughts she didn't let on. In any case, he understood her concern.

Janice approached the chair directly beside Amy but Donald waved her to another seat at the end of the bed. Francine stood beside him as he took the seat. Janice seemed slightly put off but followed his directions.

'I suppose he knows what he is doing.' She thought.

With the assistance of an oxygen tube in her nose, Amy's breathing was shallow as she lay perfectly still. Donald knew she was in a catatonic state and would not respond to direct communication. He took her hand in both of his and closed his eyes. Janice looked on with suspicion. In a few moments he matched her breathing pattern. In his mind he went to a familiar place using one of the Shamanic healing techniques he learned from Benjamin Pearlman years before.

He and Jacqueline were enjoying the final moments of a magnificent setting sun on the deck of a cruise ship while Ibrahim and Ramsey discussed a movie treatment they had received about the so called 'Indigo' children.

Just as the day met the night both he and Jacqueline were mentally transported to a theater stage. They recognized it from their life as Shakespearian actors. The only difference was the absence of an audience with the exception of two people - themselves. They sat in the audience silently watching *themselves* upon the stage.

That vision became a favorite place for Donald's deep meditation where life issues could be worked out like lines in a play. Donald felt the inner stage would be a safe place for him to reach Amy.

As he stepped onto the stage he went to a table where *life scripts* were read and edited. He sat down on one of the chairs and picked up a notepad from a pile of scripts on the table. He thought of a title and it appeared at the top of the page.

'David's Last Message'

A One-Act Play

Then he added two actors;

He mentally turned the page and wrote;

Act One, Scene One

Amy enters her living room, picks up the phone and dials David's private message service.

At that moment Donald saw Amy enter from the far end of the stage, pick up a phone that was now sitting on the script table and dial a number. Donald added;

The automatic service answers and Amy begins to listen to the messages.

He watched as she performed her part.

She presses the forward key moving through the messages until she finds an urgent message from David to Francine.

Once again Amy performed her part. She came to the urgent message Donald was looking for and stopped. Donald added one more line for Amy to play.

Amy stops and repeats the message out loud.

Immediately Amy began to repeat the message.

"Francine, I hope you get this message. I don't know how long I can talk. The guy sitting in the aisle next to me is talking to his wife on his cell phone. He's telling her 'we've heard what's happening and some of us are going to do something about it'...Yousef and I are going to help them. I know what you're thinking, 'Yousef? But how?' Its true Franny, Yousef is here, right beside me on this flight. I can hardly believe it myself. He's been with Yasmine off and on for two years. I'll explain in a minute if I have time, but first I have to tell you, Yasmine is pregnant, just as I envisioned. She's being held...by the lunatics that forced Yousef to get on this flight. He doesn't think they'll let her go..."

At that moment the nurse they has encountered early walked in the room. "What's going on here?" She demanded.

118

Donald shuddered, blinked and slowly opened his eyes. Francine turned and stood between the nurse and Donald. Donald had been voicing Amy's words in trance-like fashion and when the nurse came in, to her mind, the scene had all the appearance of a séance.

"This is outrageous! I'll have you reported Dr. Heathrow. This is not right. You just can't come in here and...."

"Thank you nurse. We appreciate your professional attitude." Janice quickly stood and took the nurse almost by force and escorted her into the hallway. She said something to her that seemed to pacify her and the nurse disappeared down the hallway.

When she came back into the room Francine was sobbing like a baby. As Jancie walked over to comfort her Donald came fully out of his trance and asked how she had managed to placate the nurse.

"If there was one thing I learned from Mr. Bryan it was how to put out fires quickly." Janice explained as she rubbed Francine's shoulders. " I simply told her Dr. Heathrow was praying and that I knew she would not want to interfere with his constitutional right to do so, no matter how strange it might seem to her."

Donald smiled. "Well done Janice, well done." Janice nodded and began gently massaging Francine's shoulders. Donald knew Francine was at a very delicate stage of inner transformation and it would take very little to sway her either backward into the madness of her years of inner torment or forward into the arms of love, his arms. What she needed most now was to be nurtured and cared for, so he was especially grateful Janice seemed to have a strong maternal concern for her, particularly at that critical moment.

"When you started speaking I too thought you must be into some kind of cult. But when your body language and speech patterns were identical to Amy's, well I knew, something very special was happening. God, I can hardly believe what I heard and saw." Janice said. When she had finished speaking, Francine turned and stared at Donald with a look of panic, tears streaming down her face.

"Oh Donald, what will we do now, what will we do? I just can't believe it, my baby Yousef on that horrible flight. Oh God, Yasmine is in terrible trouble!" The weight of what she had just learned was too much for her and she began shaking uncontrollably.

Thirty-One

1975 – 1976

Francine's graduation from the University of Oxford in the early summer of 1975 was a glorious event. Jacqueline's extended British family, which had produced a half dozen surrogate parents for Francine when Ibrahim and Jacqueline were hopping continents, virtually dominated the campus. A number of Ibrahim's friends and business associates in the UK and Europe also attended. While Abdullah made apologies for the noticeable absence of his two sons, he proclaimed, with absolute sincerity, that he would not have missed the event for any reason.

However, it was at the reception after the ceremony that Jacqueline, Ibrahim and Francine received the best news of the day. Hayfa and Micka'ill proudly announced that they were going to have a baby the following year.

Everyone congratulated the couple then Mika'ill added. "Our gift to you little sister, on this wonderful day of celebration is to make you the godmother of our first child." Both he and Hayfa were glowing from head to toe with pride.

Francine beamed and asked, "Have you chosen possible names yet?"

"Oh yes!" Hayfa said. "When my mother was alive her favorite flower was a Jasmine, so if it's a girl we will call her Yasmine."

"And if it's a boy?" Jacqueline asked.

"Then we shall call him Yousef." Mika'ill replied.

"Ah, a colorful name from Egypt's ancient past." Ibrahim laughed.

"Yes father. Another great seer like you and Jacqueline." Mika'ill added.

"Thank you my son. If that is true we should be able to see if it is to be a boy or a girl shouldn't we my dear?" Ibrahim was being facetious but noticed a familiar look of concern on his wife's face. No one else could see the expression and he wished it to stay that way. He took her by the arm and suggested they take a stroll through the campus gardens.

When they had excused themselves and were out of ear shot he said "My dear, I noticed your reaction to the name Yousef . I know that look. What is troubling you, did you see something?"

"The moment Mika'ill said the name Yousef I knew there would be a boy to fit the name." She replied.

"But that is wonderful my dear, what darkened this joyful vision?" He asked.

"Yasmine will be the child's name, dear husband. But the male child 'Yousef' will soon join the family, under a dark cloud." She said.

Ibrahim closed his eyes. Several moments later he blinked and took a deep breath. "I too have seen this cloud. We must steel ourselves for what is to come." They discussed the matter no further, knowing as they did, the danger of giving attention to dark thoughts. The following year, on February 22nd, 1976, a healthy girl child – Yasmine, was born to Mika'ill and Hayfa.

"I believe she came into the world humming *Mozart* father." Mika'ill laughed as he informed his father of the joyous event on the phone. Ibrahim and Jacqueline had just returned home from the Vivian Beaumont Theater in New York. They had been honored for an extraordinarily large donation Brarab Industries made toward the city's Performing Arts Scholarship Fund.

"Wonderful news my son, wonderful. We thank God that mother and child are well and look forward with eager hearts to welcoming our granddaughter into the Faiz family." Ibrahim handed the telephone to Jacqueline and stood by watching her drink in the rapture of the moment.

When she hung up the phone she looked at Ibrahim who was staring at a portrait of Francine on their fireplace mantel.

"Dr. Heathrow?" She said.

"Yes, my dear. The young doctor and our daughter." He replied with a solemn tone.

Two weeks later Ibrahim and Jacqueline flew back to Britain and before returning to their estate in Bath, stopped off in Oxford where Francine had taken a job as a social worker at the university. The next day Mika'ill and Hayfa came down with Yasmine for the reunion. After everyone visited with Yasmine and she had gone to sleep, they retired to the conservatory for tea.

"Father, Jacqueline and Franny, my grown up baby sister, we have some important news for you." Mika'ill said. "We wanted to wait until we saw you face to face to tell you. But knowing you two, you probably know already.

"Is it about Yousef?" Jacqueline asked.

"I told you they would know." Mika'ill laughed, addressing Hayfa. He shook his head while Francine joined in the laughter. Ibrahim, however had a faraway look on his face.

Hayfa began on a solemn note. "You all know my family was killed in the War of Attrition in 1969." Her chin quivered as she struggled to hold back the tears.

"Yes dear, we know. It has been our hope that while we can never replace your family, that you would come to feel your special part in our family. You are as dear to us as if you were our own daughter." Jacqueline opened her arms to Hayfa and she sank into them.

"Thank you so very much mummy. The love you and the family have given me could not have been dearer to me than if it were from my own parents."

Mika'ill picked up the thread. "Hayfa's parents had two faithful servants, Hakim and Maryam Khaled who survived them. They remained in Egypt and two weeks ago, to the very day of Yasmine's birth, Maryam gave birth to a son they named Yousef Amal Hakim." Mika'ill took a moment to catch his breath. "Oh God, the poor souls. They were killed in a terrorist explosion three days after the birth. So much sadness...when will it all end?"

For several moments there was silence then Hayfa broke the spell. "But their son Yousef, he survived. Friends of the family knew I was with the London Philharmonic and contacted Mika'ill immediately after it happened. As baby Yousef had no other family, we were named his godparents. We have already begun adoption proceeding."

122

Jacqueline brushed a tear from her eye as she again embraced Hayfa. "May God bless this child and his future in our family." Ibrahim proclaimed.

Francine looked on grinning from ear to ear.

Thirty-Two

November - 22 - 1997

In the fall of 1997 when Meereka received her healing from the HIV virus the family doctor and all concerned were amazed. Most doctors, at some time in their careers have either witnessed personally or learned from other physicians stories of miraculous, spontaneous healing. The word travels quickly when divine intervention occurs and Meereka's healing was no exception.

Meereka's mother Maria however, preferred not to have the medical community 'poking around' in her daughter's life and was grateful to simply have her little child healed of the scourge that killed her husband and lurked behind her own door. There was one exception to this and Benny immediately agreed when he heard who it was.

"Benito, a phone call has come today from Dr. Heathrow. He is movie person...he say his company is name *Inner Scape*. He want to meet us and talk about Meereka." Maria explained to Benny when he returned for dinner one evening.

"Inner Scape! Are you kidding!" Benny exclaimed. "That the company that made; *'Magic Mind,''Love's Last Dreaming,' 'Manhattan Shaman'* and a bunch of other great movies about far out stuff. I think we should talk with them mama."

She nodded. "After he call, The Holy Mother tells me he okay."

"Do you want me to handle it mama?" Benny asked.

"Okay Benito, you take care of doctor," She closed her eyes as if in prayer, "The Holy Mother take care of us."

Two days later Donald welcomed Meereka, Benny and Maria into the New York offices of *Inner Scape Productions* at the World Trade Center.

"Welcome Mrs. Rodriguez and Benny." Benny shook his hand.

"It's a pleasure to meet you. I love your movies!" Benny exclaimed.

"Thank you Benny, and this must be little Meereka." Donald looked into the child's eyes and gasped. Although she was just twelve months old, he knew it was the same face as the little child that greeted him when he had the experience with Chez Shift in India.

"What is it Dr. Heathrow, you look like you've seen a ghost." Benny asked.

"You could say that Benny, you could definitely say that." Donald replied. "Eleven years ago I was almost killed on a trip to India and while I was in a coma I had a really weird dream. There was a little girl toward the end of the dream. Just now when I looked into Meereka's eyes, I saw...uh...that is...it looked like...well about four years from now she could be the little girl I met."

"Wow, that *is* spooky!" Benny said. He bent over his little sister who was resting in Maria's arms and said. "What do you think of that story my little princess Meereka?" Meereka gurgled and gave him a big smile.

'Well, what now doc?" Benny asked.

"This will not be a medical examination as I promised you, I want you to meet some dear friends of mine. They own a company called *Brarab Industries,* which supplies many of the ingredients for the Wellness Industry. You know, natural foods, supplements, that sort of thing. Their company owns part of *Inner Scape* and well, if you know our company's films you know anyone involved has to be pretty tuned into the spiritual side of life."

"I bet they do. Sure thing, let's meet 'em doc." Benny said. Maria followed Benny and Donald into a large screening room that contained many posters of the movies *Inner Scape* had made over the previous twenty years. A well-dressed, elderly couple, were standing in front of the screen. The man appeared to be Middle Eastern. Something about the couple immediately spoke to Benny's heart. It wasn't a new feeling, Benny had always been able to read people, animals, birds, almost anything living. But this feeling was much more profound than he had ever experienced.

As they approached the couple, Benny noticed the woman seemed very agitated. Donald noticed it too.

"Jacqueline, are you all right?" Donald asked.

Ibrahim took his wife's hand and squeezed it gently, while he too felt the oncoming rush of the miraculous, he did not know the depths to which it would soon touch his life.

Maria saw the look of love in Jacqueline's eyes and without a moment's hesitation placed the baby in her arms. Jacqueline took the child and wrapped herself around Meereka as if she were her own. She closed her eyes as tears poured down her cheeks.

Maria whispered in Benny's ear. "Benito, this lady is with The Holy Mother. She tell me she come home soon."

Ibrahim stood silent with deep sadness in his heart. In his mind he saw himself in Jacqueline's Mayfair flat the first time he met her there. He was holding a picture of a beautiful little girl with the words, '*pink lady* - a gift from God' etched on the frame. Jacqueline told him that just before the little girl died she said she would see her mother again when it was near her time to come home. Ibrahim had always thought it would be a spiritual visitation much like many deathbed patients have in their final hours.

Little Meereka had her tiny arms wrapped as far around Jacqueline's neck as they could go. Although the child could only utter simple words and had not, until this moment talked in sentences, she pulled herself up to Jacqueline's ear and whispered.

"*Pink lady* see you again soon."

Ecstasy shot through Jacqueline's soul. She basked in it for several moments then called in her emotions. She knew it was not the time to speak of her connection to Meereka.

"Thank you so much for letting me hold your daughter Maria." Jacqueline said as she gently placed the child back in her arms.

Maria smiled as one loving mother to another. "Meereka loves you...I can feel it."

"I too love her, so very much. She is a precious child." Jacqueline said as she fought to quell her tears.

While Benny was a down-to-earth guy, his feelings about people were rarely wrong. But this time his senses went even deeper. Although Dr.

126

Heathrow had not yet introduced these people to he and his mother, he felt a strange connection to them, as if they were family.

Finally, Donald saw the moment to introduce everyone. When he finished he said. "My only wish is that my dad could have been here to witness this wonderful moment." Ramsey had passed away two years before of a stroke and Donald missed him terribly. Since Donald's ordeal in India in 1968, his dad had been his mentor, partner and his best friend.

"Your dad *is* here now Donald, I can see him standing beside the baby." Jacqueline said. Ibrahim looked at his wife's face, which was radiant. She was by far the most intuitive person he had ever known but she had never before said she actually *saw* someone from the other side. He sighed. It was a sigh from the depths of his soul, it was a sigh of resignation, a sigh of gratitude.

Donald's eyes filled with tears as he watched Meereka looking up and smiling into what seemed to be thin air while holding her hand out as if to grasp something. "I sure miss you dad." He said.

Meereka turned her head and looked straight into his eyes. In that instant he could feel his dad's presence.

Jacqueline looked at Benny and took his hand in both of hers. "Your life has changed with the coming of this miracle child. She glanced at Maria and smiled. Even greater changes are soon to come. I believe right here, in this building is where it will begin. I cannot see it clearly, but I feel it is right here."

Benny thought in some way she was referring to *Inner Scape Productions*. Donald also felt that might be the case and asked the family to stay in touch and let them know what other miracles might occur in their lives. He told them that *Inner Scape* was contemplating a television series on miracles, something people were beginning to believe in more and more as the new millennium approached. Benny told them their life had been very difficult until recently but since Meereka's healing, things were looking a lot sunnier.

"You know just the other day I was walking around these very buildings when two Doberman's cut loose from their master and came running toward me. Next thing ya know they're my buddies and I got this job walking them, for some rich guy." He laughed.

"Its only the beginning Benny." Jacqueline said. "You have a very important destiny, both you and Meereka." She turned to Ibrahim and said she was feeling tired. They excused themselves and left the office.

Again Donald asked Maria and Benny to stay in touch with him. "I have learned to just go with the flow of life, to stay out of its way and allow it to take me where it will. Everything in my life has happened with ease by following this practice." Donald said. Benny nodded, not exactly sure what he meant.

Later that night Jacqueline kissed Ibrahim goodnight and said. "I will see you soon dear husband."

"And you dear wife, and you." He replied. When he awoke next morning she had passed to spirit.

Thirty-Three

1977

Marian Anderson, a black opera diva, lived a miraculous life through extraordinary times. She dealt with social strife through her song and grace. Surrounded by prominent political, social and cultural figures, she sang on some of the world's finest stages mesmerizing millions of people. Her 75th birthday was marked by a gala concert at Carnegie Hall where she received New York City's Handel Medallion.

Ibrahim and Jacqueline attended the award event with Dr. Ramsey and Dr. Donald Heathrow. Francine, who had been spending some time in New York visiting her parents, agreed to join them at the gala. The Faiz's and Heathrow's were working with a talented young black American writer named Virgil Johnson to develop a screenplay about personalities throughout history that had contributed in a highly visible way to peace. The objective was to establish a thread that linked individuals with divergent backgrounds to the common theme of peace. Since Marian Anderson had also received the UN Peace Prize, they believed she would contribute much to the content of the docudrama.

Rather than adhering strictly to a documentary format, Donald and Ramsey wanted *Inner Scape Productions* to focus on mainstream cinema where altruistic themes could be woven into entertaining story lines. In this way they believed a larger cross section of cinema lovers would be exposed to the seeds of higher ideals without the risk of intrusion into their belief systems.

 "May we present our daughter Francine Faiz?" Ibrahim said as Ramsey and Donald joined he and Jacqueline in the theater lobby. "Francine, this is Dr. Ramsey Heathrow and Dr. Donald Heathrow, New York psychiatrists *extra ordinaire,* and…would-be movie moguls." Everyone laughed and shook hands as they inched their way toward the theater seating.

"The less visible we are the better, I think." Ramsey said. "We want the light within the work to speak for itself, unencumbered by public preconceptions."

"That is wise." Ibrahim added. "Too often the collective mind decides ahead of time what something means before the spirit in the work has an opportunity to make its mark."

"Yes, that's true." Donald added. "We want the work to have an intense inner theme, exposed to a relaxed mind. In this way, whatever pearl, which may appeal to the individual, has the chance of being picked up."

"I love your idea." Francine said. "In the short time I have been counseling students at Oxford, I have found the choices they have made, in most cases were not their own. The perception of individual choice, I think is unrealistic. It seems by the time a young person reaches the final stages of their academic education, their lives are guided by a bundle of programs so deeply hidden that what they say and do might just as well be coming from an amalgam of their parents, their friends, their political and religious persuasions, and any number of other outside influences.

Ibrahim was grateful that his daughter's insight was already moving beyond the mass mind consciousness. He and Jacqueline had given her all she required in the material sense and filled her life with the secure certainty that she was loved. Prior to her days at Oxford, most of the academic education she and Mika'ill acquired came through carefully chosen tutors who accompanied the family wherever they traveled.

Nevertheless, both she and her brother were given a wide berth in which to develop their own direction. They wanted no sense of obligation to influence the children's choices in life. Their lives were their own.

"God will fill their minds with His will, it is not for us to provide the map." Ibrahim and Jacqueline had agreed when Francine was born.

In the first year of their marriage Ibrahim and Jacqueline had also agreed that freedom of choice must be the foundation upon which they guided their children.

As they entered the theater auditorium Jacqueline glanced sideways at Donald. She could sense he was recollecting his past life with Francine. His expression was guarded. She smiled knowingly, feeling his distress. When they took their seats she made certain he sat beside her so that she could directly extend her energy to the unhealed wound he must now face.

After the presentation was finished Jacqueline asked if Ramsey and Donald would care to join them for coffee back at their brownstone. They accepted and a half hour later all were relaxing in Ibrahim's library. A subtle pressure immediately began to fill the room and Ramsey asked if anyone else was feeling claustrophobic.

"Yes, I noticed it right away when we sat down." Francine said. "But I'm not certain its coming from this room because I felt the same sensation in the theater. Did anyone else feel it?"

Donald quickly glanced toward Jacqueline then looked down at his coffee. Ibrahim had his eyes closed, which puzzled Francine. "Daddy, are you alright?"

"Be still." He said softly, and with his eyes still closed, he took in several deep breaths.

Francine thought this a strange moment to go into meditation, however she knew her father and did not question his motives. 'Something must be up.' She thought.

Ramsey apparently had not tuned in to what was happening either and smiled sheepishly at Francine and Jacqueline. Donald's head was still bowed.

"I don't know if I'm ready for this." Donald suddenly exclaimed.

"Ready for what son?" Ramsey asked.

"You don't remember dad?" He exclaimed.

Ramsey suddenly felt trapped and stood up. He began searching his mind for the source of the pressure but could find none.

"Breath." Ibrahim uttered from his meditative state.

Jacqueline was struggling to remain calm but could not find her center. 'How did I not see this before?' She thought. Francine is Twenty-Four and in all those years I felt nothing, except last year when I sensed her link with Donald. I should have known. I could have prepared her and myself. But now, here we are again. God, help us to get through this.'

Francine couldn't grasp why the others were in distress. She scanned the group one at a time and thought, 'Mummy looks more frightened than I've ever seen her, daddy is lost in meditation, Dr. Heathrow looks like he's going to jump out of his skin at any moment and his son is acting like he has gone into a deep pit.' "What's going on here you guys?" Francine asked in confusion.

"Do you know Hamlet Francine?" Donald said.

"You mean the play?" She replied.

"Remember, its all a play my dear." Ibrahim said slowly opening his eyes. When Francine studied Shakespeare in college, Ibrahim told her Shakespeare's line; *all the world's a stage* was not just a metaphor. The bard meant it literally.

"Few understood it in those days and not many more have opened to this awareness and its deeper meaning today." He told her.

"But daddy, surely you don't mean that the life we are living is not happening, I mean look around, this can't just be a play, can it?" She remembered he remained silent for a long time. She guessed it was to allow her to absorb the implications of what he had told her. "Whose play?" She asked. "And even if it is a play, how come its feels so real?"

He paused again for several seconds then replied "Its your play my dear."

"I'm sorry, I just don't get it. Its sound too crazy." She said. Since that time neither he nor Jacqueline had spoken of the concept again. They knew Francine must find the truth of it on her own, in her own way. But now, whether she was ready for it or not, an ugly scene in her play was coming full circle.

Jacqueline opened the ancient scene. "There was a fire Francine. The theater caught fire and many perished. It was long ago. We were there, Donald, Ramsey, me...and you Francine, you were there with us." Donald could not look at Francine and Ramsey seemed in a state of shock as he began to recall the horrible day.

Ibrahim, who had remained calm, spoke. "My dear, fear not, illusion cannot touch you. We all live in plays within many plays, nothing is what it seems, no matter how horrific it may appear. All is a provocation to look within, to find what we have lost." He could see that a glimmer of remembrance had seeped into her consciousness.

'Could it be?' She thought. To even think of it was too grisly to imagine. To be responsible for the deaths of so many people was beyond comprehension. She could not live with such guilt. "It has to be a dream, no, a nightmare if this actually happened." She spoke out loud as if speaking to the past. "How could I have done such a thing?"

132

"It was a dream my dear, just a dream, as is this a dream we are living now." Ibrahim said. The mass mind constructed it and still believes it is real, but it is not." There is no guilt because nothing is happening in a dream. Does the actor feel guilt when he kills in the play? No, he goes on his way to play the scene again and yet again until finally he tires of the play? What you are beginning to remember is just the remnants of an old play that has ended. No one is to blame. Each played his part voluntarily to the same end, to eventually awaken from the dream."

As Ibrahim continued speaking, Francine remembered more and more of the experience from her past life association with Jacqueline, Donald and Ramsey. She knew she had set the fire and she knew why. It was ghastly! How could she have done such a monstrous thing?

"Remember my dear one, you only played your part. Nothing really happened." Ibrahim reassured her.

Jacqueline had already poured Francine a glass of brandy. While she and Ibrahim did not drink, they kept a supply for guests.

"I think I'll have one of those." Donald said with a deep sigh. Now that the cards had been played he was experiencing the release of an ancient cellular stress.

"I think I'll stick to my coffee." Ramsey said lifting his coffee cup.

"Let me make a fresh pot." Jacqueline said. She leaned over from her seat and gave Francine a quick hug around the shoulders. "There are far worse things happening right this moment in the world dream we are living my sweet angel. None of them are real either."

Like an autumn leaf, the atmosphere in the room gently settled. "The past is dead, let us now allow it to create a peaceful present moment awareness." Ibrahim stated firmly.

Donald raised his glass and nodded. "Agreed!" Ramsey said. Francine was drained and could not yet bring herself to acknowledge the healing moment.

When Jacqueline returned, she laid the coffee pot on the table and crouched down beside her daughter. "My sweet gentle angel, you have been forgiven for the part you played in that dream. Now it is time to forgive yourself and let it go."

133

"Oh mummy, it's so hard to believe it even happened. " Francine moaned.

Thirty-Four

October -7- 2001

The day after Donald, Francine and Janice visited Amy in the hospital, she died. Donald got the call from Dr. Fitzpatrick personally as he was walking from the temporary offices of *Inner Scape* toward St. Paul's to meet with the group. He would like to have broken the news to Francine privately, but he knew all things work out for good and decided to just go with the flow.

"I've got some news folks. It may seem like a set back but we must trust that all is working out as it should."

"She's dead isn't she?" Francine said bluntly. Donald was surprised that Francine had guessed the news.

"Who?" Benny asked.

"The lady with the message." Smokie said.

Both Donald and Francine turned toward Smokie who was calmly toying with a wooden coffee stick.

"How do you know that Smokie?" Donald and Francine said in unison. They caught themselves and giggled before the gravity of the moment pulled them back.

"Cuz she told me." Smokie replied in child-like defense.

"Smokie, its okay, you haven't done anything wrong. We just want to know how...that is when, uh...did she speak with you?" Donald stammered as he grappled with the surprising possibility that Smokie was somehow connecting with Amy.

"You two look surprised. How come?" Benny asked. "After all, didn't he spend two whole days with Meereka recently?"

'He has a point.' Donald thought. Smokie was never more than halfway into the world most people called reality. Where he was the rest of the time was anybody's guess. The subject of people like Smokie had fascinated he and his dad for many years. They had even discussed the subject for a possible movie project a number of times before Ramsey passed away.

'Perhaps now,' Donald thought. 'I will be allowed a peak into the unknown world Smokie and many others like him know as their reality.'

"She's with my pop." Smokie said. He was still playing with his coffee stick and kept pointing to a sign on the wall that read *East Wing*.

"Donald, do you think he really knows something? Francine whispered in Donald's ear.

"Lets just feel the moment Franny, I don't believe we will get very far by trying to figure this out logically. By the way, how did *you* know Amy died?" He asked.

"I woke up in the middle of the night, rolled over and the digital clock read 4:44 AM - her room number. I knew then she was gone." Francine replied.

"Sounds like your perceptive antenna's reaching up again." Donald looked at Francine's face and saw something that had not been there since that awful day so long ago, the day before they were to become one.

"Smokie, did she tell you anything else?" Francine tried not to sound anxious. Her training as a counselor told her he would likely shut down and withdraw into the *other place* completely if he sensed pressure of any kind.

"Nope!" He said. Francine looked lost. Then Benny stood up and put his arm around Smokie's shoulder.

"Meereka says Amy told your dad everything Smokie. Is that true?"

"Sure did!" He giggled.

Francine and Donald understood where Benny was going with his question but also knew a detailed explanation of what Amy might have told his dad may be difficult to obtain from Smokie.

"Smokie, do ya think he might tell us what Amy told him?" Benny asked.

"I will ask my pop." Smokie whispered with a very serious tone. A moment later his eyes glazed over and he was gone.

Donald looked on as Francine stared at Benny hopefully. They waited five minutes...ten minutes...fifteen minutes, but still, Smokie had not returned. As she waited, Francine began thinking about Benny's relationship with Meereka now that she too was gone. Donald told her Benny had been in his own special space since Smokie had been rescued. 'What does Benny now know about Meereka that he didn't before?' She wondered.

"Benny, can I ask you about Meereka?" Donald took her hand and squeezed it gently. He felt, in some way Francine was being guided to open up the subject that he had been unable to touch until now. He wanted her to know he supported what she was about to do.

Benny kept his eyes glued to Smokie for any sign that he might be coming out of his dazed state. "Sure, what do you want to know Franny?"

"Benny, do you think Meereka is a *real* angel?" She asked. " I mean we all know she was, that is, she has always acted like an angel, but do you think...?" Benny interrupted her before she could finish.

"Of course!" Dr. Heathrow was there the day I found out." Benny said.

"I was? When was that Benny?" Donald asked.

"You know, the day I first met you." He replied.

A moment later Donald's mind flashed back to the sacred moments he shared with Ibrahim, Jacqueline, Benny, his mother and little Meereka.

"Mrs. Faiz knew too." Benny added.

He was pulled out of the beautiful memory by the sound of Smokie coughing. Smokie continued coughing as he turned toward Francine.

"Angry men are keeping your flowers. Pop says Mr. Yousef and Mr. David are with her, to help keep her safe. Meereka is there too."

Francine turned almost white. Donald could see she was on the verge of fainting. "Sit Franny, sit down." He said. He took her by the hand to support her as she slumped into a pew.

Benny took a seat beside Smokie. "Did your dad tell you where the flowers are Smokie?"

"No!" He said. "But Mr. Yousef said she's in sunshine state."

"That could be anywhere in the Middle East." Francine moaned.

Just then Benny looked at Donald and Francine as if he'd just been struck by lightening. "Dr. Heathrow, what is the slogan for the state of Florida?"

Donald's eyes opened wide. "The sunshine state." He smiled and laughed delighted by the sudden 'AHA'.

Francine asked. "Isn't that where a bunch of those guys were living?"

"That's right!" Benny answered.

Smokie was again playing with his coffee stick, this time twirling it toward a sign on the opposite side of the room, which read, 'West Wing'.

Benny noticed and asked, "Is she in the west sunshine state Smokie?"

"Palm trees." He replied. Benny frowned and looked puzzled. Francine and Donald were also struggling to understand Smokie's metaphoric reference.

'What could west wing palm trees possibly mean? Donald wondered. "West wing palm trees...west wing palm trees.' He rolled the words around and around in his mind. Then it donned on him, "West Palm!" He hollered.

"Well done Smokie." Benny whispered feeling proud of his new friend.

Smokie nodded. Benny stared at Smokie for a moment then got up and walked toward the folder of Meereka's drawings that he had kept with him since the group sessions began. He leafed through the pictures for a few minutes then suddenly stopped. He withdrew a single drawing, walked over to the others and laid the picture on the floor.

Francine and Donald watched while Benny knelt down beside the simple drawing.

"Look! Three palm trees and two flowers, just like the ones in the drawings we looked at the other day." He pointed to a curved line. "Then there is

138

this. It looks like a road. "And beside it, see, an orange ball, like an actual orange, with a crescent moon on the side."

"Orange crescent? Francine asked.

"It has to be! The name of the street where Yasmine is located, Orange Crescent!" Donald exclaimed.

All eyes turned toward Smokie. He just grinned.

Thirty-Five

1977 - 1978

When Francine returned to Oxford after visiting her parents in New York she found a letter from Donald Heathrow waiting for her. She had not seen him since the evening of her painful past life reunion with he and the others. That was her choice. Donald was anxious to explore their common interests, not just his connection with her parents and their spiritual passion, but also the romantic relationship they shared and cut short so long ago.

Francine was forced to come to grips with the fact that she had lived before. If that wasn't enough, she was supposedly reconnected and close to the same people she had known in her previous life, and somehow had been responsible for their horrible deaths. The entire concept was too horrible to accept, too much to understand, too much to believe. She could barely get her mind around the idea and now her parents wanted her to believe that it was all a dream, it had not really happened. Nor was she to believe the life she was currently living real. In fact, 'all life, as most people know it, is a dream,' they explained.

Despite the fact that her parents had discussed the subject of past lives with her when she was young, she had not taken any interest in the subject. If she was to accept this incredible concept, she must re-think her entire life, what it meant, and, if it meant anything. She wondered. 'How can it have any meaning if life is just a dream? Other than being a metaphor for what is occurring in one's life, what does any of it matter?

Ibrahim and Jacqueline spent the remainder of her vacation trying to help Francine understand the point to life in the dream. They knew that unless she first accepted the truth of her innate connection to an entity some called God, the purpose of the dream could not be recognized or understood. Only she could come to that knowing. It might come tomorrow, in ten years or not at all in this lifetime. They knew they must allow this knowing to emerge of its own accord as Francine did her own inner work.

'Warm greetings.' The letter began. It was hand written on a ginger colored parchment-like paper. On it, there was a peripheral watermark of a child angel. She opened the letter and her heart fluttered.

"Oh my, what's this all about?" She sighed. A wonderful feeling of anticipation flooded her solar plexus. It was familiar but she could not identify its origin.

Donald's note read, 'Franny, I hope you don't mind me calling you Franny, it just feels right. I know you have remembered some of our long lost love. I wish to speak about this. The sadness that touched us then is over and done with. Love alone remains. Please try to let the painful circumstances that ended that experience of us together, slip from your mind. It is nothing but the last fading scenes in a mournful play. What remains, as with all of life, is the essence of love. I believe together we can recapture what we once had. And so with this short note, I open the door for you my dear, for it is up to you now to take the next step."

Francine laid the letter gently on her tea tray and stared out the window, past the ancient terrace to the garden below. Ibrahim and Jacqueline had purchased and restored the old estate ten years earlier and at that moment she was intensely grateful for her graceful surroundings. 'On some level, mummy and daddy probably knew it would one day become a blessed healing retreat.' She thought.

In her years as a student at Oxford and since then as a counselor at the legendary university, she used only a fraction of the sprawling mansion. The care and maintenance of the beautiful buildings, she left to the live-in staff. She was pleased now that this quarter of the estate had been left vacant when the workmen finished their renovations.

Francine had chosen to relocate into the unused wing, which was situated on the second level overlooking a beautiful rose garden. In it, there was a quiet bed-sitting room, decorated in pastel tones of pink and lavender. The room had its own private stairway leading to a seating area in the midst of an overflowing pallet of natural colors. There, she felt wrapped in a blanket of unspoiled beauty. In its pristine state, she experienced it like a healing balm.

It was the Christmas of 1977 before she allowed herself to consider the possibility of Donald in her life again. That year, Ibrahim and Jacqueline shared the festive season with Jacqueline's family in Bath. Francine joined the party on Christmas Eve.

"You are looking well sweet angel." Jacqueline said, as she embraced her daughter tenderly.

"I am well mummy. Still feeling a little tender, but much better." Francine said.

Jacqueline smiled and gave Francine another long hug. "Bless you dear, come now and join the family."

When the two women entered the estate's enormous vaulted gallery the family had already gathered. Over one hundred close friends and relatives filled the room, which was gaily decorated with an aura of festivity. Francine scanned the room and was soon drawn to an imposing Christmas tree, standing over twenty feet tall and dressed with hundreds of tiny angels each holding a tiny white light. Her eyes were pulled to the top where a large pink angel presided over the rest. She allowed herself to drink in the grandeur of the tree as her eyes slowly slipped down the beautifully branches to a mountain of gifts at its base. There she found, bending over the packages, Donald Heathrow.

Without hesitation, she strode directly toward him and fell into his arms. Unseen, Ibrahim stood a few feet away, serene in the knowing that his daughter had just taken a giant leap toward her destiny.

The next year found Francine and Donald crisscrossing the Atlantic to be with each other. When, Ibrahim separated his business affairs with Abdullah, and soon afterward joined *Brarab Industries* in partnership with Donald and Ramsey in *Inner Scape Productions,* Francine and Donald decided it was the perfect moment to announce their engagement. On Christmas Eve, twelve months to the day after Francine walked through the door Donald had opened for her, the couple announced they would marry in the summer of the following year.

In that year the festivities took place at the Oxford mansion and as the couple announced their plans, Ibrahim and Jacqueline stood alone in front of the gallery's grand fireplace. Silhouetted in the warmth of the flames, they extended their love to Francine and Donald, knowing sadly, the couples union would first endure much heartache and years of painful separation.

Thirty-Six

September -11- 2001

"Where are we little one?" Smokie asked.

"With your poppie." The little girl replied.

"With my pop?" Smokie looked from side to side then called out into the black void. " Pop are you here?"

"I'm right here Smokie, right here!" A familiar voice replied. It came from somewhere close. It seemed to come from all around him. Not because of the darkness but for some other reason. It was as if the voice was inside his head.

"Let go son. Follow my voice. I'm here." The voice kept repeating the same thing over and over again. Smokie allowed it to pull him. First a tiny pinpoint of light appeared in his mind. Then slowly it grew larger and larger until it was the size of a silver dollar.

"Go through the light son. I'm here...right here." The voice said. For several minutes Smokie focused all his attention on the small sphere of light.

Suddenly he felt weightless and in a moment found himself on the other side of the light. At first the light was disorienting, much like the darkness had been. There was no up or down. No frame of reference whatsoever except his own body, which he could now see.

"The feeling will pass in a moment son." The voice said from behind him. He turned and there stood his father; Captain Jack Seagram.

"Pop, where are we? And where did the little girl go. Smokie asked.

"She's still with you on *the other side*." He answered. Smokie was uncertain what he meant by *the other side*.

"Pop, you're okay! The fire, we fell through the floor... I landed on top of you... you were lying on the couch...I was talking with you." Smokie felt confused. His sense of space disappeared when he lost his spatial reference point in the dark. Now he had lost his sense of time as well.

143

"I can't remember anything else pop. Why not?" He asked.

"I had to come here Smokie and you had to stay behind on *the other side*. You've been on *the other side* for ten years son. But when you are here with me, it's always now. The fire just happened a moment ago." He said.

"I, I don't really understand pop, but I'm glad we're together." Smokie hugged his dad, tears streaming down his face.

"We are always together son, you are both here and on *the other side* at the same time. Because of that people on *the other side* don't understand you. It makes you seem different because part of you is here and part of you is there.

"Pop, I don't understand." Smokie said.

"Its okay son, don't try to understand right now. You and the little girl Meereka have important work to do. She will guide you. Listen to her." He said.

"What work pop? What do we have to do?" Smokie asked.

"Remember on the couch I told you that you had a really important thing to do later?" He asked.

"Ya pop. You just told me that a few minutes ago." Smokie replied.

"That's why you had to stay in the other place. Meereka will show you when you go back. And by the way son, happy Twenty Seventh birthday." A moment later Smokie woke up and was again surrounded in blackness.

"Twenty Seven? But I'm only..."

"Smokie and Meereka help hurt people now." The little girl's voice felt like it was somewhere in front of him.

"Where are you little girl?" Smokie asked.

"Bend stick beside you." She said.

"What stick?" Smokie felt around in the darkness beside him. His hands touched what felt like a thick layer of dust. The he touched something solid. It was long and thin and felt like plastic. He picked it up.

Again the little girl said, "Bend stick." Smokie took the object in both hands and bent it. Immediately it began to glow. As the light-stick grew brighter he could see that the little girl was about five years of age. She had blond hair, blue eyes, wore a white dress and looked angelic.

"I am Meereka." The little girl said.

"Hello little girl, my name is Smokie." He looked around in the dim glow and could make out a broken box of light-sticks beside several boxes that were unbroken. His eyes began to adjust to the eerie light and he noticed the shadowy figures of other people lying in various grotesque positions. Some were partially buried beneath chunks of broken or smashed concrete. Even in the faint light and from several feet away, he could see that most had severe injuries. None appeared to be alive.

Smokie was very confused. "Over there." Meereka pointed to a pillar that had fallen sideways against another that still remained upright. Beneath it he could make out the outline of a man.

"Alive." Meereka said.

Smokie slowly got up from the floor. He had been propped up against a wall that had not collapsed. He picked up another light-stick, bent it and held both out in front of his body. He walked cautiously toward the man who was wearing a dark business suit covered in light gray dust. When he reached him he tried to move the large pillar but it wouldn't budge.

"Meereka help." The little girl said. He did not notice her come up behind him. Although he was certain she could not make the slightest difference he remembered his dad told him the little girl would guide him. He trusted his dad and decided to try. She put her tiny hand beside his on the pillar and together they attempted to move it. This time it moved easily to one side and collapsed with a thunderous crash to the floor. Dumbfounded, he looked down at the little girl who smiled at him innocently.

"Here!" Meereka said. Smokie noticed the little girl's voice now seemed to be coming from within his mind. He turned to look for her and she had disappeared.

"Meereka here. This time he knew the voice *was* coming from within his own mind.

"No time for that now." He thought. "I'll figure it out later. I must help this man and any others that are alive."

He lifted the lifeless body from the rubble and gently placed it on a nearby pile of cardboard boxes that had been folded flat. Once he removed the man he found a boy of about ten behind him and a woman beside the boy, partially hidden by several small chunks of rubble. All three people had several injuries but none of them were bleeding. Once he got them away from the debris he felt their pulse for signs of life. Each had a faint rhythm.

As he was moving the three people the dim glow of the light-sticks revealed a quantity of boxes several feet away. When he had done all could do for the people he checked the boxes. Some read driedfruit, others read protein drink mix and a few were boxes of canned vegetables. Each had a sticker on it that read: *Sunshine Health Foods.*

It was obvious there was a lot of edible food in amongst the debris. 'What about water?' He asked himself. He reasoned that if the destroyed area in which he found himself was the remains of a health food store, there must be bottled water somewhere. He decided he would look later and search for other survivors first. He broke a third light-stick and began the search. He came across several bodies, some he had seen before and others that were hidden beneath debris. With each one he found he heard the little girl's voice in his mind say, "Not live."

He decided to leave the grisly task of moving the dead until after he finished his search. Ten minutes into his search he came upon a pile of overturned storage shelves. Again he heard the little girl in his mind say, "Here."

He carefully removed the shelves, piled on top of each other, and beneath them found a large cache of cartons, each containing a dozen bottles of distilled water. After opening and downing half a bottle, he returned to the three injured people, took the rest of the bottle and cleaned their faces with his shirt and washed their wounds. Then he removed the man's suit jacket, took the lining out and ripped it into pieces, which he used to cover the survivor's wounds.

146

He then made his way back through the debris pulling the dead from under concrete, broken crates, shelving and light fixtures that had fallen from the ceiling. When he was finished there were nine bodies, six adults and three children. He laid them side-by-side at the furthest end of the destroyed shop, about 60 feet from where he had set up the provisions.

Next he went about organizing the food and water into one location while keeping an eye on the injured people for signs of movement. When he had finished he felt completely exhausted. Again he heard the voice of the little girl in his mind. She said, "Rest now." He sat down beside the three people, leaned against the food cartons and in the dim glow of the light-sticks, and immediately fell into a deep sleep.

Thirty-Seven

1978 -1979

The first indication that there was any bad blood between Abdullah's son's and Ibrahim occurred when they were conspicuously absent from the wedding of Mika'ill and Hayfa in 1975. Their father's excuse that the *House of Faiz* business kept them occupied didn't fool Ibrahim. He knew that by that time, Abdullah would never entrust *House of Faiz* business to them. Their involvement in Middle Eastern militant activities precluded any possibility of them having credibility with the moderate Muslim business and political associates that did business with the *House of Faiz*.

Ibrahim saw the boys very little since the hostilities in the region flared up in the late sixties. When he did, they showed a marked lack of respect for him as their father's partner and as their elder. He did not need to be told the reason. Many young people in the region with a shortsighted view, judged the world outside Islam as unworthy of respect. The fact that he had married an infidel, lived most of the time abroad and had openly sought a more broad-minded view of spirituality beyond his Muslim roots, labeled him nothing short of a traitor in the eyes of many.

What he did not know was just how deep the boy's vehemence toward him went. When Abdullah severed his partnership with Ibrahim in 1978 the simmering hatred within the two boys flared. In their minds there was no reason to display any false pretense now that Ibrahim - the traitor, had departed. The fact that many *House of Faiz* contracts with key clients were immediately withdrawn from the company when Ibrahim sold his half of the company exacerbated their bitterness even further.

Although many Muslim business people shared the biased view that Ibrahim had abused his spiritual heritage to further his business interests, some less orthodox members of the Islamic community honored the man for what he stood for rather than what spiritual persuasion he followed. The pressure cooker exploded when Abdullah died suddenly of heart failure a few months later. From that moment on Ahmal and Abdul poured all their bitterness into a focused desire for revenge against Ibrahim and actively sought the means to exact it.

Initially they lacked the opportunity to materialize their intentions but it would not be long before their dark passion would find an avenue to express itself. Family ties can be extremely close in the Arab culture and

148

the death of their father drew Ahmal and Abdul even closer to their mother. When the soviets invaded her homeland of Afghanistan shortly after Abdullah's death, the boys decided to join the resistance in that region. It was at about the same time Ahmal and Abdul received word that Francine was to be married to an American doctor later that year in England.

During the rebellion the typical description of an Afghan warlord was not pretty. He was ruthless, power-hungry and brutal. Mahmood Khan, a young peasant from Herat, the largest city in western Afghanistan, had declared himself warlord over that city early in the conflict and backed it up with a large number of Islamic brothers from neighboring countries that were eager to join the conflict. The wealth of the *House of Faiz*, though diminished significantly by the departure of Ibrahim and the recent death of their father, was still vast and now completely in the hands of the blood thirty brothers.

Mahmood sought to endear the brothers' and particularly their fortune to the cause. He found in their bitterness toward Ibrahim, a perfect means to do so.

"If you seek revenge brothers, Allah has opened the door for you." He told them.

"How so?" Ahmal asked with keen interest. Mahmood explained his idea to the brothers who eagerly agreed when they saw the potential to fulfill their bloodlust.

Meanwhile, elaborate plans had been arranged for the marriage of Francine to Dr. Donald Heathrow in Bath. It was to be a carbon copy of Ibrahim's marriage to Jacqueline Twenty Five years earlier. Once again, family and friends gathered from around the globe and, as large as her parent's wedding guest list had been, theirs was more than double.

Mika'ill, Hayfa, Yasmine and her step brother Yousef came in early from London and stayed with Francine at the family estate in Oxford to help her prepare. Ibrahim and Jacqueline made most of the larger arrangements in Bath through a Muslim business associate of Ibrahim's that owned an international catering company in the UK and Europe. Donald, who had never been to England, came in a week early and toured London with his parents. The wedding date was to be on the Fourth of July in honor of the American groom and his family. The Faiz and Heathrow families for the moment were enjoying the heavenly fruit of family love.

Francine had never taken to the Islamic faith and Donald departed formal religion after his transformative trip to India in 1968. As a result the couple decided to be joined in marriage through an all-faith minister so that all family members would feel, in some way, that their beliefs were not being dishonored. The night before the grand event the closest family members in the wedding party, joined for an after rehearsal dinner in the wedding reception tent. Three of the wedding caterer's employees provided the food.

The evening was light-hearted and everyone was in high spirits until Mika'ill began to complain of a stomachache. Not five minutes later Hayfa also came down with severe cramps. Jacqueline asked what they had eaten and they said that they had ordered the shellfish.

"I don't remember seeing that on the menu." She said.

"Oooh!" Mika'ill moaned. "Yes, yes it was highlighted on the menu. We were happy to see it because it is a favorite of Hayfa's and mine."

Ibrahim asked a waiter to show them a copy of the menus. When the waiter returned he said he could not find the menus but that he did find a note in the cooking area with Ibrahim's name on it. He opened the Envelop and froze.

"Jacqueline, we must get Mika'ill and Hayfa to a hospital immediately. They have been poisoned."

Jacqueline began to visibly shake. On a deeper level she knew it would do no good, nevertheless she had to make the effort. Donald and his father immediately applied their skills and encouraged Mika'ill and Hayfa to vomit their meals. Nevertheless, within an hour both Mika'ill and Hayfa were in the hospital emergency room unconscious. Everything was happening so fast that the numbing transition from merrymaking to desperation had not sunk in. However, within an hour of receiving the note the entire wedding party lapsed into a shocked state of disbelief.

Ibrahim passed the note along to the police after sharing its contents with the other dinner guests.

"The wrath of Allah has finally fallen on the head of the traitor." Repent now or expect His fury to visit the Faiz house again."

150

Two hours after eating the shellfish, Mika'ill and Hayfa succumbed to the poison.

The waiter who delivered the note to Ibrahim was taken into custody and although innocent, helped the police discover that his two helpers had only been hired the day before. Investigations later discovered that neither of the transient workers had a fixed address. They simply said that they were friends of the Faiz family and the field manager put them to work.

Instead of the bliss expected by everyone at the celebration, the guests and family who remained were obliged to endure the sorrow and loss of a double funeral. Ibrahim remained solemn but stalwart as the family head. Jacqueline, who had foreseen tragedy some years earlier, silently allowed the pain to flow through her heart, unseen by all but Ibrahim. Donald and his family were deeply sympathetic but Francine disappeared inside a shell of brooding. Although she had remained aloof from the brutality playing out in the Middle East, she did not doubt for a moment the resolve of its terrorists. Now she had ample proof of its ferocity.

No amount of persuasion from either family could convince her that she and Donald would not be next if she dared go through with the marriage. The remnants of an ancient, unresolved guilt tainted her reason influencing her to believe that as the daughter of a highly visible Islamic figure who had chosen to marry an infidel, she had brought this horror upon her family. In her mind she must sacrifice her own happiness for the sake of the family. Francine had a second motive for her decision to cancel her marriage. Now that she was the official guardian of Yasmine and Yousef, she would not jeopardize their lives as well.

For the time being Jacqueline and Ibrahim resigned themselves to her decision. They knew however her precaution could not protect the family from the insidious sickness of blind hatred.

Thirty-Eight

September - 12 - 2001

Benny walked into the station in a daze, dragging his feet. Slowly, he approached Sergeant Sarvino at the desk and whispered.

"She's gone sarge, my mom too." Benny's eyes were red and swollen. The Sergeant looked up and wiped his nose. He too had been weeping.

"And my son, Benny. My God! My son was in the building when it collapsed. He was delivering flowers…just delivering flowers. Why him, why…?"

"Oh sarg, I'm so sorry. He was such a happy kid. I can't believe it."

"Stevie just started Columbia last week. His mother and I were so proud of him. It was just a part time job. He didn't need the money. He had a scholarship…he didn't have to work…he didn't have to work.

"I know sarg. He was so excited when he told me about it last year" Benny said. Stepping around the desk Benny hugged the sergeant, trying to comfort him as if *his* loss was greater than his own.

Oh Benny, little Meereka, we all loved her here at the station. I'm so sorry for your loss." He said choking back the tears." How did you find out, I mean, how do you know, they may still find her?"

"I had a dream last night sarg. Meereka told me."

Sarvino gave Benny a queer look. He knew from several experiences over the last four years that if Meereka said something would happen or had happened that it was true. But he'd never heard Benny say anything about seeing her in his dreams.

Are you sure Benny? Maybe it was just a dream and nothing more? Sarvino asked.

"My mom and Meereka were supposed to show up at my auntie Juanita's in Jersey yesterday but they didn't arrive. Benny replied.

"Maybe they went somewhere else, maybe they..." Benny interrupted the sergeant.

"No sarge, they're gone. They were in the Towers. Meereka told me she had to go to help the children make the transition. She also said it was mama's time to go.

Sarvino wanted to believe there might be another answer. He wanted so to believe that something miraculous could still emerge from the most horrible day of his life. Maybe Meereka would be found safe in the arms of her mother under the collapsed buildings. He wanted to believe in something...something to help him hold on.

"In the dream she said more drawings would come in today." Benny added still sobbing.

The blood drained from Sarvino's face. "They uh, they...detective Thompson got some in this morning. Just like before. I, I...I mean it's so hard to believe..."

"I know sarge. My princess... she... she was so special." Benny said. He wanted to sit and reflect on his sister and mother who he loved so much, but now that he knew the pictures had arrived at the station, just like Meereka told him, he felt obligated to view them right away.

"Thanks sarge, I better go see Leroy now." Benny took a tissue from the sergeant's desk and wiped his eyes.

"Sure kid, sure." As Benny headed for the stairs something occurred to the sergeant. "Benny, if, if, that is if you speak with Meereka again, could you ask about my Stevie? I mean I'd just like to know he's okay...you know, that he's on the other side and he's okay." Sergeant Sorvino broke down and Benny walked around the desk and hugged him again.

"Sure sarge. I'd be glad to ask." Benny looked sadly into the sergeant's eyes then turned toward the stairs.

When Benny reached the top detective Thompson was waiting for him.

"I saw you come in kid, but I thought maybe it would help the sarge if he could talk with you for a few minutes. He's pretty broken up."

153

Benny shook his head and said, "Yea, I know Leroy, we all are."

"The captain told him to go home but I heard him say he owed it to Stevie to be here. "You know captain,' Sarvino said, 'in case some other parents come in who lost a child, I might be able to help, maybe we could even help each other get through this a little easier.""

"I understand. Bless him for that. This city is gonna need a lot of that kind of heart before it finds its way through this misery." Benny added.

Leroy nodded then said, "C'mon kid, I gotta show you something."

"The drawings, they're here aren't they?" Benny said.

"Ya, they're here alright." The detective put his arm around Benny's shoulder. I'm so sorry about Meereka and your mother. You knew it was coming. I just didn't want to believe it, but she was never wrong was she? Oh God Benny, I'm so sorry!"

Benny thanked the detective, then it occurred to him to ask Leroy how he knew about what happened to Meereka and his mother.'

"How did you know?" Benny asked

They walked into the detective's office and closed the door. Detective Thompson picked up the first drawing on the pile of and handed it to Benny. "Look here Benny." The detective said. Benny looked at it and began to cry. There was a drawing of two females, one was much bigger than the other and looked like she might be the mother of the smaller one. She held the hand of the little one. Both had a big yellow circle surrounding them. They were waving and smiling. Above their heads was a red heart. Inside the heart was written: *Benny*. Benny heaved a deep sigh as tears streamed down his cheeks. Leroy left the room and Benny dropped his head in his hands. It was twenty minutes before Benny joined him again.

"Have you studied the other drawings?" Benny asked, as he blew his nose in to a handkerchief Leroy had handed him.

"I've only looked at two of them so far. The one I just showed you and this one." He pulled the next picture from the pile and pointed at four stick people. "There seems to be four survivors trapped somewhere deep under the buildings. Detective Thompson said. "Look here Benny, see,

154

four people, one colored yellow and three in a muddy orange color, all standing. Then there are nine over here on the other side of the drawing in gray, all lying down. I think they must be dead." The detective said. "But I'm not certain what this pink circle is at the top."

"*Pink lady.*" Benny smiled through his tears and said. "Meereka is with them."

"I think you're probably right Benny. If we are right about this we need to figure out where the survivors are. Time is running out. There will be very little air and they probably have no water. Then there is also the possibility of a cave in."

"Leroy lets agree to focus only on a successful rescue." Benny said with resolution.

Your right kid, your right. Does no good to think about what we don't want."

Benny and detective Thompson spent some time trying to decipher the drawings. They were almost certain from the other drawings that there were definitely four survivors and that they had somehow found food and water.

"If our assumptions are correct, there is a good chance they can hold out till we find them, provided they have a source of fresh air." The detective said.

Although Benny and Detective Thompson did not discuss what might happen if a rescue team using large equipment dislodged heavy debris near the four survivors, the ominous image of it crossed their minds.

"Benny, the drawing we just received and the others must have been sent to this precinct because of you and your special connection with Meereka. And it can't be an accident that we happen to be the closest precinct to the towers." The detective asked.

"Your right Leroy. If anyone can convince the mayor's office there are survivors from information found in these children's drawings, it's definitely us. Especially after the other drawings predicted a disaster that actually happened." Benny said firmly.

Leroy was very proud of Benny's strength and endurance, even in the face of personal tragedy he was resolute, fiercely dedicated and consistently positive.

"You'll make a great detective one day Benny. I'm proud to have been the first to work with you." Leroy said putting his arm around Benny's shoulder.

Beaming, Benny thanked Leroy and gave him a big hug. "Right now those people are still alive under the Towers and need much more than two clever sleuths. They need a rescue team with a gentle touch.

Leroy told Benny he looked wasted and suggested he take a nap. Benny agreed and lay down on the detective's office couch. As Benny drifted into a twilight sleep Meereka came to him again.

Benny's heart leapt at the sight of his little princess. "I miss you so much my little princess." He said.

"Meereka still here." She said. "Come Benny." A moment later he was inside the cavern where Smokie and the other three survivors were trapped. Benny looked at the four people who appeared to be sleeping. He noticed there were three lying down covered in plastic sheeting. The fourth person was sitting on the floor leaning up against some boxes. Benny noticed the boxes read: *Pure Spring Water*. Behind them were several boxes of food. If what he was seeing was the real thing, Leroy and his hunch about the survivors having food was correct.

"Look Benny." Meereka said. Benny read the name that appeared on all the boxes he could see. They all read; *Sunshine Health Foods*.

'That's how we'll pinpoint the location.' Benny thought. 'The Tower rental agency will know exactly where this shop was located under the buildings.'

"Look Benny." Meereka said. He turned and the man who he had seen leaning against the boxes was standing beside him.

"Are you a ghost?" Smokie asked.

"No, you and I are just sleeping. "See, there you are sitting against those boxes over there." Benny replied.

156

"Oh, I see." He said in a matter of fact way. "Hi Meereka, I thought you were gone little girl. I could only hear you in my mind." Smokie said.

"Meereka here Smokie." She said.

"Is that your name? Smokie?" Benny asked.

"Ya, my dad was a firefighter. His name was Captain Seagram and he gave it to me when I was a little boy." He replied.

"My name's Benny. Are those three people over there alive?" He asked.

"Ya, they're in pretty good shape. I think the man has a concussion. He was lying on his back on top of the boy and the lady when I found him. The other two just have scraps. When they woke up none of them could remember anything that happened. They were pretty shaken up so they have been sleeping a lot. There are nine other people at the end of this room who are dead." Smokie pointed to the area where he had gathered the bodies together.

"Like in pictures Benny." Meereka said.

"Yes princess, just like in the pictures." He said.

Smokie looked perplexed and asked. "How come its not dark in here now."

"Always light on other side." Meereka said. "Smokie just forget."

"Smokie struggled to remember something about the other side but it wouldn't come to him.

"Are you gonna be okay until we can get to you Smokie?" Benny asked.

"Sure Benny, I learned a lot from my pop, he was a firefighter for twenty years before he died in a fire. He told me yesterday it was ten years ago but it seems like it was just a couple of days ago. It's been kinda confusing since I woke up in here."

"What year was it when the fire happened Smokie?" Benny asked.

"It was 1991." He replied.

157

"He was right Smokie. This is 2001. You say you talked to him here? Benny asked.

"Ya, he came to tell me and told me I had important stuff to do and to wish me a happy birthday." Smokie replied looking perplexed and sad.

Benny looked at Meereka who just nodded and smiled. "He was sure right about that Smokie, you do have very important work to do. I promise we'll get to you as soon as we can. It will be the best birthday you've ever had when we get you and the others outta here."

"Will you come back like this again Benny?" Smokie asked.

"That depends on Meereka I think. She brought me here. But I know she will be with you all the way, won't you princess?" He said.

"Meereka stay with Smokie." She said.

"Princess, where is mama?" Benny asked.

"Mama come home, Stevie too." She answered. Benny smiled, remembering what the sarge had asked of him.

It was obvious to Smokie that Benny knew Meereka. "Benny, you know little Meereka don't you?"

"Yes, she is my precious little sister Smokie." He answered.

"Is she sleeping too?" He asked

"No Smokie, She is an angel. Aren't you *pink lady*?

158

Thirty-Nine

July - 15 - 1983

Francine believed her heart could sustain no greater pain than when her brother Mika'ill and his wife Hayfa died in 1979, the day before she was to marry Donald Heathrow. She became the legal guardian of their children following their deaths and soon afterward legally adopted them. At the time she believed that by not marrying Donald her family would be protected from the wrath of the fanatics seeking revenge on her father and his family. She was wrong! Four years later, Yousef was abducted.

Francine's theory was that whoever wanted to take revenge on her father must have believed Ibrahim would suffer more if they wounded him indirectly through those he loved. The perpetrators must have felt Ibrahim would eventually regret his wayward spiritual predilection and return to the one true religion - Islam. It was insanely ironic that threats, torture and murder were used in an attempt to convert Ibrahim, a man filled with genuine love, into the embrace of a love, in this case, guided by hate.

She knew Yousef had to be either dead or snatched out of the country. Her anguish was far worse than the loss of Mika'ill and Hayfa because there was no closure. If he *was* alive, what terror might this beautiful little Seven-Year old boy be subjected to? It was too horrible to imagine.

After the boy's kidnapping Francine decided to resign from her counseling position at Oxford and move to the family estate in Bath where she would be surrounded by her mother's large family. She battled with immense guilt and depression and often disappeared for hours, just to be by her self.

The family business interests touched many areas of farming and she hoped she and Yasmine could find peace and sanctuary in that environment. She knew in the state she was in that her conduct could be harmful to Yasmine's welfare if she continued living alone with her in Oxford.

Ibrahim and Jacqueline flew in from New York as soon as they received word of Yousef's kidnapping. Jacqueline gave her full attention to Francine and Yasmine while Ibrahim made inquiries through his many friends in the Middle East about what may have occurred. Both he and Jacqueline were relatively certain Abdullah's sons were responsible for the deaths of

Mika'ill and Hayfa. There were no employment records of the two transient waiters who catered the dinner, but eventually a trail was found that led back to people connected to the Mujahideen terrorist group.

Ibrahim's learned through his investigations after the tragedy with his son and daughter-in-law that Ahmed and Abdul joined the group in 1979 to fight the Soviets in Afghanistan. And while it made no sense for them to be in the UK in 1983 when the hostilities in that region were at a peak, he felt certain there was a connection between them and Yousef's abduction. Within two month's of his and Jacqueline's arrival in Bath, he had the answer.

It was discovered Maryam Khaled, the mother of Yousef had a Pakistani half brother whom she had not seen since childhood. His name was Abdul Qahaar Khaled and he too had joined the Mujahideen. Through Ahmed and Abdul he must have learned of the existence of his nephew Yousef. It was probable that the brothers used Yousef's blood connection with Abdul Khaled to inflict further suffering on Ibrahim and his family. It was also likely Yousef would immediately be placed into a Jehad militant youth training camp.

Finding and rescuing the boy under such circumstances would be nearly impossible. Ibrahim and Jacqueline took Francine into the library, which adjoined the solarium in order to break the news to her as gently as they could. The environment was serene and conducive to the moment, setting a stage to tell their daughter the sad tidings. Ibrahim sat by himself in a chair that was positioned directly in front of a large sofa and beside a fireplace while Jacqueline sat close to Francine on the sofa.

"Beloved daughter." Ibrahim began softly. "We have all endured much pain since the death of your dear brother and his wife Hayfa. Now we have been given yet another burden to bear. Our hearts are heavy but we must place little Yousef in God's loving care for where he has been taken, we cannot go."

Almost hysterical, Francine pleaded with Ibrahim, "Why father, why can't you go after him if you know where he is? Francine wailed like a child.

Ibrahim, as was his custom, waited for the inner voice to guide his words. Francine knew he would not speak until he was ready but the pain in her heart was too great to hold her tongue.

"Tell me father!" She screamed. "Why can't you get him back, you have the power. Why won't you get him back? You have to, you have to!"

Francine collapsed into her mother's arms weeping uncontrollably. The blazing fire reflected her pain, anger, and sense of helplessness. She knew if her father had his mind set it was for a good reason and he was unshakeable, but for the moment her sense of reason was smothered by her anguish.

"Daughter, we have been told that Yousef has an uncle. Yousef is with him now, somewhere in Pakistan. Even if we could locate the boy, the uncle has a legal right to contest your adoption. The people who have him would consider you an infidel and you would not be given a fair trial even if it could be taken that far.

"But father we must try! Francine pleaded.

"Francine, he would be moved out of the area even if you somehow *won* your case. We must hand his welfare over to God. His way *is* the way."

A moment later Yasmine jumped from behind a sofa opposite the one on which Jacqueline and Francine were sitting and cried.

"Papie, Papie, I will find Yousef!"

She ran into Ibrahim's arms crying. Francine looked up from Jacqueline's embrace, her face a mask of madness. Ibrahim watched helplessly as the agony in his daughter's eyes glazed over into a cold stare. Her mind receded from the agony as she disappeared into *a far country* of madness. The flickering fire behind him reflected off her blank eyes echoing a time gone by - another fire - guilt, long buried, had resurfaced and was now playing out on a different stage.

"What's wrong with auntie Franny mama?" Yasmine asked.

Forty

1979 - 1987

The truest test of a person's resolve to live their life purpose arrives when they are confronted with an irreconcilable obstacle that challenges them to give up everything they hold dear to pursue that purpose. Francine believed this was just such a moment.

Donald did not share her belief. The loss of Francine, literally at-the-alter, not through loss of love but through love paralyzed by fear, was a senseless waste. He knew the most meaningful time to embrace love was when it is most threatened by the terror of the unknown.

He also knew that Francine believed she was protecting Donald and her family by sacrificing the union of her heart with Donald in marriage. He knew too that she was reasoning through a filter of fear and deluding her self that fear could be fought through defensive action. Love, he told himself, is the *only* antidote to fear.

He also told himself the entire Middle Eastern conflict boiled down to the same delusional thinking; the protection of spiritual identity, an identity founded primarily on peace and love, insanely defended through terrorism. The dichotomy was so obviously deranged yet completely logical to those involved. Great minds throughout the ages, from all parts of the world, taught the same basic truth; *what we focus our thoughts upon, becomes our reality.* Focus on love and that is what your world will reflect. Focus on revenge, hatred and attack and your world will be at war with itself until that focus is changed. 'So simple and yet so disregarded.' He thought.

Francine was taught this simple truth through the wise and loving nurturing of her parents who lived every moment of their lives in the spirit of this truth. She knew better. Yet the deep seeded cellular memory of self-judgment fed by guilt, had over-written all she knew to be true. The script she was playing out was forcing her to face her demons in her own way.

"My love for your daughter transcends time and space." He told Ibrahim and Jacqueline some time after the wedding was canceled. "It will not diminish. The bond of love between us is eternal. Until the moment when love overpowers the fear, as it must, I will carry the torch for both of us in my heart."

162

Donald silently bore his heartache while he and his father worked with the Faiz's to nurture their belief in the power of love to heal, through their creative projects in *Inner Scape Productions.* Gradually, the production company developed a foothold in the highly competitive world of film-making.

Within three years of its inception, *Inner Scape* had its first hit with the release of the movie: *"Magic Mind."* It was about a teenager from a poor Costa Rican family who displayed paranormal powers after a near death experience while parasailing. An advertising executive from Los Angeles discovered the boy's abilities during a holiday in the area. He saw the opportunity turn the boy's gifts into a moneymaking proposition and convinced the family to come to America. Sometime later, the executive's wife became terminally ill with cancer. The teenager's real abilities were revealed when she was spontaneously healed in the executive's presence. The next day the boy died of an aneurysm. From that moment on, the executive turned his back on his previous life and devoted him self to the study of healing.

The movie initially flopped at the box office but later gained a teen audience at the video stores. A year later, in 1982 it was re-released in theaters across the country and earned over $50 million dollars. From that time on *Inner Scape* began receiving dozens of scripts on similar topics. Some eventually made it into the theaters.

With the growing success of *Inner Scape*, Donald's primary focus moved from his therapy practice with Ramsey in New York to the day-to-day operations of the production company. *Inner Scape* had offices in Los Angeles, Toronto, New York and London. As a result Donald frequently found himself in England. When there, and as often as his heart could bare it, he visited Francine and the children.

When Donald met with her face to face he was forced to play off Francine's self imposed role of old friend, a part that kept the wound alive in his heart. A game is easy to play when one is unaware that the game is not real, but when a lie is foisted upon an awakened dreamer, the playing becomes intolerable. For this reason Donald kept his meetings with Francine to a minimum. He longed to be with her but not under false pretenses.

However, in 1983, after the abduction of Yousef when Francine sank into a semi catatonic state Donald spent a month in London helping Ibrahim and Jacqueline find the best possible professional help for her.

Finally, it was decided to place Francine under the care of renowned psychiatrist, Dr. Raymond St. John, in Salisbury, a short distance from Francine's residence in Bath. Dr. St. John practiced psychiatry in London for 30 years before discovering a unique therapy that involved working with patients in the alpha wave state. He used a technique that allowed a physician to reach patients in Francine's condition from the witness perspective, isolated from their fears. This helped remove the obstacle of self-judgment that fostered guilt. The concept worked similar to guided meditation and Dr. St. John found that in most cases it was highly effective over time.

When Jacqueline left England, Yasmine was left in the care of her two sisters. Due to her aunt's condition the child wasn't taken to visit Francine very much during the four years of her therapy in Salisbury. In 1987 Francine had recovered sufficiently to reenter normal life and returned to the family estate in Bath. Yasmine was eleven years old and was overjoyed to be with her aunt again. Nevertheless, the reunion was constrained. The family warned Yasmine that to speak openly about Yousef would put an unnecessary stress on Francine.

Since the topic of Yousef was an ever-present subject that constantly occupied Yasmine's mind, it was a difficult task for her to keep silent. She swore to her family that one day she would be reunited with her stepbrother. Nothing they could say would dissuade her from what they considered a fool hearty obsession.

In the most precocious voice she would tell them, "You just wait til I'm old enough, I know I can find him. You just wait!"

Ibrahim and Jacqueline knew all too well the power of focused thought to achieve its intentions. It mattered not whether the focus was an altruistic desire to heal the planet or a fanatical obsession to obliterate a race entirely from the planet's surface. Focused thought eventually hardened into tangible fact. As a result, they did not doubt Yasmine's firm resolve for a second.

They also knew the tie between Yasmine and Yousef went far beyond the adopted sibling relationship that brought them together. On the track Yasmine was following, that powerful bond would inevitably lead the two down a path almost no one could have foreseen.

Forty-One

1987

&

September - 11 - 2001

David arrived at the Newark departure gate for flight 93 at 7:55 am, just five minutes before it was scheduled to depart from gate A-17 for San Francisco. When he entered the plane, there were only 36 passengers on board. His boarding pass read 6C in first class but he didn't like the looks of the fellow sitting in 6B, so he took a chance that no one was likely to show up after him and sat in 6D.

Much to his surprise, a minute later another passenger rushed into the plane just as the attendants were about to close the door. Sure enough, he had seat 6D, but when he saw David in his seat, he appeared shocked, hesitated, then sat down in the seat David should have taken.

The young fellow appeared to be of Middle Eastern descent, in his mid twenties, clean-shaven with rugged good looks. He appeared nervous, as if he expected David to react to his staring.

"Hey Furuk, calm down, no harm done, okay?" David said sarcastically.

"Actually, its my fault, that seat was supposed to be mine. I just decided to sit here instead." David whispered as he flicked his eyes toward the surly looking man in the next seat.

"Yousef ignored the gesture. "My name is Yousef, not Furuk." He said firmly.

"Sorry, I didn't mean anything by it Yousef. My name's David Bryan."

The blood drained from Yousef's face. Although he was very dark skinned, David could see the fellow looked faint.

"Say Yousef, you don't look so good. You better have a stiff drink when we get airborne to calm you down."

"I don't dreenk." He said curtly.

"We'll then I'll buy ya a first class dinner." He said, laughing cynically at his little joke. "You do eat don't you?"

Yousef didn't reply. Instead, he darted a quick look at the man beside him as if he was being watched, then glanced up the aisle where three other surly looking Arab men sat. The plane began taxiing, then the pilot came over the intercom and apologized that there would be a short delay. From long experience David knew short usually meant at least half an hour. He settled back into his seat, closed his eyes and drifted into an old memory. This Yousef fellow had the same name as Yasmine's half brother and this thought took him back to the first time he met Francine.

It was the winter of 1987 and he was in London for a trade show on the future of the Internet. David's company, *GlobeTel Communications* was sponsoring a workshop on the subject and he was a keynote speaker. After the workshop ended he stopped at a display highlighting futuristic graphics.

"Virtual reality seems to be the next illusion of choice." A man standing beside him said.

"No kidding." David said. "A business associate in LA told me just the other day that actors will soon be out of business, replaced by computer characters so real that you won't be able to tell them from actual people. Its pretty amazing I'd say."

"As a matter of fact I'm in that business. I hope your friend is wrong though. It would steal the heart out of movies, the only true reality in a film." The man said.

"I agree. My name is David Bryan. I'm vice president of *GlobeTel Communications*. Nice to meet you."

"Hello, I'm Dr. Donald Heathrow of *Inner Space Productions*."

"You're kidding. You're with *Inner Space?*" David exclaimed.

"Yes, my dad and I started the company back in the 70's, but now it's half owned by the food conglomerate *Brarab Industries*.

166

"Really. What's their connection?" before Donald could answer David said, "Money I bet?"

No, not really. The couple, that own the company, Ibrahim and his wife Jacqueline Faiz are deeply involved in spiritual matters and as you may or you may not know all our movies have a spiritual essence to them. As a matter of fact, here comes his daughter and granddaughter now. Francine and Yasmine walked up to the two men and Donald introduced them to David. Francine noticed David's immediate attraction to her but ignored it. The four chatted for a while about the future of the Internet and David said to watch out for a guy named Steve Case, who owned a company named Quantum Computer,

"He'll turn this industry on its head one day soon." David's prophesy was correct, a few years later Quantum got a facelift and changed its name to AOL.

David asked Donald if he and Francine would care to join him later for dinner hoping in that way to get Francine's attention.

"How about it Francine, Yasmine is off to see that new Disney movie, *Three Men and a Baby* tonight."

"Sure, why not?" She smiled.

Later that night as the three met for dinner, Donald apologized for having to excuse himself.

"I just got a call an hour ago from the Academy Award winning screenwriter, Alastair MacPherson. He was due in later but caught an early flight from Aberdeen and wants to meet with me to discuss a book *Inner Scape* wants to adapt for the screen. Do you two mind terribly having dinner without me?"

"Go head Donald, no problem." Francine said.

"Sure, go ahead, I'll be happy to keep Francine entertained. By the way, what's the name of the book? I read a fair bit when I'm traveling?" David asked.

"It's called *The Millennium Tablets*." He replied.

167

"Ya sure, I've heard of that one. I haven't got around to reading it though. The title is catchy with the big 2000 coming up soon." David said.

"We're quite excited about it. It's got a great storyline, perfect for our audience. Well, I guess I'll see you two a little later. Enjoy your dinner."

David remembered, 'That's how it began.' His business took him to England several times a year and when he was there he met with Francine as often as he could. Although he and Donald were located in New York, he met with Donald far less. David knew about the relationship between Donald and Francine, and for that reason tried to avoid meeting with Donald as much as he could.

He was moving up the ladder quickly and by 1990, at the age of 40 he was fairly certain his next seat at *GlobeTel Communications* was president. To lock it down he needed to round out the solid image he'd been sculpting for several years. Marriage was definitely the curve that would do it. A wife, a child, a house in the country, a membership at the club was the image he needed. It all added up to a neat little package that would help put him over the top. Besides, Francine was a real beauty and he was in love with her - at least that's what he thought at the time.

David knew nothing of Francine's past emotional problems, only that she had been very upset by the abduction of Yousef. He considered that a natural reaction. Besides, it certainly couldn't hurt that she was the daughter of a rich and powerful business tycoon with global connections. On top of that she seemed very anxious to live near her parents who spent a good deal of time in New York, so the move from England was not going to be a problem for her. 'Yes,' he remembered thinking, 'its definitely the next right move.'

On New Year's Eve, 1990 he popped the question and Francine accepted. As he looked back on it he realized he had no idea what love was or how to express it in any real terms that he understood. It had never served any purpose that he could see. And, in the time he had known them both it became clear that Francine still held a torch for Donald and he for her. By marrying him she'd be closing the door on her past. The irony of it was that Donald's main residence was in New York where she was certain to come into frequent contact with him since her parents worked closely with Donald in *Inner Scape*.

He had to laugh at the insanity of it. It was like committing a crime so you could go to jail because you were in love with the prison warden and wanted to be near him.

'We were both nuts I guess.' He laughed to himself thinking about the foolish things people do because of ambition and fear. 'Seems like my entire life has been focused on winning mom's approval, and in the process make certain that I was nothing like the old man. Now she's dead and I'm hooked on power and women just like he was hooked on booze. I guess some things never change.'

Just then David was awakened from his reverie by a scream from the pilot's cabin.

Forty-Two

September - 13 - 2001

At 5:00 am, the morning after Benny's vivid dream encounter with Smokie and Meereka in the rubble under the Towers, he awoke abruptly and found he had fallen asleep on Leroy's office couch. Immediately he made a call to the detective on his private cell phone. Benny explained quickly the details of his dream encounter with Meereka and Smokie, and both men agreed what Benny experienced perfectly matched the second set of drawings they had studied the day before.

"Leroy, I'm sure now that I was right about the first set of drawings and notes. I am certain they were meant to convince us that the drawings were genuine prophesies. Perhaps some things are just meant to happen. Maybe the accumulated energy behind a possible future event takes it from *possible* to *probable* to *definite*." Benny suggested.

"I see what you mean. But if that's true, what's to say Smokie and the other survivors aren't done for too?" The detective asked.

Benny said. "I don't believe I would have had the dream with Smokie if it hadn't been for the two sets of drawings. I know it sounds incredible but its as if they drew me into the experience last night. I don't think anything is etched in stone here. If we act quickly I believe we can still save Smokie and the others."

"You may be right kid. I better call the captain right away. I'll see you at the station in an hour. "Leroy said. The detective rang off and called the captain at home. At 6:00 am the three men met in the captain's office and reviewed the details of all that had occurred since the first set of drawings and notes arrived at the precinct.

"There's no way to keep a lid on this thing boys." The captain said. Once word gets out the entire city will be galvanized around the rescue."

"Maybe that's a good thing captain." Benny suggested.

"Ya, your probably right now that ya mention it kid. God knows the city could use some good news right now." He replied.

Detective Thompson was watching Benny's face when the captain spoke of needing good news half expecting him to break down at the loss of Meereka. However, he seemed unfazed, completely normal as if nothing at all had happened to her. 'The kid must be in shock.' He thought.

"You say Smokie and the others seem to have a good food and water supply Benny? What about fresh air?" The captain asked.

"I don't know captain." Benny replied. "I didn't notice anything that might have suggested fresh air was coming in and Smokie didn't say anything to me about it."

"We better go on the assumption that they don't have much air left and move as quickly as possible." The captain picked up the phone and called the mayor's office, which even at that early hour was a beehive of activity. "Its around the clock at City Hall these days." The captain whispered while he waited for someone to answer.

Without going into detail the captain explained to the mayor that there were four survivors in the area of the Sunshine Health Foods retail shop under the Towers. He said he would explain when he got to City Hall and asked for someone from the Tower's rental agency and a representative from the Tower's architects to be present when he arrived.

"I'll convince them, no matter what it takes." The captain said decisively. "Everyone wants to believe there are survivors so it shouldn't be too difficult." That made sense to Leroy and Benny who offered to come along just in case. The captain agreed saying he wasn't going without them. Thirty minutes later they arrived at City Hall.

"I don't know what to tell you captain." An architect explained. It appears the store is located in one of the most difficult areas to reach at this point. Its still too early to tell, but my guess is it could take at least a week to get anywhere near that space, that is if its still there when we arrive."

"What do ya mean, 'If its still there.'" Benny asked.

"Well, the rubble hasn't completely settled yet. When we begin moving heavy pieces of debris, we could trigger cave-ins. It can't be helped."

The captain and Leroy nodded their heads in understanding but Benny remained silent in thought. '*Pink lady* show the way.' Benny heard in his mind.

171

"Captain, do you think you could get me into Ground Zero, I believe I can show you a way to find the survivors more quickly?" Benny asked.

The architect looked at Benny as if he were crazy. He was about to protest but the captain saw the conviction on Benny's face. He looked over at detective Thompson who nodded his head in reply to his silent question.

That was all the confirmation he needed. "When do you want to go in Benny?" The captain asked.

"What?" The architect shouted.

"Right now if its possible captain." Benny said.

"I'll be joining him captain." The detective said resolutely.

"And captain, can we find out which fire station a *Captain Seagram* was assigned to in 1991? He was Smokie's dad. I think the firefighters down at the station will want to join in." Benny asked.

"Sure thing son, I'll find out right away."

The captain stepped out of the boardroom that they had been using and spoke to a secretary. While he was gone detective Thompson said to Benny, "You got something didn't you?"

"Ya! Meereka told me she would guide us." He said

"I knew it!" The detective exclaimed. "That's good enough for me."

A few moments later the captain poked his head back into the boardroom and said, "East 29th Fire Station. Captain Roger Fox runs the station these days. Turns out their people were some of the first at *Ground Zero*. Its certain they'll be anxious to join in. I have someone calling into the station right now to have some firefighters meet us."

Twenty-five minutes later Benny, Leroy and the captain joined up with six firefighters from the 29th. Before they arrived the captain suggested they tell the firefighters as little as possible in case they became skeptical. It turned out their concerns were unfounded. When they met up with the five men and one woman from the 29th, they had already heard through

172

the grapevine a great deal about how Benny knew about Smokie and the survivors.

"So you're the kid with the psychic sister huh?" One of the firefighters said. "My sister gets visions too. She even had a migraine on September 10th and she never gets headaches. Ya don't have to convince me. I jus hope Smokie makes it - seen too many of my friends die'n the last few days."

Leroy thought about taking the firefighters aside and explaining that Meereka had also perished so that Benny would be saved the agony of that kind of talk, but Benny seemed completely oblivious to the firefighter's remarks. He decided it would probably be better not to mention the fact that Meereka was speaking to Benny from the other side. The firefighter may be opened minded to the supernatural but he and his companions were about to risk their lives and detective Thompson knew that *doubt* was the worst enemy they could have.

Benny and Leroy suited up in rescue gear and followed the firefighters to a large opening in the mangled mountain of metal debris. Smoke still billowed from the wound and they had to wear oxygen masks in order to face the dust and smoke upon entering the opening. A few minutes later their only source of light was from the high-powered flash lights they all carry.

Meanwhile, Smokie was helping the survivor with the head wound open a bottle of water. He had several light sticks glowing on the floor giving the mangled wreckage of the scene an eerie feeling. The woman's breathing was labored and she looked very worried.

The young boy cried as he lay with his head in the woman's lap. "Are we going to die?" He whimpered.

"We will be out of here in no time." The voice in Smokie's mind spoke through him.

"You sound very sure of that." The man said doubtfully.

"You will see, just hold on and try not to strain yourselves." Smokie said.

"There's no air, there's no air. We're going to suffocate." The woman whimpered. She looked like she was about to panic. Smokie knelt down beside her and put his arm around her shoulder.

"We're going to be just fine Mam. They are coming for us right this moment."

He encouraged. His confident and compassionate manner seemed to give the woman strength and she began to calm down.

The young lad and the man could also feel the calm authority in Smokie's voice and despite their misgivings, relaxed into his faith and waited patiently.

"There's an opening around that beam over there." Benny said pointing to a huge twisted piece of metal that appeared to block their way.

"How can he know that?" One of the firefighters said to his companion?" Leroy heard him and said,

"Just go look! If the kid says there's an opening, then there's an opening."

The firefighter shook his head in bewilderment and cautiously headed toward the beam. "Its here, its here! Just like the kid said. Leads almost straight down." He yelled in excitement.

"That's it, not much further now." Benny said in a monotone voice.

Leroy looked over at Benny and shone his flashlight directly into his face. Benny appeared to be in a trance.

One of the firefighters had just been lowered into the hole and shouted up through the opening, "I found a box from the health food store we're looking for."

"That's it. Right behind the smashed concrete supports in front of you. That's where they are." Benny yelled.

"You two better stay put, we'll handle this." One of the other firefighters said as they began lowering gear into the opening. Just then there was a terrific noise and the debris around them shook violently shifting the area they were in and dislodging twisted metal and smashed concrete. The smoke that had been drifting up from below suddenly exploded into a cloud blinding their vision.

"Hold on you two." The firefighter shouted over the loud din.

174

"It will settle down in a moment. Don't worry." Benny said calmly. A few minutes passed and the smoke dissipated. To be sure it was safe the firefighters waited for several more minutes before they proceeded. It took over an hour to move the concrete and rubble but the six firefighters finally shouted in excitement as they broke through. The two men shone their high-powered beams through the hole and right in front of them found the nine bodies Smokie had placed at the far end of the health food store. Immediately they thought the worst and shouted up through the opening what they had found.

"Inside, go inside! They are at the other end of the store. Go look." Benny yelled.

Five minutes later a firefighter screamed up through the opening in excitement that the four survivors had been found alive. "They were all unconscious but they're getting oxygen now so they should be okay in a few minutes."

"Thank God!" Leroy said. He shone his light in Benny's face again. Benny blinked several times then asked,

"What happened?"

"We found them kid. They're alive, they're alive!" He screamed. Benny bowed his head and said,

"God bless you little princess."

When it was discovered who Smokie was, that he was mentally disabled and that his father had been captain of the East 29th Fire Station, the entire city was dizzy with the news of the survivors and how they were found. In no way could it compensate for the incredible and tragic loss the city had endured, but even one candle makes a world of difference to those who have been forced into darkness.

As soon as Dr. Heathrow learned about Benny, Smokie and the details of the incredible rescue, he had an intuitive sense that the reason for his meeting with Benny and Meereka a few years before was about to be revealed. He called Benny and asked him if he would like to explore the deeper meaning of what might have occurred in the last several days in an attempt to help him overcome the trauma he had endured. Benny agreed and asked if Smokie could also attend.

"Despite his handicap," Benny explained, "In my dream experience Smokie seemed absolutely normal except for his disorientation with time."

Donald agreed and said he was going to suggest the same thing. He arranged to meet them the next week at St. Paul's Cathedral and said that he too would be bringing along someone he felt should join in.

Donald had already spoken to Francine about working through the trauma of her loss and after speaking with Benny he was convinced there was a connection. The name *pink lady* came up several times, and in his last conversation with Ibrahim he had been told to look to *pink lady* for guidance. Donald asked him what he meant but Ibrahim would tell him nothing more.

Forty-Three

"This will need a delicate and understanding hand." Donald said. "Benny, you had better call your detective friend. Thompson, is that his name?"

"Ya. That's him." Benny said.

"This county is on fire right now and if there is even a hint anyone connected with the towers is on US soil, there could be a lynch mob on Orange Crescent within minutes." Donald said.

Francine was in torment. Now that they were virtually certain where Yasmine was located, and so close, every fearful thought she could imagine of things going wrong entered her mind.

'Oh God, a lynch mob, Donald could be right. They'd kill everyone in sight. What if her captors have left her to die? What about the baby? Oh no! God, what if what if she's joined them, after all Yousef *was* on the plane, maybe he was really one of the highjackers." One wild idea after another passed through her mind like a parade of gremlins.

Donald waited for Benny to get off the phone with detective Thompson, while Smokie was staring at an empty spot just to the side of Francine. He had a childish grin on his face and was nodding his head. Francine began to hyperventilate and failed to notice him get up and walk over beside her. He took her hands in his just as Benny rang off with the detective. Donald turned and saw Francine's distress and was about to rush to her aid, but a sudden feeling made him hesitate. Meanwhile Benny was beaming.

"Meereka is showing Smokie what to do to help her." He said.

Smokie got Francine to her feet. In her distress she was unaware what was happening - that it was Smokie holding her hands - and simply followed his guidance. Smokie looked down at the seemingly empty spot beside him and nodded. He placed one of his hands together with one of Francine's hands on his heart then repeated the action with their other hands on her solar plexus. She immediately calmed. A few moments later she was weeping tears of joy.

The entire scene took less than a minute but in that tiny space of time Francine was transformed.

Smokie said, "Meereka say, 'old hurt healed'. Benny heard it as well and nodded.

"I can feel it. The guilt has vanished Donald." She looked at him through sweet tears of release as he too wept. At that moment Donald knew Francine's long self imposed sentence had been lifted. His beloved had finally returned.

Smokie stepped aside and Francine ran into Donald's arms. He smiled at Smokie in gratitude as Francine hugged him tightly. In blissful reunion and through an ecstatic embrace, years of heartache dissolved.

Smokie grinned at Donald and said, "Not me - *pink lady*!" Benny grasped his hand, his heart swelling with love.

2:10 PM

Two hours later Donald, Francine, Smokie and Benny were at the police station with detective Thompson. He was connected by speakerphone to a temporary command post set up two blocks away from Orange Crescent in West Palm Beach. He explained that the FBI had agents knocking on every door on the crescent posing as census takers. The area was honeycombed with special agents in unmarked vehicles while helicopters hovered just out of the range where they might alert the people holding Yasmine.

The procedure was slow and methodical in order to insure Yasmine's safety. The special agents were highly trained in the surgical removal of hostages but required precise details of the target house inside and out before going in. Two hours of painstaking canvassing left everyone's nerves frayed on both ends of the phone. Francine and the others spent most of the time praying, focused on a successful outcome where no one would be injured. Finally, at the third hour detective Thompson's contact came over the speaker phone and yelled,

4:15 PM

"They found the house!" There was silence for several more minutes then the agent came back on, this time his voice was subdued. "They must

178

have moved her, the house is empty. But I'm told they have proof she was there recently."

Francine's heart sank. Donald, who was sitting beside her, hugged tightly. Benny stood beside detective Thompson discussing the disappointing results of the search. Smokie sat across from Donald grinning. Both he and Francine noticed the far away look in his eyes.

"Donald, what do you think he's seeing?" Francine asked. Without taking his eyes off him, Donald waved Benny over to Smokie's side. Smokie was staring down at an empty space nodding his head.

"*Pink lady* says, 'Keys'."

"They're not from the Middle East." Benny exclaimed. "The people who are holding Yasmine are not Middle Eastern. They have been able to move about freely because they are Caucasian.

"How do you know this Benny?" Donald asked. "Did Meereka tell you?"

"I'm not sure, it just came to me. I don't know how, I just know."

Donald smiled and nodded. It made sense. When we focus intently on anything long enough it becomes our reality. For over four years Benny had been communicating with Meereka and *pink lady*. Now that Meereka herself was on the other side, Benny's connection with Meereka - seen or unseen must be similar to the connection Meereka had with *pink lady*. Call it intuitive, insightful, psychic or whatever feels right, the proof of the connection was in the guidance being received - guidance that had never yet failed.

Smokie too had apparently tapped into the connection, due most likely to two things; the life threatening situation he was in while buried under the destroyed Towers, and the split consciousness he maintained between the inner and outer world's. Before Benny and detective Thompson's interpretation of the drawings and Benny's lucid dream connection with Smokie when he was buried under the Towers, Smokie was communicating freely with Meereka and his father. The way Donald understood it his mind was on one side and his body on the other. In Smokie's current state of mind he was split between the two sides, which was why he appeared to people as mentally challenged.

In truth, his mind was clearer than it had been before the head injury on the day his father died. After the rescue from beneath the Towers he returned to the same childlike state of mind as before, but he brought back with him a new ability and the guidance to openly share what he was receiving from the other side.

Donald knew there was only one way to drive straight to the Keys. But which car was Yasmine and her captor's driving? How close were they now to the Keys? How would they get her safely out of the car if it were found? He knew these answers were not going to come from the authorities on such short notice. That meant it was up to the four of them to somehow connect with Yasmine's whereabouts.

It was as if the strange and powerful link between the four in the group and their connection to Yasmine, Meereka and *pink lady*, was preordained, coordinated by some unseen force to come together at precisely the right moment for a purpose they could only guess. Whatever that purpose was, it had become obvious it was for the highest good of all concerned.

Forty-Four

1990 - 1999

Ibrahim and Jacqueline knew Francine's marriage to David was a marriage of resignation. No doubt she enjoyed his company to some extent. David was a high rolling corporate climber obsessed with occupying the top seat of power in his industry. He traveled, he partied, he shmoozed with the rich and famous - anything to get his face and name in front of influential people that might be able to help him get where he wanted to go. Francine fit neatly into the puzzle he had been piecing together for most of his life. That too was obvious.

There was no doubt her however, that her feelings for Donald had never changed. The mystery for most people that knew her, was why she would marry a non-Islamic, Caucasian man who lived in New York and represented the antithesis of the non-materialistic focus of the Qur'an? For fear of further revenge being exacted upon the Faiz family she had literally run away from Donald at-the-alter, who was also an infidel by Islamic standards. Why was it now safe to marry David? If it was now safe in her mind to marry David, why not marry the man she truly loved? The answer lay in her, as yet unhealed guilt.

When Francine met David in 1987 after returning to a relatively normal life, she took frequent trips to New York to visit him. While in the states there were also dinners and outings with Donald despite his attempts to limit the painful contact with her. Somehow, she managed to persuade him to spend as much or more time with her than she did with David.

Once again, the answer lay in her guilt. On many levels, Dr. St. John had been able to help her leave the past behind and see that she was not responsible for the deaths of her brother Mika'ill and Hayfa, or for the abduction of Yousef. She had even accepted the fact that it was her father the terrorists were after. Eventually she came to realize that nothing she did was going to make the least bit of difference if the fanatics still wanted to inflict pain upon her father.

Ibrahim and Jacqueline agreed with Dr. St. John that it was the cellular guilt memory of her ancient crime that still simmered beneath the surface, repressing her sense of self worth when it came to Donald. "That wound," he said, "could take a lifetime to heal."

It was not difficult to see that her deep inner need to purge that guilt steered her into a marriage, that on some level she had to know would eventually lead to abuse, betrayal and neglect - a form of self-punishment she believed she deserved on an unconscious level.

Still, Donald would be near enough to see through the bars of her misery. To the sick mind of the guilty, it would be an exquisite pain befitting the unhealed remorse. It mattered not that all this lay hidden beneath her conscious awareness. Ibrahim and Jacqueline knew that the example of their abiding love for each other and their constant prayers for their daughter's happiness was the most powerful and real influence they could have on her. She must heal in her own way. They would be there when the ache was too severe to endure, to love and support her, but never to take her lessons away from her.

Only one thing might have held her in England, and that was Yasmine, who was at the time fourteen. However, the three years apart during Francine's convalescence and the three difficult years of guarded communication concerning Yousef since then, significantly strained their relationship. When Yasmine told Francine she was going to remain in Bath after her marriage to David, Francine was almost relieved. She loved her niece with all her heart, and believed that under the circumstances she could love Yasmine better from afar. Francine also felt a new obligation to try to be the wife David needed and allow Yasmine to mature, free of the insidious inner torment she always carried on her sleeve. Sacrifice seemed to have become her middle name despite the opulent lifestyle she had been immersed in since birth.

It was in 1993 over two years after Francine married David and moved to New York, that Yasmine entered Saint Anthony's College which was connected to Oxford University. She chose the school since it had a Middle Eastern Center and because it would permit her to remain near her family. She had been an excellent student during her high school years, focusing on languages and history and told her family that one day she wanted to be a foreign ambassador. That fooled no one. They all knew her real passion was reuniting with Yousef.

It was some time after her thirteenth birthday she announced to her family that she was no longer going to remain only a sister to Yousef. "I intend to marry Yousef one day. After all, he is not from our family's blood. I love him and I'm going to marry him." She proclaimed defiantly. Yasmine's resolve to find her brother was by then legendary. Everyone knew it was useless to reason with her through logic. Only Jacqueline was able to reach past the fire of her intent and into her heart.

"My beautiful little flower, what a joy you are. You have your grandfather's silent sense of purpose. Only his love for God attracted me more than his will."

"Nanny, you see Yousef and I are meant to be together don't you?" Yasmine pleaded.

"Yes dear, he is your true love. But are you prepared to pay the price?"

"I will pay any price to be with Yousef Nanny."

"The price may be far much more than just being with Yousef little flower." Jacqueline did not explain beyond her ominous warning. Yasmine knew her grandmother could see both into the past and the future and did not question the accuracy of what she had seen. Her Nanny's warning frightened Yasmine but she could not be stayed from her intent.

Yasmine graduated from St. Anthony's College in 1998 with a Masters degree in Foreign Affairs and Languages. The day she graduated she informed her family she was going to complete her Doctorate in Jordan. She intended to do her thesis on the Islamic question focusing on the tensions in the Middle East, Jehad and terrorism as the radical tools it employed to achieve its aims.

I only wish Nanny was here to see me graduate today Papa. She told Ibrahim and Francine. "I miss her so much.

"We miss her too my beautiful angel." Francine said. "But I am sure if she were here she would try to persuade you not to go into that tormented area of the world. There are so many dangers there. I fear for your safety."

Yasmine glanced at her grandfather then lowered her eyes. Her mother lived in fear. Yasmine would not get pulled into another argument about disaster waiting behind every corner. She knew her aunt had endured several tragedies but had she not learned anything from her parents? She knew she created her own reality with her ever-present thoughts. 'No, not today! This is my special day, one that has brought me a step closer to reuniting with Yousef.' She told herself.

Ibrahim took Yasmine's hand and squeezed it gently. In that small gesture she knew that her Papa's love and blessings went with her wherever her heart took her.

Yasmine whispered in his ear. "One day I pray I have your wisdom Papa. I have learned far more from your silent love then from anything else in my life." She hugged him and brushed away the tears.

Francine looked on, deeply grateful that Yasmine had been blessed with the same love she had received from her parents. No matter what life held for her beloved niece, that love was her rock, a touchstone that would always bring her back to her center where truth lived.

Ibrahim arranged to have Yasmine stay with a dear friend, Sulaiman al Zeid, a moderate Muslim whose family had prospered in the *House of Faiz*. He lived in Amman and since retiring had devoted his life to the study and worship of Allah. It was here Ibrahim felt Yasmine would find a balanced perspective of the beautiful heart of Islam while researching the roots of the ugly picture it portrayed to the world. Perhaps her observations would assist her in bringing a more balanced vision to light and help correct the world's picture of Islam, a wish so greatly desired by all moderate Muslims.

Yasmine used the Internet to communicate with Ibrahim and Francine and virtually every day they would receive at least a brief message from *flowerfaiz* as she called herself. Then, eleven months after leaving for Jordan neither Ibrahim or Francine received a message from Yasmine for three days. Francine telephoned her father deeply concerned about the absence of communication from her.

"Father, what do you think has happened to Yasmine. Do you think maybe she has met a boy and fallen in love?" She asked hopefully.

As usual Ibrahim knew it was best to be direct with his daughter and came right to the point. "I spoke with Sulaiman this afternoon. He told me Yasmine received a late night phone call three days ago. The next morning she left very early and he has not heard from her since.

"Oh God, what can it mean father?" She paused for a moment then almost shouted into the phone. "Yousef! Could it be Yousef?"

"Yes dear one, I believe she has found her brother. But their reunion I feel may not be so sweet as she has imagined for long." Francine knew her

184

father would not elaborate, but her own inner voice silently affirmed that he was right.

Forty-Five

June - 1998

After Yasmine graduated from St. Anthony's at Oxford University and moved to Jordan, Ibrahim returned to New York. A week later he met with Donald to discuss an important matter.

"Dear friend, how good it is to see you again." He greeted Donald at the door himself, having given the servants the day off. One of the most captivating things about Ibrahim was a profound aura of peace that always surrounded him. Today, that soothing calm experience Donald felt whenever he was in Ibrahim's presence was particularly noticeable.

"Something, I feel is very much different today." Donald said, smiling warmly as he embraced his friend and partner. "I sense that your important news bears glad tidings."

"Quite so dear friend." Ibrahim led Donald into the library where he spent most of his time when at home. "There are matters of a personal and business nature I wish to speak with you about, please make yourself comfortable and I will share with you what I wish to impart." Ibrahim had tea prepared and served Donald first then himself. He then sat in silence until he felt the atmosphere was balanced for what he wanted to say.

Donald could feel a slight sensation of sadness floating in the atmosphere. It was faint, but sufficient to disturb the serenity of the moment. He waited patiently knowing his friend's custom of going with an inner flow. Finally, Ibrahim began.

"I am leaving New York Donald and I have already bid adieu to England. While I have said goodbye to Francine, Yasmine and Jacqueline's family, they do not know that it was for the last time. I am sharing this only with you. You have my complete trust and my deepest love. I have seen your path and it very much parallel's my own. It is a path of joy and sorrow strangely mixed. A course that no man would knowing chose for himself but which his better angels know will draw him inexorably to the middle way, the way I chose so long ago. The path you too have chosen and even now have begun to see."

Donald felt an urgency to interrupt his friend but could not find the words. He knew he was seeing his beloved friend and mentor for the last time. His heart overflowed with the unbounded love of Oneness, yet ached with the very personal and human sense of impending loss. He could feel his friend's compassion and knew Ibrahim understood.

"Donald, dear friend, you have been as a son to me…no, not a replacement for my beloved Mika'il but a son no less. I count you also as a fellow pilgrim on the thorny path. Only my dear wife knew me better. Now, for a short while, we shall be separated in the realm of time, but that too is destined to end where we will once again join as the brothers we are in truth."

He paused for a moment and Donald nervously sipped some tea as he waited for him to continue. Ibrahim pulled a bulky folder from beneath the coffee table that sat between them and laid it in front of Donald. He slowly opened it and pulled several files out laying them side-by-side on the table.

"Donald, this is my last will and testament. You will find that my lawyers have prepared all the details for you which places the bulk of my wealth in your hands." Donald again had the urge to speak but knew it would serve little purpose. If Ibrahim had made such arrangements, they were well laid plans guided from a higher source and would not be changed. He listened, tormented by the agonizing thought of losing his friend.

"Powerful events will unfold over the next few years that will explain much of what I cannot now share with you. What I do say now is to follow your inner voice, as you have never done before. I entrust this fortune in your hands as I prepare to depart this world knowing that when these things occur, which they must, you will be guided as to what direction to take with the material power and influence I now place in your hands."

Donald's personal fortune was sizeable due to the success of *Inner Scape Productions'* twenty plus years of success in the movie industry. He knew Ibrahim wielded an enormous force in the business community having steered *Brarab Industries* into a key position to capitalize on the impending explosive growth in the Wellness Industry. He also knew Jacqueline inherited a vast fortune of her own anchored in the food additive industry that dovetailed perfectly with Brarab Industries' global influence. What he did not know was how Ibrahim had, for many years funded vast global business endeavors, both his own and others, through banking interests that he controlled in the Middle East. It was so like Ibrahim to be the most silent about the greatest things, 'downplaying the importance of that which eventually turns to dust' as he put it. Donald would learn some months later, after the passing of his friend in Mecca, that his fortune was in the billions.

"Tomorrow I leave for Mecca where I will lay down this mantle and take up the greater work where its influence has a broader sweep. Some years ago dear friend, you met with a great one whose words have influenced your path since that time, much more than you know. He also told you that much of what he said would be hidden from you for a time. That time will soon come to an end and when I pass this instrument of power to you, the seal will be broken and you will soon afterward come into your true life purpose, the purpose for which you were born, the purpose for which you have been prepared these many years."

Now that Ibrahim seemed almost finished speaking, Donald was speechless. Despite his feeling of impending loss, a sublime sense of peace surrounded him. He was deeply humbled knowing that a great task lay before him. What it might be specifically was a useless speculation, but since this foresight had come to him from Ibrahim he was content to wait.

Throughout the rest of their meeting the two discussed the immanent challenges the world faced, and the steadfast focus Donald would need to exercise in order to meet his part in easing the burden of it in a very tangible way. He would be required to step from behind the screen and move beyond the safety net of fantasy the world had woven.

Donald knew there was a great deal Ibrahim was not telling him, a great deal about pending world events, about the personal challenges he must face and deal with before he took his seat of power. He also knew it was useless to press his friend for details nor would he want to know those details now. In the moment of his need he knew the direction he would need would be given to him.

Three hours after arriving Donald bid farewell to his beloved friend for the last time. Two months later, Ibrahim's lawyers informed Donald that Ibrahim had passed away peacefully in his sleep.

188

Forty-Six

Ibrahim's insight was correct. He had seen that after his abduction by Abdul and Ahmed Yousef would be indoctrinated into a training camp with the Mujahideen faction. Despite his tender age, training was severe and it was soon discovered Yousef had developed asthma a short time after he was taken from Francine. As a result the ringleader assigned Yousef to menial duties around the camp.

The boy came into little contact with Abdul, Ahmed and his uncle Abdul Qahaar Khaled since they were training in a different camp in Pakistan. Later, when the three joined the fighting in Afghanistan, he saw them no more. He learned some time later that all three had been killed in an unsuccessful raid.

He was a bright and friendly boy who was favored by many. By the time he reached the age of eleven he was permanently attached to a courier named Rahman bin Hamad. Raman traveled a great deal throughout the Middle East delivering all his messages personally while using a variety of names in order to insure his security. During his travels, Rahman frequently moved about with various females that posed as his wife and later with Yousef who posed as their son.

This practice continued throughout the conflict between the Soviets and Afghans during the 80's. After the conflict ended Rahman became involved with the Taliban, which took over most of the country when in-fighting began within the Mujahideen. Then, in 1996 he became associated with the al Qaida. Yousef was twenty years old and although he had traveled widely throughout the Middle East and parts of Europe with Rahman, he had experienced no contact with females.

It was not that the opportunity hadn't presented itself. Since his health precluded his active membership in any militant activities, he was excluded from the normally celibate lifestyle many of those members adhered to. And although Rahman was connected to some very sinister people, he walked a middle road, the road that looked out for number one - himself. Since Yousef was an important cog in that wheel, he took good care of him. As a result, on a number of occasions he encouraged Yousef to sample the more delicate things in life, but always Yousef declined.

"Still holding out for that flower to come back into your life are you? Well, I think it not advisable to go there little brother. That life ended long ago and will not return. There is no escape for us Yousef." Rahman assured him.

But in Yousef's mind, as the years past he came to feel that even a single day with Yasmine would be worth the years of semi imprisonment he was forced to endure. As if written in heaven, something powerful had come over him at the age of Thirteen that told him Yasmine was much more than a sister, she was the heart of his soul.

Rahman had made himself an indispensable partner to the cause, always shifting with the definition of what the cause meant and keeping a very low profile - almost to the point of invisibility. This gave both he and Yousef considerable freedom to live a relatively normal, insulated life within the boundaries of their more ominous life. In a sense, their work became a job, a perilous and villainous job, but a job none-the-less. In 1998 during one of their 'personal freedom trips,' as Rahman called them, the two traveled throughout Europe and England. There were a number of important contacts Rahman was to make while there, nevertheless the two men had ample time to enjoy themselves.

This was the chance Yousef had waited years to materialize, and he would seize the opportunity the moment Rahman left him alone. Yousef made a number of inquiries concerning the Faiz family and easily learned of Yasmine's whereabouts. He found that she was attending her final year at St. Anthony's College and was determined to meet with her.

"Rahman, I have read that Bath has many beautiful sights, let us take a trip in that direction shall we? Yousef suggested.

"I have also heard that to be true. Let us go then little brother and forget this ugly business for a few days shall we?

Three days later he rang the college and found out where Yasmine was taking classes the next day. Rahman was in Oxford for the day and Yousef went to St. Anthony's, which was nearby. He stationed himself in a courtyard where he was certain Yasmine would pass on the way to her next class. He had not seen her for sixteen years but was certain he would know her instantly. A group of students began walking through the courtyard and Yousef sat on the edge of a fountain with a bouquet of Jasmine flowers in his hand. Even before she entered the courtyard Yasmine knew her life was about to change. The moment she stepped into the courtyard her heart swelled almost to bursting and she was pulled with a passion beyond her fondest dreams toward her waiting love.

"I have found you, I have found you my love. Oh I have found you at last." She cried as she threw herself into his arms.

"Is it not I who have found you, my once-upon-a-time sister?" He laughed - tears streaming down his face.

She looked up into his eyes remembering her promise to herself and said. "My love, you have captured my most treasured thoughts for many years. You have been the fire in my every deed. And your name has been the path my heart has followed to this moment. You are here now because I would have it no other way."

The next hour was as a gift from heaven for both she and Yousef. The years apart dissolved and the life ahead ceased to exit. They were lost in the moment, unaware of any other reality. Yasmine told Yousef of her plans to move to Jordan the following year to complete her doctorate and Yousef resolved to be at her side as much as possible.

"The work I have been called to do I have done to stay alive - for us. Now that we have found each other my every thought will be to somehow make a life for us together." He promised her.

"My love, you must take the utmost care. I know of the men you and your companion report to. No words can describe what they are capable of." Yasmine said.

"It is true dear angel of my heart, but I do not follow the lust that drives their madness. It is only you that guides my heart." He said.

"If only I could call on grandfather to help us but so much trouble has befallen the Faiz family and in my heart I know he will not remain on this earth much longer. I will miss him, he has taught me so much about the things that really matter in this world of sadness." She said.

"I have heard from time to time about grandfather Ibrahim. Those that have held the key to my chains speak with a hostile respect when his name is mentioned. It has cost me much to lose the years of wise counsel I might have had with him."

"I will share the wisdom he imparted to me with you my beloved, and the love he shared with me, which is eternal."

Yasmine agreed to meet Yousef in Jordan as soon as it was safe for him to do so. In the meantime they would communicate by Internet whenever it was possible for Yousef to arrange it. When Yasmine moved to Jordan it became a simple matter for Yousef to arrange a few hours with Yasmine each time they passed through Amman.

But their meetings were brief and the passion between them grew with each separation. Neither could contain their longing for each other and finally Yousef told Yasmine he was going to break away from Rahman.

"Beloved flower, I do not care for the consequences. I can no longer live the lie that has shackled my life - not now that we have finally found each other and the love we yearn so much to share. When I return, we will leave this place together."

Yasmine had the same resolve as her grandfather and it had been her all consuming dream since she was thirteen to be with Yousef. Yes, she would brave the unknown with her love, and so it was.

His call came late one evening and the next day, very early and with few belongings so as not to draw suspicion to her self, she left home, never to return. Rahman and Yousef had changed identities frequently over the years and he was well aware of the back streets of intrigue. Within hours after his call to Yasmine, they were on their way to America.

Forty-Seven

September - 11 - 2001

On September 11th, 2001, Yousef boarded United flight 93 from Newark to San Francisco, just moments after David Bryan. He had a choice - a catch 22 - nevertheless, a choice. He could join the doomed flight and redeem himself in the eyes of Allah, or not take the flight and watch Yasmine die - retribution for his sins. That is the way it was presented to him, by the ringleader who helped orchestrate the flight.

He was not a participant nor had he been briefed on what was to occur. He knew only that the plane was to be used as a bomb for some awful purpose that would bring the name of Allah to American soil in a powerful way that could not be ignored. He had been exposed long enough to the insanity of the radical Islamic methods of fighting what they called 'Jehad'. He knew they were serious and that the doubled edged sword he was handed meant the end of his life either way.

To Yousef there was no choice. Yasmine and their baby must be saved at all cost. He boarded the flight knowing that she would be spared provided he allowed himself to be sacrificed, along with the rest of the unsuspecting passengers and crew. Should he alert anyone of the impending fate of the flight and was found out, again Yasmine would die. When he realized who was sitting beside him, suddenly the choice he had made struck an exposed nerve.

For almost fourteen years he stood by and watched as Rahman passed messages between operatives half way across the globe, which ultimately resulted in the deaths of several hundred people. Often, his hand was directly involved although he had not planned these exchanges. He had no allegiance to his prison warden's cause. He had but two objectives; stay alive and reunite with Yasmine. Conscience was a painful luxury he did not allow himself. In the end he had accomplished both objectives. He had the sublime experience of spending two years with the love of his heart and soul, and soon, whether here or in heaven, he would also be a father.

Yasmine explained to him, "Beloved husband, love of my life, there is no death, only 'the shuffling off of the mortal coil' as grandfather Ibrahim loved to quote. We are spiritual beings having a very short physical experience all returning to a lighter dream in the blink of an eye. And there we remain until another round of physical experience allows us the opportunity to come closer to fully awakening from the dream of separation - separation from the God that lives within us all. *Every great belief system and religion has in its origins this same truth. We are one with God and we have fallen asleep to this truth.* We come again and again and yet again until finally we awaken to this great truth to sleep no more.

"Each of us is one half of one spirit - male and female, separated from that unity. We are *'Twin Souls'* my beloved husband, joined through eternity, and separated, only in the body for a time. We have been blessed in this lifetime to find each other and although our time together has been short, it has been a gift from God, for in it we were given a glimpse of the second heaven, the awakened state of our final reunion with God. Let us not grieve, for soon the dream will end."

Yousef loved to hear Yasmine speak of the wisdom grandfather Ibrahim had imparted to her. He wanted to believe, to forget the horror of his adult life and the brutal separation that took him from his home and family. But the darkness that enshrouded his life was too deep, too cold to let fall from his heart. He hated those that stole his life and corrupted it. How could he forgive such evil?

During the divine but fleeting moments he spent with his beautiful angel he learned many things that seemed so foreign to his hate filled existence. Forgiveness was by far the bitterest pill to swallow. "To forgive," she told him, " was to heal the past for it allowed the past to slip away so that it could not create an identical future."

It made such simple sense, he wanted to heal the demons that constantly lurked in back of his thoughts, but he could not forget the pain and suffering that he had been forced to endure.

Yasmine explained to Yousef, "The most important forgiveness of all my love is of yourself. You must allow the darkness of guilt to fall from your heart. To do this is to see your world become a place of beauty."

"Surely my sweet flower, without knowing it, I must have done something very right to have been blessed with your love." Yousef told her.

When he and Yasmine were found in the isolated little mountain cabin he had arranged for them in Taos, New Mexico, they thought their fate would arrive immediately. They had no idea the depths of depravity the sick mind of hatred could reach. And so it was the ultimatum was given to him, the choice that placed him in the seat next to David Bryan.

194

Yousef glanced at his wristwatch. It read 9:25 am. He looked quickly over at David and thought of the incredible coincidence. 'Of all the days and all the flights and all the places in the world David could be, here he is sitting next to me on this doomed flight. Should I speak to David, tell him of my love for Yasmine, his step-niece? No, I cannot risk it. If a message is sent from the plane that there is even a hint of betrayal by me, Yasmine and our unborn child will die.'

"No, I cannot take the chance." He whispered.

"What's that Yousef?" David asked.

"I, um, nothing...I was just talking to myself." He replied.

Forty minutes after boarding, there was a scream from the pilots cabin. Both he and Yousef flinched and craned their necks toward the pilot's cabin. For the moment they could not see what was occurring.

Yousef had never actually been involved in violent conflict, nor had he ever witnessed the consequences of his and Rahman's activities. This was different. This had a visceral reality, which he could not ignore. Now he was in the thick of a heinous terrorist attack. His body tightened as he held back the horror of what he knew was unfolding. A few minutes later, at about 9:30 am a voice with a thick Arabic accent came over the intercom and announced that he was the captain and that there was a bomb on board. He claimed they were returning to the terminal to have their demands met.

By 9:35 am, the remaining crew and passengers had been herded back into the last five rows of the aircraft. Two scowling Middle Eastern men stood in front of the small group of frightened passengers warning them to cooperate or face the consequences. No visible weapons could be seen. David wondered about this then thought perhaps the terrorists might believe an unseen weapon could have a much greater fear factor than one that could be easily identified.

Only Yousef and the highjackers knew the fate of the flight although Yousef did not know when or where it would happen. David, who had taken the seat next to Yousef, leaned back in his chair and whispered,

"Hey Yousef, friends of yours? He said half joking. "Where do these clowns think they're going? Don't they know they can't reach the Middle

East with the fuel onboard? And, there's no way they are going to get off the ground after they land back on US soil to refuel."

Yousef did not answer but wore the mask of terror he felt within. David stared at him for a moment then all of a sudden it occurred to him that he might have been correct. Yousef did know these people.

"Hey, are you a part of this? C'mon, what difference does it make now?" David demanded.

He glanced toward the two highjackers who were moving toward the first class section. They closed the curtains behind themselves and Yousef relaxed slightly. Two seats to the right of him, David noticed another passenger on a cell phone, he had a look of shock on his face. Something about the man's face pulled David into a higher perception of what was really happening. David's ability to interpret dreams was truly an intuitive gift and periodically extended into business deals - more than hunches - precognitive flashes. In an instant, he realized something terrible was unfolding and that Yousef knew what it was.

"Yousef! This is much more serious than a bunch of lunatics stealing a plane to fly to another country, isn't it?" David exclaimed.

Yousef turned his head slowly. Every muscle tensed as if he expected to be punched at any moment. In that moment he knew he could not heal all that he had done in the past, but he could not die knowing he hadn't tried to make amends. He must act despite his fears that Yasmine and his unborn child might be sacrificed. If that was to be their fate, he had to believe that Yasmine's promise of heaven was true. As he opened his mouth to speak it felt like time had slowed, his words seemed to come out in slow motion.

"I...am...Yasmine's...husband - your...nephew."

David stared at him in disbelief. "What? How...how...where did you come from?" He didn't wait for a reply. His mind began operating at hyper speed. Yasmine's email - Francine's dream - his vision of Yasmine pregnant, and now, Yousef on a highjacked plane with him. 'What fate has brought us together in this way?' He wondered.

"I was forced to be on this flight...they would have killed Yasmine if I didn't come." Yousef moaned. He looked pleadingly at David as if he wanted his approval or at least his understanding. David's higher sense was

196

in full flight now and he could see the torture Yousef's life had been, he could see the allowances he had made for his actions, just to remain alive. And, he could see the tiny pocket of love he had secreted away in his heart, giving him a reason to survive.

There was a strange parallel in their lives - sacrifices made for a dream - love for another fueling their passions - and always, the sense of feeling powerless to live a different kind of life.

"Tell me Yousef, what is really happening here!"

"Soon, they will crash this plane...to get attention for their cause." He said.

"You're not with them are you, you don't believe in their cause?" David asked.

"No! Yasmine and the baby are my only cause." The tension Yousef had been holding inside began releasing through bitter tears as he heard himself speak of his love for Yasmine and the baby.

David could feel the depth of Yousef's love for Yasmine and the child. He didn't care where Yousef had been or who he had been, he saw only who he had become. In that moment David could see Yousef's life had been worthwhile. Love had replaced hate and an ancient wound was healing.

'Could a life be reclaimed in the final moments before its departure from this existence?' He struggled to believe it could. 'Does it matter when or for how long a light is turned on before a person to sees that the fear the darkness has been hiding was not real?' He asked himself.

Suddenly, David recalled the drawing the little girl had given him on the elevator the previous evening. 'Help him.' It read. In that moment he knew he must have been destined to be here – to do something to prevent what was about to happen.

"Yousef, what can we do to stop this before its too late?" He asked.

Yousef had already been formulating a plan and quickly explained it to David. David listened carefully. Then he did something he had not done since he was a child - he prayed. 'Dear Lord, if you are real, if you still have a place for me in your heart, I ask you to strengthen Yousef and myself in this quest we have set ourselves to accomplish. Help us to save the lives of those who might otherwise perish.' When he had finished his brief
197

intercession he felt a strange sense of calm - Yousef noticed the peace on his face and smiled. It was the smile of a powerful new ally whose resolve was greater than fear.

"I must use my cell phone Yousef. I must try to help you save Yasmine and the baby." David said. Yousef's face brightened as the tears flowed.

David spent the next ten minutes on the phone, as he did he felt the plane make a steep bank changing directions. Yousef looked over at him with a face filled with terror. David rang off and nodded to Yousef that he was ready. In the ten minutes while David was leaving messages, Yousef had been speaking with the man on the other side of him who told him that several other passengers intended rushing the highjackers. Yousef explained his plan to the man who relayed it to the others planning to revolt. When David rang off, Yousef brought him up to speed on the new developments. A moment later the two men went into action.

"Filthy infidel!" Yousef screamed. "You dare to blaspheme the name of Allah!"

Yousef stood up, grabbed David by his shirt collar and pulled him to his feet into the aisle. He began shoving him toward the two highjackers who had pushed through the curtains dividing the first class section from the coach. At first they were alarmed, then, believing that at the end Yousef had seen the light and was joining them in their holy mission, that the fire in his heart had forced him to participate, called out their support.

One highjacker shouted to the other. "Look, Yousef has been touched by the flame of Allah my brother. See how he defends our God against the insults of this heathen." The other screamed his approval as Yousef continued screeching commands and pushing David toward the two men. When he and David were close enough they threw themselves at the two highjackers and all four crumpled to the floor. The rest of the revolting passengers rushed to help and in less then thirty seconds the passion of the moment turned a frightened group of passengers into a swarm of ferocious attackers. As the mob moved into the first class section the other highjacker tried to hold them off with his tiny weapon, but to no avail.

The scuffle lasted less than two minutes and as the last of the highjackers in the first class cabin was subdued the plane went into a steep bank toward the ground. The flight cabin had been left open and the highjacker piloting the plane, seeing that the game was up, must have had orders to immediately crash the plane if their mission did not go according to plan. He screamed, "Allahu Akbar - God is great."

As the ground swiftly came up to meet the plane, David grasped the hand of his savior. "Bless you Yousef."

Yousef smiled his thanks, then uttered his last words, "I love you flowers of my heart. God be with you.

Forty-Eight

October - 7 - 2001

Several hours before the FBI showed up in West Palm Beach Yasmine and her two captors left the rented house on Orange Crescent and headed for the Keys. The nondescript bungalow was acquired in late August, a few days after Yasmine and Yousef were discovered and captured in New Mexico.

Yasmine and Yousef were in a bookstore in Taos, New Mexico where they had a small mountain cabin on the outskirts of town. Yasmine was looking for a copy of her grandfather's book; *The Same God* to replace the copy she brought with her. Somehow it managed to find its way into their fireplace and since it was a constant source of philosophical conversation between her and Yousef, she wanted to replace it as soon as she could.

"The little one in your belly hears us reading from grandfather's book my dear. I fear he will miss the inspiration." Yousef said. He was completely serious and Yasmine said. "I have heard that the fetus can feel and hear while in the womb. If that is true then we can be certain our child will benefit from the influence of grandfather's wisdom, even before *she* enters the world of illusions. Our baby will need every advantage possible to remain awake in a world determined to teach every newborn the errors of the collective beliefs system about fear.

When she arrived at the bookstore she found that the book was temporarily out of stock and had to be ordered. "What name shall I reserve your order under Mrs...?" The clerk asked.

"Faiz." Yasmine said without thinking. Normally, she and Yousef were very careful not to give out any information that might lead Yousef's old connections back to them. She always gave the fictitious name Yousef had made up on their faked documents. This time however she was momentarily distracted when the clerk asked for the author's name. When Yasmine told her it was Ibrahim Faiz the name slipped out when the woman asked for her own last name. Even after the slip she had no suspicion that anyone would be tracking people who ordered her grandfather's book. She was wrong.

Had she thought to mention the slip to Yousef he would have immediately told Yasmine to begin packing. He knew all too well the meticulous

200

determination of these people to exact retribution on anyone who betrayed them. Hadn't grandfather Faiz found that out the hard way? First his son and daughter-in-law were executed, then he himself was abducted from a playground when only six years old. From personal long-term experience Yousef knew that the insanity of hatred had no limit. When one has been poisoned by hatred, nothing stands in their way.

When Yasmine picked up the book three days later, she was followed home. Ten minutes after she arrived, She and Yousef were taken from their home, bound, gagged and blindfolded. Only the intervention of Rahman prevented the two from being executed immediately. It was he that cleverly devised the ultimatum that would allow Yasmine and the unborn child to live. He argued that Yousef's love for Yasmine had turned him from his loyalty to Allah.

The fact that Yousef had never even once been swayed by his natural male instincts made Rahman's argument all the more convincing. Yousef had been a reliable assistant for many years and deserved a chance to redeem him self, and save Yasmine and the baby in the process. The ringleader capitulated but would not allow Yousef to speak with Yasmine again. He was spirited away to a small airport where he was flown to New York State, about fifty miles outside New York City. Yasmine was driven by the couple who would be watching her for the next several weeks, directly to West Palm Beach where they stayed in a motel for a few days until the Orange Crescent house was contracted.

The couple guarding Yasmine, were married, in their early thirties. Neither were Middle Eastern, which gave them a low profile. Nevertheless, the nation's attention was focused on its wounds after 911 and it was decided by the ringleader to lay low and not move Yasmine for at least a few weeks after the hand of Allah's faithful fulfilled their insane dream. Both of her captors seemed to be very familiar with the needs of a woman close to giving birth. They treated her kindly and insured she did nothing to exert herself needlessly.

In the six weeks she spent in the house with the couple, she became convinced they had nothing to do with the events of 911. She had an intuitive sense that in some way they too were being held hostage - pawns in a twisted game within a game. Nevertheless, they were involved somehow, in a plan that resulted in the forfeit of Yousef's life. Until she knew what that involvement was, she decided to keep her thoughts to herself.

Her heart told her to forgive. She could almost hear grandfather Ibrahim coaxing her to let the past go, 'be grateful for the two bliss filled years you shared with Yousef and forgive those who took him from you.' She knew the heartaches her grandfather had endured were always met with forgiveness and love. She remembered his guidance to her one day after she spoke to him about a particularly brutal terrorist incident in the news.

'Forgiveness is the greatest healer of all sweet angel. You may witness the ravaging effects of hatred, judgment and bitterness on the faces, in the diseased bodies and in the horrendous circumstances of people everywhere. The world reflects exactly what is hidden within and never what it would merely like it to be.'

Love was his answer to everything the world seemed to bring against him. "Forgiveness is forgetting - allowing the past to dissolve into the nothingness that it is. Only this moment is real - only *Now* is real. The future is also an illusion and for most people it simply mirrors and repeats their past. Repeated thoughts, words and actions can only result in the same effect that caused them. Live *now* beloved child of my heart. Live *now* and love much. These are the simply keys to a peaceful and joy filled life."

His beautiful words and loving memory were all that kept her heart from breaking - that and the thought of the new life that she was about to bring into the world. Her Nanny also had a great influence on her life choices but grandfather and she were cut from the same cloth. Grandmother was like an older loving sister. It was as if the lessons that could be learned with her had been completed in another time and were already integrated into her soul.

For as long as she could remember Yousef had been her reason for living, her driving passion, her very existence, and now he was gone. So it was that Yasmine resolved that the journey to the Keys would be the beginning of a new life - a life that left the past behind - a life that allowed the unknown to guide her steps - a life where love replaced fear.

As the dark blue van left the outskirts of Miami heading south, Yasmine decided she would risk speaking with her captors.

"Do you two mind if I ask you a question?"

The woman turned and gave Yasmine a strange look. She could not detect any hint of malice or deceit in Yasmine's voice or face. She glanced at her husband who nodded once then said.

"Go ahead."

"Are you two involved with these people because you want to be, or because like Yousef and I, you are compelled to be?"

Yasmine could feel the mood in the van become very tense. Were they angry at the audacity of her question or were they frightened they were being tested? Yasmine wasn't certain.

Yasmine could see the man's hands grip the steering wheel so tight that they began to turn white. She knew she had pressed a very sensitive nerve. For several long seconds there was complete silence while the man and woman seemed to grapple with the question. Finally, the man spoke.

"Oh what the hell, lets tell her Joanne! She's suffering too!" He glanced from the road to his wife who he could see was on the verge of tears.

"All right Derek, go ahead tell her." She said. Derek took a deep breath as his wife fished in her purse for a tissue.

"We have been holding you prisoner because at this moment the lunatics that were behind 911 are holding our children hostage in Afghanistan." His voice trembled and he took another deep breath. Joanne is a nurse and I'm a doctor. Six months ago we were traveling in the Middle East as volunteers with *Doctors without Borders*. Foolishly, we were on the road alone one day when our van was stopped by a group of militants. There was a white cross on our vehicle and when they stopped us they said they had several wounded men at their camp and needed our help. There was no violence, just an urgency to take us to their injured men. At first we were a little frightened but once we saw their intentions were genuine, we were quick to cooperate."

Derek picked up a water bottle he had stowed beside his armrest and took a drink, then offered the bottle to Yasmine. Joanne turned and leaned over the seat. It appeared as if an enormous weight had been lifted from her shoulders. She smiled sweetly then picked up the story from that point.

"God works in mysterious ways. We should never have been traveling by ourselves that day but when we found ourselves with these people - people many would call fanatics, all we saw was a bunch of young men, some just teenagers, tired, scared and wounded, wounds that obviously went much deeper than just the physical. We saw it as an opportunity to extend the common language of love and perhaps in the process, leave with them a

203

different impression of people in the West, different from what they had been told about us."

"That was until the ringleader of this group rejoined them." Derek added. "He was a fierce and clever character who obviously hated anyone not completely loyal to Allah. As soon as he saw the work we had done to care for his men he recognized an opportunity to attack and humiliate infidels by using them against themselves. None of his men who we had helped dare defy this barbarian. It would have meant certain death."

Yasmine's heart went out to the two brave souls who had placed all their skills and love in God's hands and found themselves the apparent victim's of the people they sought to help. She knew there were no such things as victims in this world. All create their own reality. But it took this revelation from her captors to bring to her memory the words of her grandfather.

'Nothing real can be threatened my beloved.' He told her. 'Only the illusion is vulnerable to the changing tides of good and evil. There are no opposites in Truth. All is one, all is now, all is love.'

When Derek and Joanne had finished releasing the dreadful burden they had kept to themselves for over six months, Yasmine repeated her grandfather's words to them.

"We knew you were not one of them." Joanne whispered. "We could feel there was more to what was happening to you and Yousef than just the reparation for his defection."

"But we couldn't take a chance of speaking with you. If there was any chance you were with these people and were being chastened for breaking their code of loyalty, well..." Joanne's words were interrupted by sobs, "they have our children...we just couldn't take a chance."

Yasmine nodded sadly. "I understand. I understand. But we must think of a way to save your children and ourselves." Joanne looked at Derek for an answer.

"She's right sweetheart. She's right." He said.

Yasmine peered through the tinted glass of the van at the ocean in the distance. Her mind was racing. She had not yet told them that one evening, when they were not watching her closely, she had used their computer to risk sending an email through David Bryan's office to her mother. 'Maybe she received it and even now is looking for me. It's a long shot but not an impossibility.' She thought.

"My mother's family is very wealthy." Yasmine said. "They know many people in the Middle East. If we could just reach them and let them know where we are, they may be able to help us find your children and bring them to safety."

"We are supposed to meet up with our contact in Marathon in the Keys this evening. If we don't show up or if they suspect anything, our children will be sacrificed. We can't risk using the cell phone we have because it's likely tapped." Derek explained. Yasmine nodded in agreement. After the incredible way in which she and Yousef had been found she had no doubt Derek was correct.

"And we don't even know if we are being watched right this moment, so if we stop and use a pay phone we could be running the same risk. We need a miracle, nothing less will help us out of this." Joanne said.

Yasmine took her hand and squeezed it affectionately. "By ourselves we are nothing, but with God, all things are possible. Let us surrender this into his hands. Grandfather always told me that there is no order of difficulty in miracles."

Forty-Nine

4:35 PM

When it was discovered the house on Orange Crescent was abandoned Donald and the others returned to St. Paul's. Francine was down hearted. Donald walked from the precinct to the church with his arm around her shoulder. Since he created the little group, the void that divided he and Francine had dissolved. The uncertainty and anxiety about Yasmine's whereabouts and safety dredged up every fear she had locked up inside since that terrible day when her brother Mika'ill and his wife Hayfa died. Now, at this darkest hour, Donald was certain he and Francine would soon be together again. 'How ironic,' he thought, 'Tragedy so often bridges differences and heals ancient wounds. Hasn't this city learned the truth in that on every corner of every street and in every heart these last few weeks?'

Benny was lost in thought wondering why he could no longer connect with Meereka. When the four regrouped at the church he decided to voice his troubling thoughts.

"Something strange has happened everyone. Since Meereka's miraculous healing four years ago she and I have had a silent link with each other. Often, there was no need to speak or even be in the same room together. I somehow knew she was in a different world from this one and we met somewhere in the middle - between the two. I have never understood it I just accepted it as another miracle about her. After we lost her on 911 I seemed to be pulled more into her world - off center from the middle point where we had always connected. That is up until the last few days." He paused for a moment mournfully staring into space. He shook his head back and forth slowly and with a tone of sad resignation said.

"I guess now, she really is gone."

"She's not gone Benny." Smokie laughed. "She is with me."

Everyone stared at Smokie who was grinning. Benny came over to Smokie and crouched beside him.

"You mean she speaks to you now Smokie?"

206

"No Benny. She speaks through me."

Francine gasped as a light began to glow around Smokie. Donald hugged her tightly, surrendering to the peace that filled the room. He could sense something sublime was happening. Tears filled Benny's eyes as he watched in awe. Smokie stood and slowly walked across the room to where the wooden angel was now leaning against the wall. The light surrounding him intensified. He turned and his face had transformed to that of a beautiful woman. A moment later his entire body resembled a living version of the wooden statue. Everyone watched in amazement.

"I am *pink lady*, the angel of Harmony. Throughout the ages I have manifested in the innocent for a brief time. I radiate the essence of harmony through simplicity, humility and unconditional love then depart having planted these seeds of Truth. It is for each one who has benefited to nourish these seeds in order to reap the harvest of harmony's blessing. The children's drawings you received were an aspect of how those seed have grown. Your response has nourished them.

"The world has arrived at the crossroads of transformation, a time when the subtle influence of inner conflict has risen to the surface of the world's collective mind, soon to be swept away. Everywhere, it appears your worst fears have come upon you. In truth they have come to pass away through your awareness of them. You no longer need to fear the arrow that flies by night. For the light of understanding is dispelling the long dark night of mankind's deceit. The hidden is now being revealed. The lie of separation is being exposed. Harmony is being restored to the plan of mankind's awakening.

"Dark clouds are appearing everywhere around the world only to be swiftly blown away by the winds of true understanding and forgiveness. Each of you here has a task in the great awakening. You will take your skills, your experience and your transformed fears and through the power that has been placed in your hands you will share the truth of mankind's undivided unity with God. I will soon come again. The child you seek will grow to maturity and join many others from the realms of light beyond the veil of tears and sadness that have shrouded your world for eons."

The angel stopped speaking and the light that surrounded Smokie gradually faded as he regained his normal appearance. He fell to his knees and Donald and Benny rushed to his side lifting him to his feet. His head was bowed and as he slowly raised it they could see he was still in a trance like state - still connected in some way to *pink lady*.

"You need no longer fear for your niece." He said looking at Francine. "The collective love of you and your friends has helped to save her. Now you must save the two boys who are in great danger." He turned and looked at Donald and Benny. "In time you will understand. They will be found in the mosque of Masjid Quba." With these last words Smokie fell unconscious. Donald and Benny carried him to a pew and stretched his body out on it. Donald stood and looked over at Francine whose face was glowing.

"I'm not afraid any more Donald. I'm not afraid. I could feel Yasmine's presence when *pink lady* spoke. It was as if *pink lady* was here and in Yasmine's baby at the same time. I just know she will somehow pull through her ordeal. We must save the boys Donald, somehow they are connected to what has been happening to all of us - to what *pink lady* said we would be doing to promote world harmony."

Donald smiled and nodded. "I too felt the fear disappear my love." He left Benny with Smokie and walked back to Francine.

Francine said, "From now on my darling, all that we do we will share together."

Then she kissed him and buried herself in his arms. After several bliss filled moments where the two let the years of lonely separation slip from their hearts, Donald pulled away.

"I must do what I can to follow *pink lady's* instructions." He bent down and picked up his cell phone from his briefcase. He opened his telephone directory and Francine stopped him.

"Darling, when *pink lady* spoke her last words I sensed we should begin with Sulaiman al Zeid in Jordan where Yasmine was living when she disappeared. I know that he and my father spent a great deal of time traveling together with the *House of Faiz*. Other than his partner Abdullah, for many years he was father's most trusted employee and friend. I believe he will know who can be trusted to help us." She opened her bag and extracted her own telephone directory and a few minutes later Francine had Sulaiman on the phone.

4:55 PM

She apologized for the late hour due to the time difference then introduced Donald who she said would explain their reason for calling. Donald spoke with the man for fifteen minutes bringing him up to date regarding Yasmine and Yousef then, without trying to explain, he told him about the two boys that were being held at the mosque of Masjid Quba. Sulaiman said he knew it well and that many years ago he had spent many wonderful weeks with Ibrahim in Medina, where the mosque is located. He told Donald not to be concerned, he knew a holy man in Medina that he could trust. He would get details of the situation and deal with it as Allah guided him.

In gratitude, Donald rang off and told Francine and Benny that Sulaiman promised to get back to them with whatever news he could find as soon as possible. Despite the fact that they had only just heard of the boys' desperate circumstances, they all felt intimately connected. After receiving Sulaiman's assurance he would handle the situation with the utmost discretion, the three felt somewhat relieved. *Pink lady* did not say all would be well with the boys, only that they were to save them. They had done what they could for the moment and turned their attention back to Smokie.

Donald and Francine stepped over to the pew where he lay. Benny was already kneeling on the floor beside the pew. Smokie had the smile of an angel on his face and Donald instinctively reached down and grasped his wrist. His heart sank. There was no pulse. The other's saw the look of shock on his face and knew what it meant. His first impulse was to immediately attempt to resuscitate Smokie but a powerful influence inside told him Smokie had fulfilled his life purpose and he had returned home. Benny and Francine felt no urge to interfere. The look of peace on his face said it all.

Benny took Smokie's other hand in his and held it gently like a child's while Francine stroked his hair. Silence filled the room where minutes before *pink lady* had graced their lives with her presence. In that moment the three knew that death could not separate them from their friend and that their lives had forever changed.

5:15 PM

Fifty

October - 7 - 2001

For some time after the Johnson's revealed their forced involvement with the terrorists, they silently questioned the wisdom of sharing their awful secret with Yasmine. As the van sped toward Marathon in the Keys they were lost in a sea of 'what ifs'.

'What if we really are being watched, or worse, what if the van is bugged'? "Oh God!" Joanne whispered.

'What if the authorities tracked us down at the Orange Crescent house and are after us at this very moment? With the fever of the nation at a peak they might just shoot and ask questions later.' Derek thought in anguish.

Yasmine could feel the wretched agonizing the Johnsons were experiencing. It hung like a thick cloud in the confined atmosphere of the van. Again she recalled the words of grandfather Ibrahim when she was in terror about a particularly difficult exam she was facing.

"Fear, associated with loss is a terrible burden dear heart. When the possibility of loss is connected to a special relationship that fear can become a monstrous entity in the mind poisoning every thought. Held in mind and repeated long enough, the thoughts crystallize into the circumstances, people and things we call our reality. Of course positive and beautiful thoughts similarly manifest but with more agreeable results. Both are dreams in the world people call reality but the latter at least is *'a happy dream.'*"

"We must resolve to keep our spirits up you two - no use lamenting over what might or might not be." Yasmine said. Joanne turned and bravely nodded in agreement. Derek followed with a loud bang of his hand on the steering wheel.

"You're right, you're right! We must stay positive!"

"Ooooh!" Yasmine laughed while moaning. That was a high kick."

"The little one." Derek said.

210

"She may not be so little." Yasmine giggled. "I feel she's anxious to join in the party."

They all laughed. " Some party, Joanne said gloomily."

"Did your doctor tell you it was going to be a girl Yasmine?" Derek asked.

"No. I just feel it." She replied confidently. "

Derek looked at his watch. "It's **5:15 PM**, we'll be in Marathon in about twenty five minutes or so. Our contacts are supposed to meet us there at **6:00 PM**. After that, we don't know what to expect."

Derek's shoulders were hunched as he drove. Joanne placed her hand on his neck and massaged the tension knots. "God be with us." She sighed. He nodded and she leaned over and kissed him gently on his cheek.

Meanwhile the baby in Yasmine's belly continued to make its presence known. Despite the ominous circumstances, she could not help feeling a sense of blissful wonder at the thought that a part of Yousef's essence would soon be in the world with her again. As she rolled the wonderful feeling over in her mind she drifted into a peaceful reverie that took her back to the little cabin where she and Yousef shared their love for two years.

When Yousef settled the two of them into what he referred to as 'our safe house' he asked Yasmine if she thought she could leave her past behind - completely behind. She told him that her life had only just begun the day she met him in the courtyard at St. Anthony's the year before. She asked him the same question and she could still see the look of despair on his face.

"I don't know my lovely flower. I will try. Perhaps you can show me how."

Her life had been focused, determined and driven with but one purpose; to reunite with her beloved Yousef. His life had been an endless passage through the dark corridors of secrecy and deceit and the cruel consequences of having to live with the suffering his activities inflicted upon others. It was true he had endured it all when instead he might have terminated his own life. But he remained. Staying in the horror of it while holding to the dream that one day, by staying alive he might be with Yasmine.

For both he and Yasmine the new life together, although isolated and remote, was a dream come true. It showed them the deluding influence time and space could have on the mind. Neither time nor space had the slightest effect on the limitless sense of freedom they now shared despite being closed off from the rest of the world.

Yasmine's musing slipped into the blissful moments of intimacy that she shared with Yousef. It filled her heart with joy as she remembered the divine moment of her baby's conception. Near midnight, locked in the ecstasy of her lover's embrace, free of every past demon or future fear, she and Yousef stared passionately into each other's eyes. In the dim light of a single candle he said to her. "Flower of my soul, in this moment we are three in one: you, I and the child within." She wept tears of joy and drifted into a heavenly sleep. In the morning she awoke to find a single pink rose on the pillow beside her. She had never told Yousef pink roses were her favorite. She delighted in his insight.

"My love, for many years I have dreamt of a pink rose - nothing more, just a single pink rose - vivid and pure like my love for you. Throughout the dark and lonely years of my life, just you and that beautiful dream have given me the only peace I have ever known."

The van pulled to a stop and Yasmine blinked, plucked from the glimpse of her season of rapture, back into the cold reality of the moment.

5:55 PM

"The Barracuda." Yasmine read the sign above the restaurant. "How appropriate."

Derek laughed uncomfortably and turned the engine off. "Well, here we go. May the angels be with us?" He walked around the vehicle and opened the door for Joanne then opened Yasmine's door and helped her out. He took one look at her and his expression immediately changed . It was the look of a doctor sizing up a situation he'd often seen. Yasmine nodded. "I think so Dr. Johnson."

Joanne looked from her husband to Yasmine then back to her husband, then it dawned on her what was going on. Their rendezvous at the Barracuda was about to take on a new dimension. The three smiled at each other and clasped their hands together.

"It's going to be all right. It's going to be all right. " Yasmine said.

212

Ten minutes later they were seated in the restaurant and about to order when two surly looking Middle Eastern men entered the building. They glared at the Johnsons with malevolence.

"That's them!" Derek whispered. The two men indicated to the waitress that they were joining the Johnson's table and headed toward them. When they were within ten steps of the table Yasmine suddenly let out a loud moan.

"Oh God! She's coming." The waitress standing beside the table had just asked Yasmine not a minute before when she was due, and Yasmine laughingly answered.

"Any minute now!" Now that it was actually happening the waitress shouted,

"Wow, she wasn't kidding. She's having a baby right now!" The waitress looked confident, like a young woman who had delivered more than one baby herself. "I'll call a doctor."

"No need miss. I'm a doctor and my wife is a nurse." Derek said. Just help us get the young lady to one of those booths in the back. Oh, and I'll need a few things. I'd appreciate it if you..." The waitress cut him short and said,

"I know just what you need doctor." While Yasmine was being helped to the back of the restaurant the two Middle Eastern men followed and sat down at a nearby table as close as possible. They appeared angry and frustrated but clearly recognized they would have to wait.

While Derek and Joanne helped Yasmine deliver her baby the miraculous moment of new life filled the room. Although they had delivered many babies, the euphoric sense of God's creative power was always present. Their spirits soared and the courage they needed to face their fear came upon them. "It's no good my love, we must not allow ourselves to be the victims of tyranny. If we are to trust God we must do it fully. We must not allow these two men to escape. For us, the madness must end here and now."

Tears streamed down his face as he took hold of the desperate fear in his heart. Joanne's face was also stained with the tears of courage.

"Follow your heart darling." She said.

"I must call for help!" Derek yelled. "There is a complication." The waitress pointed to a telephone a few feet away near the washrooms. Derek stepped toward the telephones glancing at the two men to see if they had been alerted to what he was up to. They weren't. He dialed the police and in less than three minutes explained what was happening, then hung up and returned to Joanne and Yasmine.

Ten minutes later, just as Yasmine's baby uttered her first cry of life, two men dressed as paramedics walked into the restaurant and directly over to the two Middle Eastern men. They grabbed their arms pulling them above their heads so that they could not reach for any device or warning signal they might be carrying. Instantly, a half dozen plain clothed police joined the scuffle and the two men were whisked away in an unmarked car.

7:40 PM

Less than two hours later Yasmine lay sleeping in the Marathon hospital. Derek and Joanne sat down beside her just as she opened her eyes. They gently placed Yasmine's baby girl in her arms. She beamed with a radiant glow that seemed to light up the room. Seeing the joy in their eyes and sensing it meant more than the beautiful blue-eyed wonder she was holding, she said,

"So…tell me about the good news you two are wearing on your faces." Yasmine whispered.

Joanne began crying and Derek squeezed her hand. "They're safe Yasmine. Our boys are safe." Derek said as he too began to weep. The baby gurgled and kicked its feet beneath her blanket. A moment later tears of joy flooded Yasmine's eyes as well.

"Tell me, tell me. What happened?" She asked.

When the police got your name from me on the telephone they found an; 'all points bulletin' on us in their computer issued by the FBI. From that information they were able to reach your aunt Francine and found that she and some friends somehow already knew about our boys. Apparently, they had contacted a friend of theirs in the Middle East who they believed could help. Through his contacts the boys were easily located. They were lightly guarded because their jailors did not think anyone could possibly know about the boys or their whereabouts. It was only just an hour ago that they were rescued. We spoke to them just before you woke up and they're okay.

214

Fifty-One

October - 8 - 2001

When the men holding the boys in the mosque of Masjid Quba were interrogated about the Johnson's involvement with Yasmine's abductors, one of them came clean right away. Like Yousef, he was working with a terrorist cell against his will. And, like the Johnsons, he had been threatened that his family would be harmed if he did not faithfully perform his duties to Allah. An unwilling pawn in their game, he was anxious to cut a deal. As a result, the Johnson's were released from custody immediately.

Donald, Francine and Benny flew down to Marathon on the *Inner Scape* corporate jet the day after the balloon went up in Marathon. Donald rented a large villa near the water and Yasmine joined them a day later. A few days after that, the Johnson's boys arrived in Miami on a government transport and joined their parents later that night at the villa where they all shared an intimate dinner together.

The reunion reflected a moment of rare beauty. The Johnson's had their own lives and their boys' back safely. Donald and Francine were lost like two teenagers in love. Yasmine, with her beautiful Bashira by her side, was glowing from head to toe in the bliss of new motherhood, while Benny had again connected with *pink lady* through the newborn baby.

In contrast to the joyous gathering, a torrential downpour swept across the Gulf of Mexico, punctuated by deafening thunderclaps while shocking webs of lightening lit up the night sky every few minutes. The entire scene looked and felt like a war zone.

After dinner Francine snuggled in beside Donald on a sofa while Benny started a fire in the hearth. Yasmine cuddled up with Bashira in a love seat beside them and the two Johnson boys huddled outside in the shuttered lanai with their parents - all exchanging stories about their incredible adventures.

Despite the ear shattering racket going on outside the atmosphere within the villa was sublime. It was as if the tension and torment, the agony and pent up anxieties of each one's worst nightmares were being released in one incredible spectacle.

"Somehow, I feel like the horror of 911 is a larger mirror for the weather this evening darling." Francine said. Benny turned from the fireplace and nodded.

"Meereka told me just a few weeks before that terrible day something very much like that. She said, 'too much pain Benny. Moma earth is crying'."

"Ibrahim explained to me not long before he died that the planet had reached a breaking point - a point where the poisons of accumulated darkness from the negative and hate filled thoughts of mankind must be released. He said, 'nevertheless, there is so much goodwill dotting the globe now that much of the apocalyptic destruction that might have occurred has been transmuted. Events now occurring are the toxins of disharmony being released in small bursts rather than through cataclysmic events that could send the world back into another dark and primitive age. When these bursts do occur they will *not* be seen as small tragedies, but, by comparison to what could have been, they will be minute.'"

"I think I know what he meant Dr. Heathrow." Derek said as he stepped toward the fire Benny had made." The two boys sat beside Yasmine and inspected the new life cooing in her arms while Joanne poured herself a coffee and sat on a thick rug at her husband's feet in front of the fireplace.

"Joanne and I have been protestors for years. If we saw injustice anywhere, we were the first to join a March or picket line. Our every thought, word and deed was *against* something we found offensive or unfair in the world. Then when the boys were taken and we were forced to help those awful people it was as if our worst fears had come upon us. I believe our motives were correct but our methods were off balance. We should have been focused on how we wanted the world to be instead of protesting the way it was." Derek said, as he sat down beside Joanne on the carpet.

"People should tell the world to talk about good stuff." One of the Johnson boys said. He and his brother joined their parents on the carpet and Joanne stroked the boy's hair and put her arm around his brother, hugging him tightly.

"That would be like asking the newspapers and television media to spread the good news instead of all the high crimes, gossip and dramas that fill their pages and new reports." She said.

Suddenly Donald's body shuddered and in a flash he was transported back to the experience he had with the holy man while at the home of Chez

Shift in India. He knew it had really happened. It wasn't just the hallucination he thought it was all these years. The holy man told him, 'the day will come when my words will return to your awareness - that day your life will be transformed.' He remembered. The words came back to him just as if they were being spoken to him in that very moment.

"Invest the entire force of the great Spirit now available to you behind the healing of the planet. Speak to the minds of the children first. They will be the most receptive. Mold their minds with gentle care and show them that true happiness can only be found through loving their world and all that is within it. The mold can only yield what is poured into it. Teach harmony, and show the world that there is only one God - *The Same God* with many different names and that he lives within the hearts of every living soul."

"What is it darling? Francine said. "Are you okay?"

He stared out into the storm, laughed and shook his head. "Now I remember. Now I understand!"

"What Donald? What do you remember, what do you understand?" Francine asked. Benny and the others looked on expectantly for what he would answer.

"Ibrahim knew what was going to happen." Donald blinked and broke from his semi trance. He looked at Francine then to the others. "I don't mean specifically, but he knew that there would be a turning point late this year. The Trust Fund Francine, your father's Trust Fund as you know stated that it was to be closed until the end of 2001 when I would have complete access to it. Besides the sizeable provisions he made for you and Yasmine, the total Fund is over three billion dollars."

Derek and Joanne gasped looked at each other in amazement.

"Wow!" Benny shouted. "That's a lot of zeroes."

"It's a lot of good news is what it is Benny." Donald said.

"I think I see where you are going with this doctor." Derek said with growing excitement.

Francine cuddled closer to Donald and sighed. " Oh Donald, I see it too, but its such a huge responsibility to take on. Do you really believe it can be done?"

217

"'By ourselves we are nothing.' Grandfather Ibrahim used to say when he echoed the great Master teacher." Yasmine said.

Just then Bashira let out a laugh, large enough for all to hear above the cacophony of the racket outside. All eyes turned to her. Benny's face shone from the reflection of the fire. The child was holding his baby finger in her hand. In their minds each one heard,

'*Pink lady* says, with God, all things are possible.'

Epilogue

2095

"What did Dr. Heathrow and his friends do with the money in the Trust nanny?" Huriyyah asked.

"You see the emblem on your school tunic little angel?" Nanny Bashira said.

"Yes nanny." She replied

"Do you know what the symbol means Huriyyah?"

"I think the three triangles inside each other mean that no matter how big or how small something is in this world, God is there. All is in the One God." She answered.

"That's right my little angel. And what about the letters - TSG - inside the triangles, what do they mean? What do they mean?" Nanny Bashira asked.

Huriyyah thought for a moment then said, "I don't know nanny, they are everywhere at school; on walls, on plagues, above doors, but no one ever told me what they mean."

Nanny Bashira smiled. "That's all right little one, people often forget their roots. More important, is the life that flows through those roots. You have done well to drink deeply of the life that flows through the roots of your school."

Huriyyah grinned then asked, "But what about Dr. Heathrow and his friends. What did they do?"

"The letters stand for *The Same God*." Nanny Bashira said.

"Wow!" Huriyyah exclaimed. "You mean they started our school nanny?"

"Much more than that sweet one. During the following year, after the confused people from the Middle East made the Towering Angels fall in New York, Dr. Heathrow and Francine, who had become his wife, Benny, Yasmine and their new friends the Johnson's, created a world wide

219

organization called *The Same God Foundation*. It was just like hands that reached out to all the people of the world to form a circle of Oneness!"

"And my school is one of those hands?" Huriyyah asked.

"Yes!" In fact it was the first hand. After Dr. Heathrow remembered what the holy man told him to do many years before, he and his wife and their friends began by setting up a special school - your school - to teach very young children that God is in everything and everyone. It also taught them every great religion is connected by the same truth, though told in different ways. Do you know what that truth is?"

"That's easy nanny, its love. We learned that on our first day when I was just two years old." She laughed.

"Right again. And did you also learn that everything in the world is made of love?"

Huriyyah nodded her head.

"The people that lived before your school started didn't know that. Their scientists told them that everything in the universe was made of energy and information. But they had to wait for your school to begin to find out that energy and love, are the same thing. They had to learn that because everything and everyone is made of love, that everything and everyone are connected. Everything and everyone *are* one.

"Because people had not yet learned that they were made of love, they lived in a big dream thinking they were not one with everything and everyone in their world. In their big dream they believed they were separate beings and in their dream they started a thing called *polarity*.

"I know what that word means nanny. My life instructor told me it means *opposites*." Huriyyah said.

"That right little angel. People in the world of the big dream saw everything as different from themselves and began to make everything and everyone opposite. Some things they called good and some they called bad and when they did, it was called *judgment*. Judgment is what caused all the *static* I told you about static before I shared the story with you. It is how in the big dream people lived without harmony."

"Now I understand nanny. So when people learned from the children in our school that they were all One, is that when they woke up from the dream?" Huriyyah asked.

"Not right away. People were afraid to let go of their dream at first. Nanny Bashira said.

"But that's silly nanny. Why would people want to hold on to a dream where all they had was static?" She asked.

"Because they didn't know anything else existed. They thought their dream was real." Nanny Bashira said.

"What does it mean to be afraid nanny?" Huriyyah asked.

"It means to have fear little one, just like you have, from what remains of your memory, when you say you see scary things. In the big dream, in the world of opposites they made in their dream, fear was the opposite of love." She said.

Huruyyha looked out the kitchen window at the rose garden while she thought about the story Nanny Bashira had told her. Then she noticed something she had not noticed before. "Nanny, all the roses in your garden are pink, just like in your story."

Nanny Bashira smiled. Huriyyah looked at her nanny then back to the rose garden, then back to her nanny. Suddenly, she realized what it meant. Her eyes opened wide and she exclaimed, "Nanny, you are *pink lady* aren't you?"

"Yes little one. But you too are an angel." She said.

Huriyyah thought about that for a while then said, "If everyone is made of love and angels are messengers then a message of love is from an angel. Is that right nanny?"

"That's right sweet one. The more love we extend to everyone and everything in the world the more we are all expressing the angel within. And when *everything* we do, all day long, is extend love, then we are angels all the time."

221

Huriyyah smiled because of all the things she wanted, the most important thing was to be just like her nanny. "Then I will love everything and everyone all day and I will really be an angel just like you nanny."

Nanny Bashira beamed as she felt the determination in her grand daughter's heart and soul. Then Huriyyah realized something.

"Nanny, you called those big buildings that fell down; Towering Angels."

"Yes, that's right little angel." Nanny Bashira said.

"Was it because everyone in those buildings *was* an angel that didn't know they were?" She asked.

"Yes Huriyyah. From all the hands in *The Same God* circle, the most important thing taught is to see the angel in every face you meet. In that way, gradually everyone awakens from the dream. And so it is today, people everywhere are starting to realize that they too are angels - messengers of love. They *are* love itself - One with God"

About the Authors

John McIntosh

John is a dynamic speaker and has been an entrepreneur and leader in the field of sales management, marketing, training and motivation for 35 years. During that time he has risen to the level of national sales manager in two separate companies, founded two companies for which he acted as president, and for 23 years operated a highly successful, international natural health distributorship. Over the last 35 years, he has trained thousands of people internationally presenting his material with high energy and conviction based on personal experience and success.

He has been a student of metaphysics, inspirational and spiritual philosophy during his entire career, successfully incorporating the truth he learned into his own daily life and that of his inspirational training.

Jo Ann "Ananda" McIntosh

Jo Ann is a remarkable intuitive healer, spiritual counselor, Reiki Master and All Faith Minister, teaching "A Course in Miracles" for the last 9 years. She is also a spiritual channel for beautiful prose and a photographer with a perceptive eye for the spirit within all life. For over 15 years she had a strong background in theater in New York successfully performing virtually every function within the framework of producing a play and used these highly tuned skills to help teach children Self Empowerment.

She has also worked within the Aids community in a variety of capacities while sharing her unique healing ability with many miraculous results.

Other books by the Authors
The Millennium Tablets
Living Abundantly through Inner Guidance
356 Days of Inner Guidance Inspiration
Loves Last Dreaming (also a screenplay)
The Hughes Legacy

Contact
www.awakendreamer.com
createmiracles@aol.com

www.ingramcontent.com/pod-product-compliance
Lightning Source LLC
Chambersburg PA
CBHW070109260626
47160CB00004B/1388